"Just play dumb, Jessie.

"That shouldn't be hard for you to do," Lee snarled.

"I've never met a man as rude as you, Lee Kincannon. And if I'm so dumb, and you're traipsing around after me like a pet dog, then what does that make you?"

"I guess that makes me pretty dumb, too."

She twitched her shoulders in satisfaction.

"A pet dog, Jessie?" he asked.

"That's what I said." Jessamine crossed her arms, realizing too late her little act of defiance forced her more closely back against him.

His tongue traced the curve of her ear.

Jessamine's eyes widened. "What are you doing?"

"Your pet dog is licking your pearly little ear, Miss Jessamine," he whispered. "Isn't that what pet dogs do?" And he proceeded to do it again.

Dear Reader,

Thanks to the success of our March Madness promotion during 1992 featuring four brand-new authors, we are very pleased to be able to, once again, introduce you to a month's worth of talented newcomers as we celebrate first-time authors with our 1993 March Madness promotion.

Teller of Tales by Laurel Ames. When free-spirited Jenner Page captures the eye of the bored nobleman, Lord Raines, their reckless affair causes a scandal that Regency London is likely never to forget, or forgive.

Riverbend by Mary McBride. Despite their differences, Lee Kincannon and the fiesty Jessamine Dade seem destined to cross paths at every turn, but the jaded gambler still can't believe that fate has finally dealt him a winning hand.

Snow Angel by Susan Amarillas. Katherine Thorn never expected to find herself stranded at the ranch of her unfriendly neighbor during a Wyoming blizzard, and she was even more surprised to discover that Logan McCloud was definitely not the man she thought he was.

Romance of the Rose by Claire Delacroix. Though Armand d'Avigny vowed that he would never again allow the lovely Alexandria de Fontaine to be taken from his side, Alex knew that as long as her enemy remained alive she would never be safe—even in the arms of the powerful knight.

We hope that you enjoy every one of these exciting books, and we look forward to bringing you more titles from these authors in the upcoming year.

Sincerely,

Tracy Farrell
Senior Editor

Riverbend

MARY McBRIDE

Harlequin Books

TORONTO • NEW YORK • LONDON
AMSTERDAM • PARIS • SYDNEY • HAMBURG
STOCKHOLM • ATHENS • TOKYO • MILAN
MADRID • WARSAW • BUDAPEST • AUCKLAND

Harlequin Historicals first edition March 1993

ISBN 0-373-28764-X

RIVERBEND

MARY McBRIDE

Mary McBride comes by her romantic streak naturally—what else from the daughter of two people who met on a blind date on Valentine Day? Her affinity for riverboat gamblers flows directly from the mighty Mississippi in St. Louis, Missouri, where she lives with her husband and two young sons.

For Leslie, of course

Prologue

Autumn, 1860

"I don' know if this here fountain was such a good idea, Mr. Lee. Folks been drinkin' the champagne like it was water," the majordomo observed, shaking his grizzled head.

Lee Kincannon plunged an Irish crystal goblet into one of the rivulets of pale liquid, letting some of it wash over his fingertips. "Folks are having a good time, Fayette," he drawled. "The war's gonna start soon. They're making hay while the sun shines."

The old man's ebony face distorted in disapproval. "They ain't makin' hay, Mr. Lee. They makin' asses o' themselves."

Lee grinned down at the wiry former slave. "Since when do you care about white folks acting like horses' behinds, Fayette?"

Fayette's expression went blank for a moment, and then he blinked. "Don't s'pose I do," he said as his gnarled black fingers eased the cork from another bottle of champagne and he emptied it into the fountain.

Lee reached out and caught some of the stream in his glass. "No. Nor do I, Fayette," he said. Taking a long draft of the champagne, he gazed around the crowded ballroom of the Imperial Hotel, where New Orleans' finest—the cream of the social crop—were waltzing, flirting, gossiping and drinking.

"Besides, Fayette," Lee said, "a goodly portion of these asses will be too drunk to make their way home tonight, and they'll be settling their nether parts upstairs in our beds." He winked broadly at the old man and lifted his crystal goblet. "Good champagne is good business, Fayette."

Lee Kincannon stood there for a while, listening to the delicate splashing of the fountain. He was a head taller than most of the men in the room, his shoulders broader, his waist more trim. He wore his black frock coat, white silk shirt and black neck cloth like a French marquis, but always with the awareness that those fine clothes covered a body with more scars than anyone present—soldier or slave.

Fools, all of them, he thought. These Confederate gentlemen believed they could actually win a confrontation with the rich industrialized North. Hell, they might as well set fire to New Orleans, Natchez and Louisville tonight and get the whole thing over with. War, when it came, was going to last a sight longer than the few months everybody predicted, and be far bloodier than anybody dared imagine. Worst of all, it was going to play hell with his business. Traffic on the Mississippi would slow to a couple of steamers trying to play river tag with scores of Union boats. His riverboats would be empty, and so would his hotels. Or they'd all be commandeered by iron-assed generals for the comfort of their boys.

"Damnation!" Putting down his glass, Lee extracted a thin cheroot from the breast pocket of his coat and bit off the tip. Then, before he could reach into his pocket once more for a match, a flame appeared, mere inches from his face.

"You're swearing into thin air again, Lee," Alpha Parker said as she touched a wooden match to the end of his cigar.

"Who are you thinking about this time, darlin'? Abolitionists or secessionists?"

Lee blew out the match with a hard stream of smoke. "All of them," he snapped. "The ignorant devils."

Alpha stood as close to him as her wide emerald green skirt allowed, leaning her upper body against his arm, gifting him with a full display of her splendid cleavage. "Well," she said, "speaking of devils, we have a little problem with one of them right here."

Lee eyed her keenly. "Somebody been bothering you, Red?" It wasn't unusual at one of these fetes for a so-called gentleman to get liquored up and suggest that the luscious redhead resume her infamous career as Riverboat Red. Lee Kincannon shifted his relaxed stance, ready to discourage the gentleman.

Alpha laughed. "Settle down, Lee. Nobody's so much as patted my backside."

He slid his hand along the gathers at the rear of her skirt. "Too damn much silk here between a gentleman and temptation," he said.

"You're no gentleman, Lee," she said as she raised her eyes to meet his knowing gaze. They had been together for a dozen years, since the night a twenty-year-old Lee had won the *Delta Star* in a poker game. The next morning he had Alpha measured for a high-necked dress of blue velveteen and lace and informed her she was through hustling gamblers for a living. "Are you asking me to marry you?" she'd asked. "No, Red," he replied, "I'm going to do better by you than that. I'm going to make you rich."

And he had. Alpha Parker had received a percentage of each riverboat and hotel Lee had acquired, in return for her talents as a financial advisor, administrator, hostess and decorator—not to mention her favors as a mistress. Lee had done very well by her indeed, but Alpha was still waiting for him to marry her.

Her hip jutted against his now. "This skirt's not a permanent fixture," she purred, "if temptation's on your mind."

Lee smiled down at her as he tucked a stray red curl back behind her ear. "Always, Red. You know that." Then he sighed and looked out at the ballroom. "But it's going to be a hell of a long night."

"I know," said Alpha. "They haven't even dragged out the virgins yet."

Lee grinned wickedly. "I believe they're called 'debutantes,' Miss Red."

Her reply was a snort. "Five'll get you ten most of them aren't virgins anyway."

She was probably right, Lee thought, recalling the less than ladylike behavior of several of the young women present this evening. With green-eyed Alpha, however, that subject was best avoided. She was more than a little possessive where he was concerned. "Any devil in particular you wanted to discuss, Alpha, or was it merely deviltry in general?" he asked her.

"Hell, I nearly forgot about her."

"Her?"

"Miss Jessamine Dade," Alpha said.

Lee recognized the name—not hers so much as her father's. Judge Levander Dade was a political bigwig from Missouri. In fact, Lee had been keeping an eye out for the judge all evening, hoping to get a little help with permits for some fancy brickwork on the sidewalk around his hotel in St. Louis. "And just what about this Miss Jessamine Dade?" he asked.

"Seems the little dear has disappeared."

"What do you mean 'disappeared'?"

The redhead retrieved Lee's goblet and downed a good portion of its contents. "I don't know, Lee," she snapped. "Gone. Disappeared. Not where she's supposed to be. Her papa's fit to be tied, 'cause he came all the way down here just on her account. Now she's up and vanished.''

Lee's dark eyebrows drew together. He didn't like problems, especially problems with women. In this case, a young one. ''Is she one of the girls to be presented tonight?'' he asked.

''Yup.'' Alpha's kohl-rimmed eyes twinkled at him over the crystal edge of the goblet. ''And this one probably is a virgin, mad as her daddy is about her disappearance.''

''Where is the judge?'' Lee asked, scanning the ballroom for signs of a distraught father.

Alpha pointed to the series of arched windows that opened onto St. Charles Street. ''Outside. The judge and his three sons. They've already turned the hotel inside out. Now I guess they're combing the whole Vieux Carré. I pity that poor girl when they find her.''

''Where's the mother?'' Lee was thinking he might better spend his efforts consoling Mrs. Dade than roaming up and down St. Charles Street trying to locate four irate men and one damn addlepated girl.

''Dead,'' said Alpha. ''Emerald LaPaix, the girl's aunt by marriage, claims little Miss Jessamine's a wild one. Says the girl wasn't raised right 'cause the judge was too busy grieving for his wife.''

''That's a shame,'' commented Lee distractedly.

''According to Mrs. LaPaix, the judge's grieving consisted mostly of bending his elbow. And she also says—''

Lee cut her off. ''Are you planning to write a biography, Alpha, with all this gossip?''

The woman glared at him. ''Well, everybody's talking about it, Lee. I mean, the girl's gone. And if she's not located pretty soon, this whole affair's going to fold up quicker than portulaca at sunset.''

''Damnation!'' Lee dropped the remains of his cigar on the marble floor of the ballroom and ground it out with a glossy black boot. "What does she look like, this little motherless tart?"

"Pretty. Or so her aunt says. Black hair. Blue eyes. 'Bout this high." Alpha indicated a height several inches shorter than her own.

"And what was she wearing?"

"Well, white of course." Alpha grinned. "Just like all the other virgins."

Lee swore again. "You make sure nobody leaves this party, Alpha. And see that Fayette keeps this damn fountain flowing. I'm going out to retrieve the brat myself." With a yank on the sleeves of his coat, he strode off in the direction of the lobby.

Alpha Parker raised the goblet to his broad retreating back. "Good hunting, Lee," she said. "And bring her back a virgin, you hear?"

Lee shouldered his way through the crowd. His large body dwarfed the bankers, lawyers, gentlemen farmers, and fops—men his ambition had run up against more than once.

There had been a time Lee's ambition was completely satisfied by being the damnedest gambler on the Mississippi. Not so bad for the son of a Natchez whore and a rum-sotted, iron-jawed cotton grower who'd just as soon kick his bastard son as lay eyes on him. Not so bad for a ragged boy who had sometimes figured curling up and dying might be a better fate than his own accursed life.

The boys who'd tortured him like a stray cat had been the first to teach the young Lee Kincannon that there were few limits to his physical abilities. He hadn't meant to kill Willy Bradshaw with the knife he wrested from his hand, but Lee was quicker and smarter and more desperate than Willy had ever been.

Then Deuce Barnett had discovered Lee, ten miles up river from Natchez, bloody, rope-burned and cowering be

ind a bale of cotton on the *Natchez Belle*. He had taken the
oy under his wing, taught him how to play cards, then fol-
owed the lessons by teaching him how to cheat. By the time
ee was seventeen, even Deuce hadn't been able to best him
at cards, whether the game was crooked or straight.

But it was Riverboat Red, lying in his arms after he'd won
he *Delta Star* with a stony expression and an honest pair of
reys, who had taught him about ambition. Lee was aiming
o turn the steamboat over to the first fool he met who had
a couple thousand greenbacks.

"How much money do you think this old boat brings in
n a month?" Red had mused while she toyed with the hair
on his chest.

"I don't know. A thousand at most. Much of that can't
be profit," he'd replied.

Red had sat up, the sheet crushed to her breasts. "Two
housand," she'd said. "And half of that goes right in the
owner's pocket. It'd be more if the damn boat was run
ight."

Lee, too, had sat up then. "What do you mean, 'run
ight'?"

"I mean right—clean, on schedule, with proper advertis-
ng and food that's fit to eat. Nobody books passage on the
Delta Star more than once, you know. Well, that's great for
he gamblers. You boys always have brand new sheep to
hear. But it don't do much for profits." Red tugged the
heet around her. "It's people coming back time and again
who make money for a riverboat."

"How do you know so much about it, Red?"

"Honey, I've been working on these boats since I was
ifteen. There's not a lot about 'em I don't know."

So Red had proceeded to teach Lee everything she knew
about Mississippi steamboats, and it hadn't been long be-
ore the student surpassed the teacher. Not only was the
Delta Star run right, she became the premier steamboat on

the Mississippi, accompanied in quick succession by the *Delta Queen* and the *Delta Princess*. Then, because it irked Lee to see travelers disembark to spend their money elsewhere, he'd acquired his first hotel.

Now, as he crossed the inlaid Georgia marble floor of the ballroom of his newest hotel, Lee's jaw was clenched in anger. He had gone all out for this debutante ball—from the champagne fountain and the Irish crystal to brand new uniforms for his staff—in order to win over New Orleans society. Their patronage alone would guarantee the hotel's success. It meant a great deal of money—money he needed badly, for as his empire had grown, so had his debts. His New Orleans hotel had to make a handsome profit, or he would be in deep trouble.

If this ball was a failure, there would never be another one. New Orleans society was as fickle as it was loyal. If they went home early, they wouldn't be back. His entire future was threatened, not by catastrophic weather or an act of God or even the impending war, but by some damn snippet of a girl.

His dark eyes smoldered as he approached the brass-and-etched-glass doors to the lobby. His determined stride was suddenly halted by a wall of white organza. A white kid glove clamped down on his arm.

He wanted to curse, but tamped down his ire to drawl politely, "You're looking very fetching this evening, Miss Marsh."

Before the young woman could acknowledge his compliment, Marybelle McKenzie inserted herself between them by nearly breaking Lavinia Marsh's arm. "I haven't seen you in the longest time, Mr. Kincannon. Where on earth have you been keeping yourself?"

The scent of orange blossoms was potent as Marybelle, a strawberry blonde, edged closer to him.

"Ah, but I've seen you, Miss McKenzie. Weren't you shopping on St. Charles Street just last week?"

Marybelle McKenzie flushed and stammered. "I was. Indeed I was. And just last week."

"Marybelle, don't be such a simpleton." Ruthellen LaPaix sneered and dug her elbow in the young woman's side. "We were all shopping on St. Charles Street last week. Everyone shops on St. Charles Street every week. Mr. Kincannon knows that. He's just leading you on." Ruthellen turned her mud brown eyes up to look into Lee's face. "My mama said to be wary of you, Mr. Kincannon. Why is that, do you suppose?"

Lee bowed slightly, his face nearing hers. "I haven't a clue, Miss LaPaix. Have you?"

Ruthellen fussed with her carved ivory fan as her cheeks turned a vivid crimson. Then, suddenly, a figure in frothy pink descended on the girl like a nervous guardian angel. Mrs. Emerald LaPaix raised her chin to Lee's dark face.

"Have you heard the awful news, Mr. Kincannon?" she asked. "Ruthellen's cousin has disappeared."

"As a matter of fact..." Lee began, only to be cut off by Ruthellen.

"That hussy! Don't let's talk about her. She's practically ruining our evening." Her ivory fan snapped open and sent the white ruffles on her bodice flying, and her mother's agitated fingers attempted to smooth them back in place.

"Hush, dear," Emerald LaPaix said. "Jessamine is a willful child, but your cousin is not a, well... not that."

Marybelle McKenzie sniffed. "Our mamas say we might have to go home before executing our *tableaux vivants*. And we've worked so hard. Try to guess what I was planning to portray, Mr. Kincannon."

Tableaux vivants were the current rage, though Lee had a hard time fathoming why people enjoyed posing as living pictures. "Wouldn't be some sort of Greek goddess, would

it, Miss McKenzie?'' he asked, offering her a slow and sly grin over the head of Mrs. LaPaix.

Marybelle's gloved hand rose to conceal her blush. ''You flatter me, Mr. Kincannon.''

''He's teasing you,'' Ruthellen told her with another sneer. ''And besides, nobody's going to be anything now that Jessamine's gone and ruined it all. How I despise that awful girl!''

''Now, now, dear,'' her mother said soothingly. ''She *is* your kin.''

''I don't care. I hate her.''

Lee shifted his stance, drawing his boot safely away from Ruthellan's stamping foot. ''Why don't you ladies just proceed with your *tableaux*,'' he suggested. ''I'm sure everyone would be most charmed.'' And distracted, he added to himself. Perhaps they would even forget about the wayward brat.

''We can't,'' wailed Lavinia. ''My mama said it would be sinful, with Jessamine maybe lying in a gutter somewhere, or floating facedown in the river or with her clothes all torn and—''

''I believe we grasp your meaning, Miss Marsh,'' said Lee. ''Is there any reason to believe Miss Dade might have been abducted? Does she have a special beau?''

''All of them,'' wailed Marybelle.

''Oh, hush, Marybelle,'' snapped Ruthellen. ''The Cartland boys were just sparkin' her 'cause they think she's fast. And as for James Valentine, he wouldn't know a good woman if he fell over one.''

Emerald LaPaix's prim mouth twitched in silent agreement.

Lee was putting together a clearer picture of the situation. He shuddered for the future of his hotel if these princesses had a bad time at the ball.

Wherever this Jessamine was, he knew he had to get her back posthaste. Finding her would undoubtedly be the easy part; it was getting her back that might prove sticky. But Lee intended to do it, using whatever means necessary. He'd sling her over his shoulder if he had to. And then he was going to see to it that the brat made the proper apologies. After that, Lee thought, these harpies were welcome to her hide.

The Imperial Hotel's lobby was paneled in teak and carpeted with rose-and-cream Persian rugs. A golden light fell from massive brass chandeliers, warming the crimson satin of the settees and wing chairs. The room that Alpha Parker had designed so well usually gave Lee a feeling of well-being, but now, as he strode across the lobby toward the hotel's entrance, he felt contentious and as mean as an alligator.

Fayette beckoned him from a door that led to a back hallway. When Lee waved him off, the grizzled old man began gesturing wildly with both arms.

"Mr. Lee. Psst. Mr. Lee."

Unable to ignore his majordomo and unwilling to have the old man break into a shout, Lee turned in his direction.

"What is it, Fayette? I was just on my way outside." Lee tried to keep the irritation out of his voice, but he wasn't entirely successful.

"There's hants, Mr. Lee," Fayette whispered urgently.

"What?"

"We got hants in the hotel."

Now Lee noticed the panic in Fayette's eyes. "Hants? You mean ghosts, Fayette?"

He nodded vigorously. "Yessir. Ghosts. Up on the fourth floor. Magnolia done seen 'em." Fayette gestured behind him and called over his shoulder. "Magnolia, you get over here, girl, and tell Mr. Lee what you seen up there on four."

A diminutive woman with her dark hair woven in several stiff braids appeared from behind Fayette's back. She was wearing a maid's uniform—a long black dress adorned only by a crisp white apron. The starched white cap on her head was askew.

"You tell him now. Don't be 'fraid. Tell Mr. Lee what you seen."

She glanced up at Lee, who towered above her, then stared at the floor again. "I didn't see nothin', Mr. Lee." Her voice dropped to a whisper. "I heard somethin'."

Lee, by now, was making a heroic effort at patience. "'Nolia, tell me what you heard. Don't be afraid. Just tell me what happened."

Magnolia raised her big brown eyes and this time held Lee's gaze. "I was up on four, smoothin' the linens on the bed. There wasn't no blanket, so I was goin' to fetch one out of the wardrobe, but when I pulled on the latch, a hant spoke out."

"And what did he say?" Lee asked.

Magnolia shook her head. "Wasn't no he. It was a she. And she said, 'Git out o' here,' so I got."

Fayette stepped forward. "What you want me to do about it, Mr. Lee?"

Lee's full lips curved in a slow smile. "Nothing, Fayette. I'll take care of it myself. What room was it, Magnolia?"

"Four-one-two, sir."

"Thank you. Fayette, why don't you take Magnolia back to the kitchen and see that she has a cup of chamomile tea and some of those macaroons?"

"Yessir. I'll do that. What you goin' to do, Mr. Lee?"

"I'm going to catch me a she-ghost, Fayette."

With the key to room 412 clenched in his fist, Lee mounted the wide marble staircase from the lobby. He hadn't yet decided just how he was going to capture young

Miss Jessamine Dade, but he didn't for a moment question his ultimate success.

It occurred to him as he climbed the stairs that the little witch had so far been quite successful herself. She had stolen the attentions, if not the hearts, of several young men. She had made enemies of at least three debutantes, one of whom was her very own cousin. And she had managed to elude what was most likely a rather impassioned search party, while scaring the drawers off a superstitious maid.

Lee had to laugh. Stair by stair, his curiosity grew, and the edge wore off his anger. He wasn't going to fling open the wardrobe and lunge for her—although that was exactly what he would do were Miss Jessamine Dade a man. But it had been Lee's experience that females tended to fight like cats when cornered, and having been scratched once or twice in his youth, he had no intention of tangling with one at his advanced age of thirty-two.

There had to be a better way to smoke her out. Well, that was it, of course. He'd smoke the little hellcat out. Put a good scare into her, too, then yank her downstairs to make amends.

On the second floor, Lee located a metal trash basket and a bucket of sand, one of several on each floor to be used in case of fire. He continued to the third floor, where he purloined a copy of the *New Orleans Sun* from a guest's door, then crumpled several sheets and dropped them into the trash basket. Then, with his props in hand and his jaw set like granite, he mounted the stairs to the fourth floor.

The door of room 412 was ajar, most likely left that way by the frightened 'Nolia. The lamp was still lit inside, and he could see the fresh white linen on the tall four-poster bed, as well as the cabbage rose paper on the walls. And there was the wardrobe—tall and dignified, its double doors closed. Lee slipped the brass room key in his pocket, then

quietly placed the paper-stuffed trash basket by the open door.

Slowly, as if he were a man with little to do and ample time in which to do it, he reached into his pocket for a cheroot and a match. The fine Virginia tobacco rated an appreciative sniff before he popped the wooden match with his thumbnail. After his cigar was lit, Lee took several leisurely puffs, and, with a devilish smile, he dropped the live match into the basket.

A tongue of flame licked up one side of the basket, then the other, and it wasn't long before the paper was curling and blackening and Lee was grinning as he fanned the smoke into the room.

As a gray haze began to build, he kept an eye on the tall wardrobe. Nothing happened.

When nothing happened for several more minutes, it occurred to him that the girl might have fled the room on 'Nolia's heels and taken up a new hiding place. He really had no way of knowing she was still inside. His devilish smile changed to a scowl. Damnation! Wouldn't he feel a fool and a half if the little witch was now watching him from another room.

Suddenly the wardrobe door swung open. A long, slim, white-stockinged leg emerged. It was quickly followed by another leg, and then by yards and yards of white muslin and ruffles and bows. The she-ghost!

Her back was to the door, and her hair hung in a loose chignon, raven and netted with pearls. The massive wardrobe dwarfed her. She couldn't have been but an inch or two over five feet. The girl looked as delicate as a teacup.

And when she turned fully toward him, through the haze Lee saw two of the biggest, most violet eyes he'd ever seen. Soft, velvety, huge. And very, very frightened.

His first instinct was to wrap her in his arms and tell her she was safe. His second, which he followed, was to relish

the sight of her panic as she stepped forward and was yanked back against the wardrobe by her skirt. Clamping the cigar between his teeth, Lee picked up the bucket of sand and poured it into the wastebasket, extinguishing the blaze. Then he entered the smoky room and slammed the door behind him.

Jessamine Dade was tugging on her skirt with both hands and cursing a blue streak.

Lee did more than simply stand in the doorway. He had drawn himself up, all six feet, two inches of him, and imposed himself on the threshold. The cigar remained clenched in his back teeth, and his lips were pulled back in a grin.

The girl's violet eyes cut through the haze. "I could use a little help," she snapped, "or are you just going to stand there grinning like a jackal and watch me roast?"

"I was thinking about it," Lee drawled, taking the cigar from his teeth and stepping forward as he removed a silk handkerchief from his pocket, unfurled it and handed it to her, along with his cigar. "Here. Hold this while I see what's got you battened down." He lowered himself to his knees beside her, then shouldered her legs aside in order to lean into the wardrobe.

"Well?" she said. "Come on. Be quick about it."

Lee brought his wide shoulders out of the walnut wardrobe, eased back on his heels, and looked up at her. "Take your damn dress off if you're in such a confounded rush." He crossed his arms and cocked a single eyebrow. "Or would you rather perish in all that virgin white?"

Jessamine dabbed at her eyes with his handkerchief a moment, then flung his cigar to the floor. "Fine," she said. With both hands, she ripped the bodice of her dress to the waist. Pearl buttons flew across the room, several of them hitting Lee's astonished face.

He stood up as she struggled to undo one of the catches at her waist. "Whoa... Settle down, little girl. There's no

fire," he said, stomping out his cigar before it could burn through the carpet and grasping her firmly by the wrists.

"Let me go," she snapped, trying to wrest herself from his powerful hold.

The front of her dress was open, inviting Lee's gaze to the spills of soft flesh above her lacy corset. The more she struggled, the more she spilled. He was enjoying the view immensely—until she kicked him in the shin.

He howled and brought her wrists around her back, holding her tight against him so that she couldn't do him any more damage.

"Damnation!" Lee gritted. "If you'd hold still for a minute, we'd both be a lot better off. Just hold still. You're not going to fry, Miss Jessamine. There's no fire. It's only a little smoke."

She did hold still then, but it wasn't the stillness of calm. He could feel her body building up a blistering head of steam.

"Let me go," she demanded, her face pressed into the frills of his white silk shirt.

"Not until you promise to behave," he said, rather enjoying the feel of her in his arms, the fragrance of heliotrope in her dark hair, the flutter of her heart against his ribs.

"I promise to scratch your eyes out." She tried to wriggle out of his arms, but he only tightened them. "My father put you up to this, didn't he?"

"Nope," he drawled, his lips brushing the top of her head. "I thought of it all by myself. And you'd best save all the eye-scratching for the young ladies lying in wait for you downstairs. They mean you a lot more harm than I do."

Her body slackened within his arms. "All right. I promise. Just let me go."

Lee loosened his embrace slowly, releasing her wrists when he was fairly sure the fight had gone out of her. One

look at her face, and he knew he had won. The fire in her violet eyes had gone out.

Jessamine dabbed at them again, stepping back. "I trust you had sense enough to extinguish whatever it was that created this infernal mess."

He nodded, savoring the sight of five feet two inches of female panic and fury reorganizing itself into icy disdain.

"Well, then," she sniffed, "do you imagine we might open a window now that all the excitement has transpired?"

Lee crossed the room, pushed back the velvet overdrapes and the lacy sheers and eased up the heavy sash. A cool northern breeze rushed in. About as cool as Miss Jessamine Dade was trying to be, he thought, as the breeze swirled the smoke and blew the wardrobe door soundly against her back.

"Let's get you uncoupled from this piece of furniture," he said, jamming his shoulders once again into the wardrobe and finding the place where her skirt was snagged. As he jerked the fabric free, a splinter gashed him. Lee swore as he backed out and stood up, his finger in his mouth.

Once freed, Jessamine went immediately to the dresser, with its rose marble top and carved-leaf pulls. The tall Dresden pitcher was empty, so she touched her tongue to Lee's silk handkerchief and proceeded to wipe a spot of soot from her cheek. Lee, meanwhile, was gathering pearl buttons from the floor. When he had a handful, he put them on the bedside table, then gave the tasseled bellpull a firm yank.

He'd been watching her out of the corner of his eye, his reflexes still on a hair-trigger, but she seemed totally absorbed in wiping her face and patting her hair into place. Lee wondered if she had forgotten about the front of her dress, or more exactly its lack of a front. She wasn't brazen so much as natural, as if those firm mounds of flesh above her

corset were of no more interest than her pert nose or her elbow.

She caught his gaze in the mirror. "I have three brothers, sir. Modesty is impossible, but please do not take my disarray for more than it is."

Lee cleared his throat and was about to inform her that he took no interest at all in her snowy cleavage when a hesitant knock came on the door. "Come in," he called.

The door creaked slowly open, and 'Nolia's dark face peeked in.

"Magnolia, we're going to need a pitcher of water, and some white thread and a needle," Lee said.

"Yessir, Mr. Lee." The little maid's head bobbed and disappeared from the door.

"You act like you own the place," Jessamine sniffed.

"I do," Lee replied. Stretching out on the bed, he leaned back against the carved headboard, his arms locked behind his neck. His boots were black against the white linens.

"Oh, *that* Lee," she said. "I might have known."

"Your girlfriends told you some tales, did they, Miss Jessamine?" He thought she probably didn't need a corset at all; her tiny waist nipped in all by itself, and those breasts would ride high on her with or without the benefit of stays.

"They're not my girlfriends, Mr. Kincannon. I barely know those silly young women." She glanced at him in the mirror, one shapely brow quirked upward. "But they did have a tale or two to relate."

"Well, don't believe everything you hear," he said dismissively. "Especially about me."

There was another knock on the door, and the maid walked in hesitantly, her eyes locked on Jessamine.

"That's your hant, 'Nolia," Lee laughed. "Here. Just put the pitcher on the dresser and give me the needle and thread."

Magnolia moved quickly, and was quickly gone in a swish of black skirt.

Lee pulled a long piece of thread from the wooden spool and bit it off. He threaded the needle at arm's length. "Now," he said, patting the bed beside him. "Let's get all these buttons back where they belong. Come over here, Miss Jessamine."

"I'm quite capable of sewing on my own buttons," she said, edging next to him on the bed.

"I wouldn't doubt it at all," said Lee, "but I aim to see this gets done." Not to mention, he thought, making sure her buttons wouldn't fly off once she was dancing, giving some young swain a lovely eyeful. "Sit up straight," he said.

She did, and Lee reached for the loose halves of her bodice, pulling them up. With one hand still on Jessamine, he reached to the bedside table for a pearl button and then began to sew it back on what had once been her collar.

Jessamine raised her chin. "You're going to stab me with that thing," she said.

Lee pursed his lips in concentration. "Shh. Only if I have to." He continued to weave the needle in and out of the soft muslin fabric, smiling to himself.

"You seem to find this all very amusing, Mr. Kincannon."

"A little," he said. "Don't you?"

She took in a deep breath, unconsciously expanding her chest and causing the back of Lee's hand to brush across the top of her breast. "I've been carted eight hundred miles downriver to meet a legion of pale and shiftless boys in the hope that one of them will marry me and get me out of Missouri and off my father's back. The judge—my father—has no love for me. He hopes an eligible New Orleans boy will feel otherwise. If that strikes you as amusing, then you have a very peculiar sense of humor."

Lee thought of the bevy of belles downstairs, any of whom, he was certain, would happily travel thousands of miles to trap one of Louisiana's young dandies. "It strikes me as different," he said, breaking off a thread and reaching for another button. "What is it makes you so different, Miss Jessamine?" he asked as he began on the button right at cleavage level. And how could the judge, or any man, he thought, fail to love those velvet eyes?

"I'm not different," she said. "I'm simply needed at home. At Riverbend. I have a hundred acres of hemp that's been harvested and, depending on the weather, could be ready any day for gathering and shocking."

She leaned away, and Lee pulled her closer with a firm grip on the muslin. "Surely there's someone looking after the place in your absence," he said.

Jessamine shrugged her shoulders, causing Lee to yelp as he pricked his finger. "Sorry," she said. "Oh, I have help. There's Eamon Dobbs, my overseer, who only works when I threaten to fire him. And then there are a dozen slaves, ten of whom only work when the overseer threatens them life and limb. The two other slaves are the sole hard workers, other than myself. By now they have probably run off in sheer disgust." She sighed. "In short, Mr. Kincannon, I have many obligations, and very little time for foolishness." She looked down at his agile fingers. "Are you almost done?"

He ignored her. "You have brothers. Don't they take their share of the responsibility?"

Jessamine's mouth drew into a taut line. "My brothers, like our father, confine themselves to whiskey and lengthy political discussions. They take little interest in the running of Riverbend."

Lee searched her deep violet eyes, pricking his finger again, but paying it no mind. "You're mighty young to be taking on such burdens. You can't be a minute over fif-

teen," he said. Two years less than half his own disreputable age, he noted silently.

With her chin at a defiant tilt, she said, "I was seventeen last week. And Riverbend is not a burden. It is my heritage."

He proceeded to the next button, just below her breasts. "Your heritage is in some jeopardy with this war coming on, Miss Jessamine. Have you taken sides, or are you not politically inclined like your father?" She looked about as politically inclined as a wildflower, but then, wildflowers didn't run plantations single-handedly.

"I haven't time for politics, but I intend to see that Riverbend survives, no matter who succeeds if this hateful confrontation comes to pass." Jessamine angled her head, seeking his dark eyes. "Are you a rebel, Mr. Kincannon?"

He laughed softly. "I blow with the wind, Miss Jessamine," he said. "Last button. Sit up straight and don't breathe." He held the needle in his teeth as he used two hands to adjust the fabric at her waist. "Actually," Lee said, beginning to sew again, "I am a businessman, and, like you, I intend to see that my businesses survive, even prosper, during this war."

He put his head nearly in her lap in order to bite off the last piece of thread. "That is," he said, grinning, "if my businesses survive your preposterous behavior. Do you mind telling me why it takes a whole ballroom full of agitation, a posse, and a near-conflagration to get one little girl ready for a party? What the devil was it you hoped to accomplish this evening by causing such an uproar?"

For a moment Jessamine looked somewhat chastened, but then her chin once again assumed an arrogant angle. "My father refuses to listen to me. He's been ignoring my pleas to go home. I thought this might be a rather vivid way to impress him with my seriousness."

"Vivid indeed," commented Lee.

"If I've failed," she said, "I shall book passage on a steamboat and return to Missouri alone."

Not on one of my boats, Lee thought. He nearly always appreciated a headstrong female, but not when she threatened to bankrupt one of his hotels or possibly even sink one of his boats. He stood up, put his hands under her arms, and lifted her feather-light body up. He began buttoning the delicate fabric, slowly, from the bottom.

Lee glanced at her firmly set mouth. It had not escaped his notice that, while she had explained her perverse behavior, Jessamine Dade had by no means apologized for it. Oddly, she reminded Lee of himself at the same age—defiant, determined to do things her own way whatever havoc she wreaked. She might look like a porcelain doll, but this little girl was all Missouri mule.

When he started to speak, he discovered that his mouth was dry and his throat constricted. Damned if his hands weren't trembling as he pressed each button through its proper hole. All for this little violet-eyed girl.

He placed his hands on her shoulders, as much to steady them as to survey his handiwork, then looked into her eyes. He swallowed hard. "Is that what you want, then?" he asked huskily. "To go home?"

She didn't blink. "It's the only thing I want," she said.

He could do it, of course. One telegram to a friend in St. Louis. One telegram back to Judge Dade in New Orleans, begging his assistance in some fabricated political crisis. Then the judge would be headed back north—bag, baggage, sons and sole daughter. The question was, did Lee want to let this woman-child get away from him so fast?

As he deliberated, Jessamine took his hand in hers. "You have a splinter, Mr. Kincannon," she said softly. Without another word, she lowered her head, took his finger in her mouth and gently sucked, then slid her lower teeth along his flesh and sucked again.

"There," she said, inspecting her handiwork and picking a sliver off her pink tongue. When she looked up into his face, her eyes were soft and as innocent of guile as spring blossoms. "Better?"

Lee's heart was battering his rib cage, and his blood thundering through his veins. He was bewitched by the innocence of those eyes, and at the same time rocked by the sensual promise of that pink mouth. He took in a deep, ragged breath. He'd never wanted a woman more. Or less, he thought to his surprise, to his complete and weak-kneed amazement, as he inched away from her.

He wanted to wrap himself around her, to protect her from the claws of the debutantes downstairs, from the worries that etched her delicate brow, from the hard privations of the coming war. He wanted to protect this pansy-eyed child from everyone and everything that might seek to do her harm.

Damnation! What he needed to do, above all else, was to protect her from an inveterate rogue named Lee Kincannon, whose hardened heart could cut her own to shreds.

His voice was thick with desire and regret. "If home is what you want, Miss Jessamine," he said, "I'll see what I can do."

And fast, he thought. For your sake, little girl.

Chapter One

Autumn, 1864

Eamon Dobbs stomped out of the tavern, slapping his felt hat against his leg, mindful of the laughter at his back. He was drunk, and the heel of his left boot was missing. When he stumbled on the uneven pavement, he appeared to be doing a three-step jig.

"God dang it. What is it you want with me at half past five in the evening?" he bellowed to the woman standing before him on the sidewalk. "It's after quitting time, I'll have you know."

"Quitting time! You quit a day and a half ago, Mr. Dobbs, and it's taken me this long to find you," Jessamine bellowed back at him. "Now if you . . ."

The tavern door opened, and a stout man in a soiled frock coat came out, grinning. He tipped his hat with exaggerated politeness.

"Evening, Miss Dade. Eamon. I see she found you again."

"Go on home, Floyd," snarled Dobbs, "before your old lady comes looking for you."

"Last time she did that was twenty years ago," the stout man said. "She's still sorry she found me." He continued

down the sidewalk, chortling, trying to get his hat to stay on his head.

"Mr. Dobbs," said Jessamine, only to be interrupted again.

"Aw, go on back home, will you? I'll get there when I'm good and ready."

"Our hemp is good and ready, Mr. Dobbs. If I don't see you out in the fields with at least six men at first light tomorrow, you needn't bother to come back."

"The judge hired me. I expect he'd be the one to fire me," he shot back.

"I expect he would, but the judge is in Jefferson City right now, as you well know." Jessamine pulled on her butter-colored kid gloves, pressing down between each of her fingers. Then she tightened the bow knot of her gray silk bonnet. "Are you coming with me in the wagon, Mr. Dobbs, or do you prefer to walk?"

Eamon Dobbs cast furtive glances up and down the sidewalk to make certain there were no witnesses to his capitulation. "I expect I'll ride. Did you drive that wagon all the way to town alone?"

Jessamine glared at him. How she hated having to rely on such a lazy, slovenly good-for-nothing. "No, Mr. Dobbs. I left Riverbend with a coachman and three footmen, but they joined up with a rebel outfit at Walnut Creek," she said sarcastically.

"I thought the judge told you..."

She turned, gave her stiff petticoat a kick, then strode to the buckboard, ignoring the rest of the overseer's remark. If she did everything the judge told her, Riverbend would be in an even sorrier state than it was right now. There was no need to look over her shoulder to see if Dobbs was following. She knew he was. They had played out this charade innumerable times before.

Jessamine hiked her gray plaid skirt to climb into the front seat of the wagon, and then she waited, her violet eyes trained on the gathering clouds overhead, her gloved fingers drumming on her lap, until she felt the thump that meant the overseer was sprawled in back. She gave the reins a shake.

"Come on, old Daniel. You can go back to the barn now."

The roan gelding shook his head and began the five-mile journey back to Riverbend.

Moments after the buckboard crossed the bridge over Walnut Creek, six Union soldiers rode out of the elm grove behind them. They spurred their horses hard, and it was only a matter of minutes from the time Jessamine spotted them until one of them had caught Daniel's bridle and the rest had surrounded the wagon, pistols drawn.

"Afternoon, ma'am," said the soldier who was restraining Daniel. "I'm Major Thomas Harding of the Third Ohio Fusiliers. I'd like to ask you a few questions."

"Certainly, Major," said Jessamine. "You could have just called out for me to stop, rather than put on this display of military might. And you may release my horse."

"Yes, ma'am," he said, letting go of the bridle, then touching a finger to the brim of his hat.

He wore a regulation dark blue uniform whose brass buttons were either new or recently polished, Jessamine noticed. His boots, too, were polished to a high gloss. He had a wide copper-colored mustache and full sideburns—cultivated, no doubt, to make him appear old enough for his rank. Jessamine would have been surprised if he was much older than her own twenty-one years.

She noticed, too, that the major was riding a white stallion with a salt-and-pepper mane and tail and two black patches on his forelock. Pepper. The horse had been a gift

from her brother, Charles, before he had left to join the Confederate Army in the summer of '61. Jessamine had been forced to sell the animal a year ago to put a new roof on the barn.

"I admire your horse, Major," she said now.

"Thank you, ma'am."

A soldier called from the rear of the wagon. "Major, there's an old geezer passed out back here under a blanket."

"Is he armed?" asked Major Harding.

"No, sir."

"I assure you, Major, Mr. Dobbs is not armed. Nor is he dangerous—except to himself." Jessamine looked up at the sky. The sun was slipping into a far bend of the Missouri River, casting the clouds overhead a deep purple. The air began to smell like rain. "I'd like to get home before the weather breaks, Major," she said.

Major Harding, too, regarded the sky, his coppery mustache turning down at the edges. "Our camp near Foley was attacked last night by some irregulars, ma'am. I lost five of my men, and managed only to wing one of theirs."

"Foley is better than twenty miles away," Jessamine said.

"Yes, ma'am. But we're pretty sure they rode this direction."

"Well, I haven't seen anyone suspicious between here and Riverbend. Not even a turtle crossing the road."

"Riverbend?" he asked, nudging the stallion closer to her.

"My plantation, Major. It's about three miles west of here. On the river." She pointed. "See right there, where the rain's already coming down?"

One of the soldiers, whose horse had drifted sidestep from the rear of the wagon, interrupted. "Ask her if she's got slaves, Major."

Jessamine ignored him and spoke to the officer. "You needn't ask. When Mr. Lincoln issued his proclamation, all of our people were given their papers. Most of them chose to remain. I can assure you, sir, Riverbend is well within the law."

"You a rebel, lady?" the soldier asked. He twisted in his saddle and called back to the others. "Hey! We got us a female rebel!"

"That will be enough, Corporal," snapped Major Harding.

The young soldier turned his horse and retreated to the back of the wagon.

The major looked apologetic. "I'm sorry, ma'am, but I have to ask. About your political leanings?"

"I do not lean, Major. I grow hemp."

"Do you have a husband?" he asked.

There was something in his pale blue eyes that led Jessamine to conclude that his question was more personal than political. "I do not," she said briskly. "I reside with my father, Judge Levander Dade, and I have three brothers, one of whom was killed at Pea Ridge, and another of whom is in a Confederate prison at this very moment." Jessamine omitted the fact that Charles had been wearing Confederate gray when he died.

"I'm sorry, miss," Major Harding said. "It's just that you never know who you're talking to in Missouri. Whether they're for the Union or against it."

"So I understand," said Jessamine. "But I can assure you that no one currently at Riverbend is politically engaged on either side. As for Mr. Dobbs back there, I think you can see for yourself."

Major Harding appeared reluctant to let her go. He shifted in his saddle and seemed to be searching for words.

"A lone woman oughtn't to be so far from home. Especially one as pretty as you. May I offer you an escort back

to your farm, Miss Dade? I would be happy to drive your wagon for you."

Even in the waning light, Jessamine could see that his cheeks had flushed beneath his coppery sideburns. She was flattered but uninterested. "Thank you, no. I know the road quite well, Major. I would, however, like to be on my way before the rain begins." She smiled sweetly.

"Perhaps I could call at Riverbend tomorrow," he said, "just to see that you've made it home safely?"

"Perhaps," said Jessamine.

He touched the brim of his hat again, then called to the soldiers at the back of the wagon. "We're riding on, men. Let's look sharp."

Jessamine lost no time in picking up the reins and flicking them to make Daniel take off like a shot. "Goodbye, Major Harding," she called over her shoulder. "Best of luck in your search."

Twenty minutes later, cold and drenched, Jessamine arrived at Riverbend. The tall, sapling-thin Sampson greeted her with a tarpaulin.

"We were starting to worry about you, Miss Jess. Here. Give me those reins, and you scurry on in the house." He draped the cover about her head and shoulders as he helped Jessamine down from the wagon.

"Thank you, Sampson. That wet lump of blanket in back is Mr. Dobbs. See that he gets to bed, will you, please?"

"I surely will, Miss Jess. You get on inside now."

Jessamine picked up her wet skirt and raced for the back door. Rain was pouring off the eaves so hard that she had to walk through a wall of water to enter the kitchen.

Maisie turned at the sound of the downpour. "Oh, child, you is one wet, bedraggled sight."

Jessamine stood silently and let the woman minister to her. Maisie always smelled like bacon grease and molasses,

with just a hint of sour mash on her breath. For Jessamine, they were the fragrances of comfort—for the mountainous, black-as-midnight Maisie had nursed her, diapered her, bathed her, and sung her to sleep.

When the gray plaid dress lay puddled at her feet, Maisie said, "Now you get on upstairs and take off them wet things and put on that yellow wrapper."

Jessamine planted a wet kiss on the woman's cheek. "What would I do without you, Maisie?"

"Catch your death, I 'spect," she huffed. "You find that derelict Dobbs?"

Her mouth thinned in disgust. "I found him. I almost wish I hadn't."

Maisie clucked her tongue. "Who else gonna work for such piddlin' pay? Bad as he is, least he's stayed by you since times got bad."

"You call working two days and drinking five 'staying by me'?" Jessamine snapped.

"Two days beats no days at all, child. Now you get on upstairs."

After struggling out of her wet corset and pantaloons, Jessamine put on dry underwear and the yellow muslin wrapper Maisie had laid out on her high four-poster bed. She pulled a towel from the cabinet beneath the washstand, held it to her face and breathed in the distinct fragrance of sunshine. It made her feel happy and carefree for a moment, as if the war had never happened. Then, as she bent forward to wrap the towel around her hair, there came a knock on her door.

Without waiting for a reply, Maisie backed into the room, her arms cradling a large silver tray. "I knows you too distressed to eat supper, Miss Jess, so I brung you some tea and cinnamon toast." She put the tray on a butler's table in front of the fireplace.

Jessamine eyed the array of plates. "Tea and toast, Maisie?"

Maisie planted her fists on her hips. "That li'l ol' thing? That a soft-boiled egg."

"And this?" Jessamine pointed to a flowered Haviland plate.

"Them put-up snap beans you so crazy about," said Maisie. "Now you eat.

Jessamine sighed. "You take good care of me."

"Somebody got to, child," Maisie said as she closed the door behind her.

Jessamine listened to the woman's heavy tread down the stairs. Thank God for Maisie, she thought. Without her, it was entirely possible Jessamine wouldn't have survived. When her mother had died, three days after Jessamine's birth, the judge had intended to send the tiny girl away. But Maisie, who had just given birth to Sampson, would not stand for it, and had made the judge's existence hell until he handed over his infant daughter to her care.

And here she was, twenty-one years later, with Maisie still caring for her. Jessamine sighed and picked at the food on her tray. It wasn't like her to mope and feel sorry for herself, but tonight—with Dobbs and the Yankees and the infernal rain—she felt entitled to a minute or two of self-pity.

The rain drummed on the roof and spattered the windowpanes. A shutter thumped against the side of the house, and Jessamine made a mental note to have somebody fix it. Fix it. Fix it. Riverbend was falling apart. The white paint was peeling off the boards of the two-story house. The railing on the wraparound porch was wobbly. A hinge was loose on the front door, and the screw had been misplaced. Inside, her mother's furniture still glistened with Maisie's lemon oil, but a shabbiness lurked just under the surface. And the outbuildings were a disgrace.

Her room turned a ghostly blue as lightning flashed, then thunder rattled the windows and the glass chimney of the oil lamp beside her bed. This horrible war, she thought, jamming a fist into the pillow. How she hated it, hated everything about it. It was ruining Riverbend, and there didn't seem to be anything she could do about it. And it was ruining her family, too. Or what was left of it.

The judge had gotten elected to the state legislature in 1861, and since then had spent most of his time at the capital. Her brothers had all left right after the hostilities commenced—dashing Charles riding off to join the Confederate forces in northern Arkansas—quiet Caleb, the youngest, crossing the river into Illinois to ride with the Fourth—and Louis, rifle in one hand, whiskey jug in the other, taking off west on Hecuba, Riverbend's prize mare.

Such changes. Charles was dead now, shot through the heart at Pea Ridge in '62. Caleb, if he was still alive, was moldering in a rebel prison in Georgia. And Louis, when last heard from two years before, had been in Colorado, most likely drinking himself into an early grave.

But despite all the changes, despite the war ripping Missouri to shreds, Jessamine was still at Riverbend, still trying to hold the place together as she always had, with hard work, a shrill tongue, and the tears she never let anyone see. Not even Maisie.

With such thoughts tumbling through her mind, Jessamine dropped off into a fitful sleep.

"Wake up, child. Sampson says you got to get out to the barn quick," said Maisie.

Jessamine rubbed her eyes. "What? Is it the storm? What time is it, Maisie?"

"Here," Maisie grunted, pulling her up to a sitting position. "I got your wrapper. The rain's done let up some."

"What's happened?" Jessamine asked as the big, powerful woman threaded her arm through a long sleeve of the robe.

"There's trouble, Miss Jess."

"What trouble? Is it a fire? Is someone sick?" Jessamine wracked her brain for possible tragedies.

"It's rebels," whispered Maisie. "One down in the kitchen, and one out in the barn. That one's been hurt bad."

"Oh, Lord!" she said, standing up and finding her other sleeve. "You go on downstairs. I'll be there as quick as I can."

"You hurry now," said Maisie from the door.

Jessamine lit the lamp by her bed and carried it to the washstand. Splashing a good dose of cool water on her face, she then quickly twisted her hair and pinned it.

"Rebels," she muttered. Just what she needed. She lowered the wick on the lamp and trotted down the stairs.

Maisie had stoked the fire in the kitchen, and a fat tallow candle burned in a saucer on the table. Sitting there sipping a cup of coffee, was a young man with wet clothes and slicked-back blond hair. He couldn't have been much past his seventeenth birthday, Jessamine thought, noting the few blond whiskers on his upper lip. His boots were muddy and his plaid shirt was torn. A pistol lay on the table in front of him.

"This here's Mr. Nathan Anderson," Maisie said, gesturing to him with her thumb. "And he ain't the only one."

Jessamine could see that Maisie was ready to take on the whole Confederate Army. "All right, Maisie. We all just need to be calm right now. I believe I'll have a cup of that coffee, please."

"Keep you awake." Maisie snorted. She didn't make a move toward the stove.

Jessamine rolled her eyes heavenward. "It doesn't look as if there will be much opportunity for sleep tonight, does it?" She headed for the big enamel coffeepot herself.

"All right. Set down. I'll get it for you."

"Thank you," Jessamine said stiffly. She pulled out a chair at the table, then asked, "What is it you want with us in the middle of the night, Mr. Anderson?"

The young man ran his fingers through his wet hair. "I don't know your leanings, ma'am—whether you be for or against the Union. Me, and the men I ride with, we're Confederate soldiers. Well, not regular army, exactly, but our captain takes his orders from General Calvin Buford. Are you a secessionist, ma'am?"

"No, I am not. Nor am I pro-Union. I suppose you could say I am neutral."

He fixed her with his weary, bloodshot eyes. "Just what does that mean, ma'am?"

Maisie put a cup of coffee on the table in front of Jessamine. "It mean what she say it mean, rebel."

"Thank you, Maisie." Jessamine gave her a hard look before turning back to the young man. "It means, Mr. Anderson, that I spend all of my time and energy just trying to keep this plantation going."

"Then will you help us?"

"In what way?" Jessamine asked.

Young Anderson leaned forward. "My captain's been shot, ma'am. He's doing real poorly. Your man's seeing to him out in the barn right now, but if I can't find a doctor for him real soon . . . well, he's like to die."

The boy looked frightened to death, Jessamine thought. "There's a doctor in Newton. Why didn't you take him there?"

"You don't understand, ma'am . . . ."

"Who you sayin' don't understand, you young pup?" Maisie snapped.

"Please, Maisie," said Jessamine. "Let's let him finish."

"There's Union troops all over three counties looking for us. And they know one of us caught a bullet. Most likely every doctor around is being watched right now or, if he ain't, he will be soon."

"Oh, I see," said Jessamine.

"Please help us, ma'am."

"Well, I would never send a sick or wounded man away from my door. But what would you have me do? I haven't the skills to care for him myself. No one here does."

"I figured you could send for a doctor, tell him it's you or one of your loved ones needs him."

"And when he arrives and discovers the circumstances?" Jessamine asked, looking pointedly at the pistol lying on the table between them.

He followed her gaze. "I guess we'll just deal with that when the time comes."

"Yes. I see." Jessamine sipped her coffee, then, deliberately, set it down on the table again. "Perhaps we should go out to the barn and see how your captain is doing before we make any decisions."

Anderson stood up, pushing back his chair. "That'd be fine, ma'am." He picked up the gun and stuck it in his belt as he followed her out the back door.

The storm had blown east, and a few clouds were scudding across the sky, lit silver by a waning moon. Jessamine lifted the hem of her robe as she walked the muddy distance from the back door to the barn. Nathan Anderson held her elbow lightly, tightening his grip when she slipped in a puddle.

Jessamine tried the side door. It was locked. She rapped softly.

"Who's there?" Sampson called from inside.

"Sampson, it's me. Jessamine. I'm with the other rebel. It's all right. Unlock the door."

Inside the barn, the air was warm, heavy with the smells of hay and horse. Daniel nodded in his stall. A lantern hung from a low rafter, shedding a cozy yellow light on the floor.

"Where is he?" whispered Jessamine.

Sampson angled his head to the right. "Over there. In Old Pepper's stall. Keeps passing out and coming to."

She didn't know why she felt compelled to whisper, but she did. "Sampson, what are we to do?" she asked him.

"Depends on you, Miss Jess. That rebel needs a doctor, that's for sure."

"The only one close is old Doc Ferguson in Newton. What if we get him out here and then he refuses to help?"

Sampson shrugged his narrow shoulders. "Miss Jess, I'd say we ought to cross them bridges as we get to 'em. We don't even know if he'll come yet, do we?"

She heard a raucous snort. "Is that the captain?"

Sampson grinned. "No. That's Dobbs. He's up there." He pointed to the hayloft. "Pretty near killed hisself tryin' to get up there, too."

Dobbs! It seemed an eternity ago that she'd carted him back from town. "We can't let him know about this, Sampson. Eamon Dobbs can keep a secret about as well as a mynah bird. Perhaps we'd better get the captain into the house."

"Best do anyway, Miss Jess. This night air don't do no-body no good."

Jessamine took a deep breath and followed Sampson toward the stall. She could see the wounded rebel's legs—one extended, the other slightly cocked and listing away from his body. She saw his light gray breeches and tall black boots spattered with mud. Or was it blood? she wondered. Jessamine's stomach knotted. She wasn't used to dealing with

sickness or injury. Maisie had always seen to the fevers and broken bones at Riverbend.

She became light-headed when she stepped inside the stall and glimpsed the captain's shirt. She grabbed for the wooden partition to steady herself as she stared at the blood.

"He doesn't look too good," she heard Nathan Anderson whisper to Sampson.

"Lost a lot of blood," Sampson whispered back.

She took in the rebel's spread form as he lay on a hay-littered blanket, one arm folded across his chest, the other by his side. His fists were clenched, the knuckles white. His head and shoulders were propped on a pile of hay.

Then Jessamine looked full in the captain's face. His eyes were half-closed, barely focused. His mouth was taut with pain, but it flickered into a weak grin.

"Evening, Miss Jessamine," he drawled.

Chapter Two

The color drained from Jessamine's face. "Oh, my God," she cried. "Oh, dear Lord."

"What is it, Miss Jess?"

"Sampson, I know this man." She sank to her knees, taking Lee Kincannon's hand in hers.

Nathan Anderson leapt in the air, whooping. "Hot damn! I knew this was a lucky place to stop, Captain. Didn't I tell you?" He slapped his hand against his knee. "Hooray!"

"How do you know him, Miss Jess?" Sampson asked suspiciously as he studied the rebel stretched out on the barn floor. "He's not from around here. I never seen him before."

"He's from New Orleans," she said, reaching out with her other hand to smooth the dark and sweat-damp curls from Lee's forehead. "Can you hear me, Mr. Kincannon?"

Lee thought for a moment he was dead, that the Yankee bullet had sent him straight to heaven, to the sweet, unforgettable face of that pansy-eyed child. But he hurt too much to be dead. And heaven was the one place Lee Kincannon was certain he'd never see. When she repeated her question, he tried to focus on her eyes as he attempted a grin. "I'm shot, Miss Jessamine. Not deaf."

Jessamine laughed, despite herself and despite the grim situation. "Yes, and still a varmint, too, as near as I can tell." And as near as she could tell, Lee Kincannon would die if he didn't get medical help. He was pale and soaked with cold sweat, and even now the wound on his shoulder seemed to be pouring out blood.

His lips moved soundlessly. Jessamine leaned close. "The Yankees," he murmured. "You can't—"

"Hush," she said. "You're at Riverbend. You're going to be fine. Now just hold on tight till we get you some help." She gave his hand a reassuring squeeze before standing up.

"First things first," she said, surprised by the steadiness of her voice. "We must move Mr. Kincannon into the house."

Sampson looked down at the sprawled, muscular, six-foot-two Lee. "He's too big for me to tote all by myself," he said.

Jessamine knew they had no time to waste. "Then you get his legs, Sampson, and Mr. Anderson, you pick him up under the arms, but take care not to hurt him."

"Yes, ma'am," said Nathan Anderson, still beaming at their unexpected good fortune. He squatted down beside Lee. "You just let out a yell, Captain, if I don't do this right."

Lee gritted his teeth as they lifted him and struggled to maneuver him out of the horse stall. Suddenly he was floating, and his wide-eyed Jessamine was gone. Or perhaps she had never been there at all.

Jessamine scurried through the kitchen door well ahead of them. "Maisie, we're bringing the wounded reb inside," she said, looking for obstacles that might impede their passage.

"You what?" shouted Maisie.

With her hip, Jessamine shoved the table aside. "You heard me. I said we're bringing him in." She pushed a chair under the table. "I believe we'll put him in Charles's room. That's closest to the stairs. And we're going to need—" Jessamine stopped, her hands dropping lifelessly to her sides. "Oh, Lord, I haven't the least notion what we'll need."

"Miss Jess, you cain't just bring some stranger in this house. And a rebel, too. Your daddy gonna have him a fit."

"But I know him, Maisie. He's the man I told you about from New Orleans. Remember?" She leaned her head a moment on the older woman's broad shoulder.

"You mean that black sheep hotelman? The one what's seven foot tall and handsomer than God?"

"That's the one," Jessamine said as the door opened and the two men carried Lee in feetfirst. "Careful now, Sampson," she said. "You watch that table, you hear?"

Sampson rolled his eyes.

As they carried him past her, Maisie peered down at Lee. "Don't look no seven foot tall to me," she sniffed. "Sampson, you put him in Mr. Charles's room up top of the stairs."

"Yes, Mama," said Sampson, winded by his half of the burden. "The stairs are a mite beyond the door, Mr. Nathan. I'm ready if you are."

Anderson, too, was breathing hard. "Just keep walking. If we stop, I'm gonna drop him."

"You go easy on them stairs," said Maisie as they passed out of the kitchen. "Lord almighty, I hope they don't get that reb's blood all over my carpets."

Jessamine swayed against Maisie's side.

"And you—" Maisie clasped her around the waist and led her to the table "—set down 'fore you fall down. Won't do nobody no good having you pass out, Miss Jess."

Jessamine wilted into a chair, and Maisie put a steaming cup of coffee in front of her. She folded her hands around the cup and felt the warmth seep up through her wrists and arms. "We need to send someone for Doc Ferguson right away. I have to make up a good lie, Maisie. What do you think?"

"Ol' Doc Ferguson believe anything you tell him. What I wants to know is, what you gonna tell your papa?"

Jessamine scowled. "He's not due home for three more days. I'm not going to worry about the judge now. Not with so much else to worry about."

Maisie pointed upward. "That reb look bad, Miss Jess. He ain't gonna be up and about in any three days." Then she gave Jessamine a quizzical look. "He wind up here on purpose, or was it a accident?"

"Accident, I suppose." Her face brightened. "But wasn't it lucky, Maisie?"

The big woman shook her head. "Oh, yes'm. Real lucky. You be seein' just how lucky when them Union soldiers rides up to the door." Maisie turned from the table and began pumping water into a pitcher.

Jessamine placed the pitcher of fresh water on the washstand, then stood over Lee's unconscious form a moment before motioning to Sampson to join her in the hall.

"Sampson, I want you to ride into town and get Doc Ferguson," she said, speaking fast, her thoughts racing ahead of her tongue. "You tell him there's been a hunting accident out here—that my...my cousin is visiting from New Orleans and we were out duck hunting by the river and my gun misfired."

"That ain't no bird shot in his shoulder, Miss Jess. The doc's gonna know that right away."

Exasperated, Jessamine said, "Well, can you think up something better?"

The lanky young man leaned back against the wall and wiped the beads of sweat off his forehead with the back of his hand. "The huntin' part's all right, I 'spect. I'll just tell him it was deer you were huntin'."

"And we need to do something with their horses, I suppose."

"They just rode in on one. Mr. Nathan's horse went lame on him."

"All right. Well, let's just put the captain's horse in Pepper's old stall and say it belongs to my cousin."

Sampson nodded. "Need to clean up in the barn. Lot of blood out there."

Jessamine chewed her lower lip. She hadn't thought of that. "While you're gone, Mr. Anderson or I will see to that." Her eyes searched Sampson's face in panic. "Is there something else we should be doing, Sampson? Help me. I can't think anymore. Is there anything I've forgotten?"

He pushed off the wall. "Can't think of nothing, Miss Jess. Seems like this reb is mighty important to you. He the one you come home from New Orleans all a-twitter about before the war?"

"I was a child then," she said defensively.

Sampson started down the stairs. "Yes, ma'am. And now you a woman, and you all a-twitter again."

It was nearly four in the morning. The bedroom was lit by a few crackling elm logs in the fireplace. The small banjo clock over the mantel ticked softly. Jessamine's skirt swished as she rocked back and forth, her fingers keeping restless time with the clock.

Lee was sleeping now, as he had off and on for the past two hours, never peacefully, and never for long. When he woke and asked for water, Jessamine raised his head and held a glass to his lips. When he moaned, she held his large

hand in both of hers. Now she sat quietly and watched him in the firelight.

His hair was as lavish and dark as she remembered. Four years had merely touched it with silver at the temples. His eyes were still dark and deep-set beneath his finely shaped brows. Profiled in firelight, his jaw was strong, shadowed with more than a day's growth of dark whiskers. His...

Jessamine bade herself stop. She closed her eyes. She was not, as Sampson had so smugly put it, all a-twitter. She had spent the past hour relishing every detail of a night she had tried for so long to banish to a distant corner of her memory. But the visions kept returning. Lee standing in the smoky doorway like a dark and dangerous specter. His strong arms around her like iron. His long, agile fingers weaving the needle back and forth through her bodice. The film of perspiration on his face as she had brazenly teased the splinter from his finger.

He had taken her downstairs after that, and never let her out of his sight, never let her out of his arms, laughing at any man who attempted to cut in as they waltzed.

And when it had come time to say good-night, Jessamine hadn't wanted to leave. He had kissed her hand, and when she asked him if she would be seeing him on the morrow, he had smiled that slow and cagey smile and said, "I expect you'll be twenty miles upriver by supper time tomorrow, Miss Jessamine." And she had been.

The judge had been none too happy to be carting his unbetrothed daughter back north, and he had been furious when the hastily arranged secession assembly proved to be a hoax. In no time at all Jessamine had been home, at Riverbend, right where she had told Lee Kincannon she wanted to be. But it had taken her a while to find any happiness or comfort in it.

Lee stirred now, and Jessamine rushed to the bed, grasping his hand tight in both of hers.

He whispered something she couldn't understand. She bent down, and felt his breath hot on her face as he tried to speak again.

"Jessamine," he said. "My pistol. In my saddlebag."

"You want your gun?" she asked.

"Now," he rasped. "Go get it. And promise me...if they come, you must say I forced you, that Anderson..."

"I'll do no such thing, Lee Kincannon. Now you just lie still and don't worry about anything except getting better."

He gripped her hand even harder. "Damn you, Jessamine. Listen. You could be hanged for helping me. I won't—" His eyes tightened as pain overtook him.

"I'll get your gun," she said softly. Extricating her fingers from his, she tiptoed out of the room.

It was just after dawn when the sound of a wagon woke her. Jessamine rushed from the rocking chair to the window to see Sampson helping Doc Ferguson down from the high seat. She glanced to make certain Lee was still sleeping, then picked up her skirts and raced downstairs to the front door.

The doctor looked as if he had jumped from his bed right into the wagon. His blue-and-white-striped nightshirt was tucked loosely into his pants; one brown suspender was twisted over his shoulder, the other sagging at his hip. His white hair was mussed, and he wore no hat. But he walked toward the door as if he were paying a social call, breathing in the fresh morning air and smiling broadly.

"Oh, hurry, Doc," Jessamine called.

"Morning, Jessamine," he yelled cheerfully. He had some difficulty with the wide front steps—his seventy-year-old joints must have stiffened up on him during the ride from town—so he shuffled his feet as he took one step at a

time. "There's nothing like a crisp autumn morning to get the heart ticking and the blood running," the old man proclaimed. "How are you, dear?" He kissed her on the cheek when he reached the top of the steps.

"I'm fine, Doc, but—"

"Glad to hear it," he said, entering the vestibule and dropping his black leather bag on the Queen Anne library table. "How's your father these days?"

"Well, he's fine, too, but . . ."

"I don't suppose he's home much now that he's a legislator." The doctor's voice boomed in the hallway. He spoke like a man who assumed everyone's hearing was as diminished as his own. "I'd like a cup of coffee, if that wouldn't be an inconvenience, Jessamine. Where's that Maisie of yours?"

"Who's that callin' me?" asked Maisie, appearing suddenly from the kitchen hallway, wiping her hands on her white apron. "Mornin', Doc. Why don't you come on in the kitchen and let me fix you up with some strong chicory coffee. Meantime, Miss Jess, you is wanted in the front parlor." Maisie pointed with her chin.

"But I—" Jessamine stammered. Help was at hand, in the form of Doc Ferguson, and suddenly everyone was behaving as if this were a tea party rather than an emergency.

"In the parlor, Miss Jess," Maisie said firmly, as she took Doc Ferguson by the arm and walked him into the kitchen, extolling the virtues and healing powers of chicory.

"In here, Miss Jess," whispered Sampson.

"What's going on around here?" she asked as she whisked into the parlor.

Sampson slid the paneled oak door closed. "We was detained by some bluecoats on the road a ways back. They questioned the doc up one side and down the other."

"Oh, Lord." It was probably the same patrol that had stopped her yesterday, she thought. "Did they suspect anything?"

Sampson laughed. "I don't rightly know. That Doc Ferguson, he can jus' say good-morning and get you so confused you don't know which way the sun comes up. They asked him why was he rushing out to Riverbend, and he told them a visitor got shot. I can't say whether they believed him or not. Anyway, they rode off east toward town."

Jessamine sighed. "Well, that's a small blessing."

"How's the captain doin'?"

"About the same. Worse. I don't know." Jessamine lifted her chin, and her violet eyes riveted his. "I won't let them take him, Sampson. I want you to know that."

"I figured that right from the start, Miss Jess," he said.

"If the Yankees come, there could be trouble."

"Seems like there's always trouble at Riverbend, one sort or another." He put his hand on her shoulder. "If you're asking me am I with you, Miss Jess, you don't have to ask. And my mama, too. I can't say about the others."

Jessamine's eyes clouded with tears. "Thank you, Sampson. You've been a better brother to me than my own flesh and blood."

"Go on, Miss Jess," he said, his dark face coloring even more. "You and me, we don't need to say these things. We just know them in our hearts."

She sniffed. "I expect you're right. Still, it doesn't hurt to say so every once in a while."

There was a soft knock on the parlor door. When Jessamine called come in, Nathan Anderson's head appeared between the sliding panels.

"Hope I'm not interrupting," he said.

"Not at all. Come in, Mr. Anderson," Jessamine said, astonished that she already felt at ease with this straw-haired boy, when only hours before she'd regarded him as an in-

truder in her home. She supposed it meant that she was a rebel now herself. What was it Lee had said in New Orleans, when she'd asked him if he were a rebel? That he blew with the wind? Well, maybe she did, too. And a hot, strong wind had just blown up from the south.

"I cleaned up the barn," Nathan said, then added sheepishly "and caught me a few winks. I woke up when I heard the wagon. Is the doctor here? How's the captain doing?"

"The doctor just arrived," Jessamine said. "And the captain is doing the same." She paused, thinking how her politics had changed in a single day—how her life had changed. "Mr. Anderson, I want you to know that I intend to do everything in my power to help you and your captain."

"Thank you, ma'am," he said, grinning crookedly.

"Well," she said, as if concluding a meeting, "I believe it's high time we got the doctor upstairs, don't you?" Though her tone was calm and cheerful, Jessamine felt sick with fear and dread.

Upstairs in the bedroom, Maisie had opened all the drapes and the early-morning sunlight warmed and colored the room. The fire had burned down to a bed of white ashes. When Jessamine came in, after stealing a few moments to wash her face and re-pin her hair, Doc Ferguson was sitting on the bed beside Lee, jabbering away while he removed the bloody cloths packed against the wound.

"From New Orleans, are you? I was there once, in '45. Or was it '46? Oh, well. Don't suppose it matters much."

Lee was barely alert, his dark eyes half-closed, his face nearly as pale as the pillowcase.

"Pretty city," the doctor continued, his hand now pressing firmly against Lee's forehead. "Hot, though. Don't know as I'd like to live there."

"How is he, Doc?" asked Jessamine, picking up the blood-soaked cloths the doctor dropped on the floor.

"Right poorly," Doc Ferguson replied. He pointed to his black bag at the foot of the bed. "You want to hand that thing up this way, Miss Jessamine? Careful now. It's a mite heavy."

Jessamine picked up the worn double-handled bag and carried it over to him, then resumed her vigil as Doc Ferguson fished through the bag and mumbled to himself. He laid various items on top of the quilt, one by one.

"Is that gal Maisie here?" he asked without looking up.

"I's here."

"We're going to need lots of cloth, Maisie. I don't suppose Miss Jessamine would mind if you tore up some of her bed linens, would you, Miss Jessamine?"

"No, Doc."

"You leave some of them whole, Maisie, and tear me a couple dozen real long strips. 'Bout as wide as your hand. You got that?"

"Yessir," said Maisie obediently.

"And don't be too long now," he said.

"No sir." Maisie patted Jessamine's arm. "You give me them rags you got, Miss Jess."

Jessamine looked down. She'd been twisting them without even realizing it, and now Lee's blood was on her hands.

"Thank you, Maisie," she said, handing her the bloody cloths.

"That's all right, honey."

Suddenly Jessamine felt useless. "What can I do, Doc?" she asked.

"Well, Miss Jessamine, I recall your papa is a drinking man. Is that right?"

"Yes, that's right."

"I'll just ask you then to go and get a bottle of brandy or some such." Doc Ferguson turned his watery blue eyes on Lee and winked broadly. "How's that sound, young man?"

"Like I've died and gone to heaven, Doc," said Lee.

Jessamine threw up her hands. "Is that all you two can think of? Drinking? At a time like this? I'm ashamed of you both. Especially you, Doc."

Sampson took her arm and ushered her to the door. "Miss Jess," he whispered, "the whiskey's just for the captain. The army done confiscated all the doc's chloroform." He nearly pinched her arm to make his point. "You understand? This ain't gonna be no picnic for him."

Jessamine returned quickly with a bottle of the judge's finest brandy and a cut glass tumbler. "I believe this will do just fine," she said, pouring out a shot, the bottle clinking against the glass as her hands trembled.

"You drink that down right quick, young man, because I'm obliged to start feeling around on that shoulder to see just where that lead is," said Doc Ferguson.

Jessamine lifted Lee's head and held the glass to his lips. He took one good swallow, then coughed.

"No reflection on your papa's brandy, Miss Jessamine," he said weakly. "Let's try it again."

"Are you sure?" she asked. The coughing fit had twisted his features in agony.

"Oh, yes, ma'am."

She held his head with one hand and the glass in the other until he had drained the tumbler and his lips and chin were wet with brandy.

Doc Ferguson had rolled up the sleeves of his striped nightshirt and was cutting away what was left of Lee's blood-soaked shirt. The old man's bushy white eyebrows pulled together in a frown. "How long ago did this happen, Miss Jessamine? Looks to me like some of this blood is mighty old."

"Late yesterday, Doc. Then we got held up by the storm."

"Hmmm," he murmured. Then he said, "Soldiers are out lookin' for a man got shot two nights ago. Don't suppose you'd know anything about that, Miss Jessamine, would you?"

"Not a thing, Doc," she said.

"Didn't think so," he said as he peeled the last of the white cotton shirt away from Lee's chest. "You're lucky to have a cousin who is not only beautiful, but a mighty poor shot, as well, young man. I don't believe anything vital was hit. But let's just take a feel, shall we? You just go ahead and curse if you like. I'm sure, living with the judge and his three boys, Miss Jessamine's heard plenty of cussing." With that, he pressed two crooked fingers against the wound.

Jessamine winced when she heard Lee's quick intake of breath. His chest heaved upward and then sagged back. His lips paled and tightened. She reached for his hand, and silently withstood his crushing grip while the doctor pushed and probed.

"Yup. There it is," said Doc Ferguson. "Almost a shame you're so muscular, son. On a puny fella, that lead would have passed clear through. Well, that's all the poking I need to do. You just knock back another glass of that brandy while we wait for that Maisie." He stood slowly, straightening his knees with difficulty. "I'll be needing to use the necessary, Miss Jessamine. Point me in the right direction, will you, dear?"

"I'll show you, Doc," said Sampson, who had been quietly standing at the window with Nathan Anderson, both of them peering off into the distance, keeping watch.

"Well, now, thank you, boy." Doc Ferguson pursed his lips and regarded Sampson closely. "Aren't you the rascal broke his leg tumbling out of Mrs. Bohling's apple tree?"

"You got a good memory," said Sampson.

"Hell, it's the best thing a man's got at my age," said the doctor as he followed Sampson out of the room.

The bottle chattered against the glass as Jessamine poured another tumbler of brandy.

Lee rolled his head toward her. "Might not be a bad idea to take a taste of that poison yourself, Miss Jessamine," he said. "Your color's off."

She looked bleakly at the glass in her hand. "I expect you're right," she said, quaffing a healthy dose, then closing her eyes and letting the brandy slide a burning path down her throat.

"Now," said Lee, "if you'll prop another pillow behind me, I'll just handle that glass myself. And don't you go anywhere with that bottle, you hear?"

"You don't want to make yourself sick now," she cautioned as she stuffed another pillow behind his shoulders as gently as she could, all the while trying to avoid looking at the torn flesh on his shoulder.

As soon as she handed him the glass, he downed most of its contents. "I'm courting oblivion, Miss Jessamine," he said, licking a drop of the brandy from the corner of his mouth.

"So I see," she said.

"You don't approve," he said, taking another drink. "Would you rather I were courting you, little girl?"

"Such talk. I think you're drunk already." Jessamine could feel the color rising in her cheeks.

Lee took another swallow. Some of the liquor dripped down his rough chin, and Jessamine dabbed at it with a corner of the sheet. He gazed at her, his bleary eyes straying from her hair to her eyes, and then to her mouth. He smiled lopsidedly. "How old are you now, Jessamine? You were hardly more than a baby in New Orleans. Before the war. Remember?"

"I remember," she said softly, thinking she had done little else but remember, especially these past few hours. "Seems like a hundred years ago."

"A thousand," he said as he continued to drain the glass. "Prettiest damn ghost I ever saw."

Jessamine smiled and refilled the glass.

"You were a sight, climbing out of that big old wardrobe. Those long, white, shapely legs. Little delicate ankles." He craned his neck to see her better. "Is your waistline still so tiny?"

"Probably not," she said, a little stiffly, holding the brandy bottle in front of her as if it would hide her from his inquisitive gaze.

"Looks like it to me," he murmured. "Tiny. And all those pearly buttons down the front of your virgin white dress. Your eyes haven't changed, Jessamine. They're still just like pansies bloomin' in the summer shade."

"You'd best not talk so much, Lee."

"Best drink," he said, taking another swallow and spilling more than before. Jessamine blotted the spilled brandy again as he continued to ramble on about buttons and virgins. "Prettiest damn little girl I ever saw, Jessamine. Damnedest little girl. There wasn't a man in that ballroom didn't want to take you away from me." He grinned sloppily, crooking a finger to motion her closer. "I told you I'd get you home, Jessie, didn't I?"

"Yes, Lee, you did." She poured the last of the brandy into the tumbler.

"Had to," he murmured. "Had to let you go. God, how I wanted to keep you." He closed his eyes with a sigh. "I'm tired."

Jessamine eased the glass from his hand. "And about halfway to oblivion, I'd say," she whispered.

She watched him then as he dozed—the faint twitch of his wet lips, the heavy rise and fall of his bare chest. He said he

had wanted to keep her. For four long years Jessamine had thought he'd sent her away without a second glance, like a toy he'd finished playing with. Still, she cautioned herself, he'd had a lot of brandy. And Jessamine knew from long experience that liquor loosened tongues. For all she knew, in his drunken state Lee might have imagined he was talking to someone else. A man wouldn't send away a woman he wanted to keep. Oh, but still . . .

Lee's eyes opened dully as the door creaked and Doc Ferguson reappeared. Maisie was right behind him with an armload of clean sheets and torn rags.

The doctor hummed tunelessly to himself and proceeded to inspect his instruments on top of the quilt—a long pair of tweezers, a metal clamp, a fat sewing needle, black thread, scissors, and a straight razor.

Jessamine upended the brandy bottle and drained the last few drops.

"How you holdin' up, child?" Maisie asked her.

Jessamine didn't know. She just looked at Maisie as if in a daze.

"You kin do it," the big woman said. "I knows you, Miss Jess. You kin do anything you has to. And you has to." Maisie plopped the fresh linens and bandages down on the foot of the bed. "What you want us to do, Doc?"

Arms crossed over his chest, Doc Ferguson stood by the bed, surveying the room. "The light's all right, I guess," he said, "but the bed won't do. Too soft. We'll have to get him on the floor. Maisie, you spread out one of those sheets down here. And you boys, Sampson, you and the other one, lift the young man down on it."

Jessamine just stood while everyone else snapped into action, Maisie shaking out a sheet, Sampson and Nathan taking a stance by the bed and planning how best to transfer the large, unwieldy Lee from mattress to floor. "What can I do, Doc?" Jessamine asked.

"Well, nothing right now, Miss Jessamine."

Lee reached for her hand. "You just give aid and comfort, little Jessie, to this suffering soldier of the South."

"Hush, Lee. You're drunk. You don't know what you're saying." Jessamine looked to see if Doc Ferguson had heard, but he appeared to be busy directing Maisie with the sheet.

"I'm saying, Jessie, you've got the sweeteest eyes."

"Well, that's all right. You can say that," she answered, flustered now.

"I'm saying you've got the shiniest raven hair, and the tiniest little waist, and two of the most shapely—"

"You can't say that, Lee," she snapped. "And you shouldn't even be thinking such things. You're intoxicated."

"Not enough," he rasped, struggling up on one elbow. "This is taking a hell of a long time, Doc. Can't we get it over and done with?" Lee fell back, his eyes closed tight.

The doctor signaled Sampson and Nathan, who picked Lee up and laid him on the floor, where Maisie eased a pillow under his head.

"Now, if you boys will assist me and my old knees . . ." said Doc Ferguson. They held his arms while he lowered himself to the floor. "And put my instruments right down here beside me now," he directed them. "Right there. That'll do just fine."

Jessamine thought she was going to swoon right onto the bloody sheets that Lee had just left.

"Miss Jessamine, I need you now," Doc Ferguson called.

Her knees quaked as she walked around the foot of the bed. "Yes, Doc. I'm here," she said.

"Now I want each of you boys to hold a leg down, and Maisie, you take the young man's good arm. You sit on it if you need to, gal. He's a strong fella, in spite of his condi-

tion, and he can't be flailing around, or I'll hurt him worse than he already is."

Jessamine's stomach turned over as Sampson and Nathan and Maisie all took up positions around Lee's prone body.

Doc Ferguson turned his pale blue gaze on Jessamine. "Now," he said, "what I want you to do, Miss Jessamine, is hold down his injured arm. You must be gentle but firm. Do you think you're up to that, young lady?"

She had to be, Jessamine thought. After all, this was her Lee. This was the man she'd dreamed about, the man she'd thought never to see again, until fate and this confounded war had dropped him on her doorstep. He was here, and he was alive, and she had no intention of losing him. Not to death or the Yankees, and not to anything or anyone else. Her skirt billowed out as she knelt. Then she reached for Lee's arm, which was crooked, almost defensively, across his chest. It wouldn't budge.

She leaned close. "Lee, you must relax. Let me take your arm."

He skewered her with his dark eyes, as if to say, "Go to hell."

"Please." Jessamine pulled again, but he wouldn't let go. She sat back on her heels a moment, frowning. Then she leaned close to him, so close her breasts were brushing his bare chest as she whispered in his ear. "Close your eyes, Lee. Imagine it's four years ago, and you have a little splinter that needs to be eased out."

His mouth quirked into a roguish grin. Then he sighed. "All right, Jessie. Here. Take my hand, little girl."

"That's better," she said, gently pressing his arm down on the floor, all the while noticing how badly it was trembling. Or was it hers? She couldn't even tell.

"All right, then. We are about to begin." Doc Ferguson took a white handkerchief from his bag. With great care and

deliberation, he folded it several times. "This is for you, young man. If you would care to bite down on it, it may give you some comfort." He placed the handkerchief between Lee's teeth, then picked up the straight razor. "This won't take long, son. And, Lord willing, you will faint before we are done." His gnarled hand moved quickly and sliced into the shoulder.

Lee's body bucked, and it took all the strength of Sampson, Nathan, Maisie and Jessamine to hold him down. Sweat broke out on his face and chest as the doctor opened the wound to search for the bullet. He bit down on the handkerchief, his lips turning from white to blue. Lee's eyes searched wildly about the room, held for a single moment on Jessamine's wet violet eyes, and then rolled up in sweet unconsciousness.

Chapter Three

They were riding out of the night and slashing at the blue-belly camp like wolves. He could see them—boys mostly, raw recruits—tripping out of tents, fumbling for their long underwear and their muskets, their eyes wild with panic, while his own youngsters loosed their rebel yells and forgot to keep their damn-fool heads down as they swept through the camp.

He could smell the acrid smoke of gunpowder and see the muzzle flashes like bright tongues of flame.

And he could see the copper-haired Yankee officer calmly pouring powder into his muzzle, then ramming down the charge with grim deliberation before slowly raising the musket and taking aim. For Nathan's head. No time to warn him—only time to stand in the stirrups and lean, as if he could provide a buffer between the boy and the bullet.

"Nathan!"

"Just hang on now, Captain."

He was. He was hanging on with all his might.

Jessie, then. Her violet eyes moved in and out of his line of vision. He had tried so hard not to follow her up the river after he arranged her departure, but here he was anyway and he couldn't recall how he came to be here or why he was in pain. Was it Alpha? Had he called out Jessie's name just once too often from his incessant dreams? Had she finally

*shot him in a jealous rage? If she had meant for him to go
to hell, her aim had been disastrous.*

*He was in heaven with his Jessie. He couldn't feel his right
arm. He didn't care. He was sprouting wings. But it hurt like
hell.*

"Jessie!"

"I'm right here, Lee."

"I'm right here, Lee." She said it again and again as she
sat with him after everyone else had gone downstairs for one
of Maisie's enormous breakfasts.

It had taken Doc a long time, a terribly long time, to find
the bullet and then get a purchase on it with his tweezers. By
the time it was all over—Lee stitched up with coarse black
thread, his wound packed over with folded pieces of sheet,
his arm bound to him so that he wouldn't be able to move
it—Jessamine and Doc Ferguson had been nearly as bloody
as he was.

And then she had just watched over him, watched Lee
Kincannon breathe, never in her life so glad for something
so simple as breath. If pain could kill, he'd had enough to
take his life and then some. But a bit of color had returned
to his face. He even appeared peaceful, now that he'd
stopped fussing about the bindings on his arm and moaning about wings.

She left him long enough to say goodbye to Doc Ferguson. Then, as she lingered out on the front steps, Jessamine
turned her face up to the midday sun. The worst was over.
She was certain of that. And reasonably sure Doc Ferguson
believed that Lee was her cousin from Louisiana. Most important of all, the doc had said Lee would live. Knowing
that, she could deal with whatever happened next—whether
it took the form of a Yankee major or Eamon Dobbs, her
overseer, who was stomping around the side of the house
right now, slapping his hat on his leg.

"I can't find that Sampson anyplace, Miss Dade. Damn fool boy. You seen him?" Dobbs put his hat back on, then hooked his thumbs through his belt.

Jessamine knew very well where Sampson was—in Caleb's bedroom, getting a well deserved rest—but she wasn't going to tell Dobbs. "Morning, Mr. Dobbs," she said brightly, shading her eyes from the sun. "I've asked Sampson to do some work for me in the house."

The overseer sneered. "Don't know how you expect me to get anything done when there's nobody to work for me. Hell, the hemp's too wet to shock, anyway."

"Another day or two of this sunshine will take care of that," she said.

"Prob'ly rain tomorrow," Dobbs muttered. He gestured toward the barn. "I see you got a visitor."

Maybe they should have hidden Lee's horse after all, Jessamine thought. But this was Eamon Dobbs, for heaven's sake. She could outfox him using only a tenth of her wits. "Yes, that's right. You left shortly before my cousin arrived from New Orleans. He's been here several days. Long enough, I'm afraid, to have had a terrible accident. Doc Ferguson only just left a while ago."

Dobbs squinted in the bright sunshine. "From New Orleans, you say? He ain't no Johnny Reb, is he?"

Jessamine laughed. "That's quite amusing, Mr. Dobbs. You'd see the humor, too, if you knew my cousin. He's even less interested in politics than I am."

The overseer scratched his unshaven chin. "Is that a fact? I thought all them Southerners was rebs."

Jessamine was tired of the man. "You thought wrong, Mr. Dobbs," she said curtly, then stood up and shook out her skirt. "Good afternoon to you."

"Afternoon, Miss Dade. Guess I'll just wait till that hemp dries out, then."

"Yes, you do that, Mr. Dobbs," she answered back over her shoulder, surprised to discover that what would have been considered a minor tragedy only yesterday seemed hardly a trifle today. But it wasn't a trifle at all. More rain could set them back days, could even ruin the crop as it lay in the fields waiting to be gathered and shocked. And then where would they be?

But as she mounted the stairs on her way to sit with Lee, little else seemed to matter.

Jessamine stirred in the rocking chair at the sound of kindling crackling. She rubbed her eyes and saw Maisie squatting down by the fireplace, placing an elm log atop the vibrant flames.

"Oh, Maisie..." She yawned as she stretched her arms above her head. "How long did I sleep?"

"A couple hours. You go on and git to bed, child. I'll sit with Mr. Lee."

Jessamine walked over to the bed and looked down at Lee's sleeping face. "He hasn't stirred for quite a while, Maisie. That's not a bad sign, is it?"

"He just wore out, that's all. You be glad he's sleepin'. He ain't gonna feel too good when he wakes up. That arm's gonna hurt him plenty."

"Don't we have anything to give him?" Jessamine asked.

"Doc give me some salve to put on him, but it ain't gonna help the hurtin'."

"Maybe I should get another bottle of brandy."

"Don't you be turnin' him into no drunk now, Miss Jess."

Jessamine studied Lee's face. "Isn't he handsome, Maisie?"

The big woman grunted as she put another log on the fire. "He's all right for a white man."

"Oh, Maisie, you—" She stopped in midsentence. "I hear a horse coming up the front drive," she whispered, rushing to the window and pulling back the heavy drapes. "Oh, my God. It's Major Harding."

"Who?" Maisie joined her at the window.

"Major Harding. He and his men are out searching for Lee. What are we going to do?" She closed the drape, overlapping it to make certain it remained closed.

"I's goin' to Mr. Caleb's room and roust Sampson and that boy, that what I's goin' to do. And you, if you got any sense, will brush out your hair, pink up your cheeks, and greet that Yankee with a big ol' smile."

"I suppose you're right." Jessamine looked at Lee. "I just hate to leave him."

"He'll be awright, child. Maisie'll look in on him."

Several minutes later, with her hair brushed and a little color rubbed into her cheeks, Jessamine was at the front door in time for the major's resounding knock. She opened the door smiling.

"Major Harding! Well, isn't this a nice surprise? Won't you come in?"

The major took off his hat, exposing a head of wavy copper hair that matched his full mustache and sideburns. "Thank you, Miss Dade. I was worried about you yesterday," he said. "Did you make it home before the storm?"

"Nearly. I only got a little wet."

"I'm happy to hear that." He looked around the vestibule, craning his neck a bit to see into the front parlor. "This is a lovely place, Miss Dade."

"Thank you, Major." Her face was beginning to ache from smiling so hard, and she found his wandering gaze extremely unsettling. She had to get rid of this man. Now. "I hate to be rude, Major," she said, touching the back of her wrist to her forehead, "but I was just about to lie down for a while. I suffer from occasional headaches."

His light blue eyes widened, and his countenance melted with sympathy. "I'm so sorry, Miss Dade. I never would have come calling if I had known you weren't well."

Calling? she said to herself. The major was calling on her? He was acting as a man, rather than a soldier? And here she was encouraging him with all her simpering.

"Perhaps some other time," she said. "Although I don't suppose you'll be in this county long."

"On the contrary," he beamed. "Our garrison has just moved a few miles east of Newton. We'll be here for the foreseeable future."

Jessamine fingered her collar. "How nice," she said. "Well, I trust you'll call again sometime. Of course, I know how very busy you must be."

"That's true. We have been lately, what with those murderous rebs on the loose."

"Oh, you haven't caught those varmints yet?" Her heart was beginning to hammer.

"Not yet. But we will," he proclaimed confidently. "Oh, by the way, Miss Dade, how is your cousin coming along?"

"My cousin?" What was he asking her, she thought frantically. Just how much did he know?

"I spoke with Doctor Ferguson as he was rushing out here this morning. I believe he said your cousin was wounded in a hunting accident."

"Yes, my cousin was hurt, Major, but he's much improved."

"That's odd," Major Harding said.

"I beg your pardon?"

"Oh, I was just saying it's odd. The doctor insisted that it was you who had accidentally shot your cousin while deer hunting. Of course, I knew that was impossible, since I had seen you just before sundown yesterday." He grinned, showing his perfectly square teeth. "Unless you Missouri folks hunt deer in the dark."

Jessamine could barely contain her heartbeat now. She was sure, if he listened hard enough, the major would hear it thumping against her ribs. "He told you it was I who shot him!" she exclaimed. "That Doc Ferguson gets up confused with down. And I can assure you, I don't hunt, Major Harding, during the day or after dark."

"It was me shot Miss Dade's cousin," said Sampson, coming down the stairs.

As Major Harding turned at the sound of his voice, Jessamine noticed that his hand moved cautiously to the hilt of his sword.

"My name is Sampson Fry, sir," he said as he crossed the vestibule. "It was my gun accidentally went off yesterday."

"Sampson works for me," said Jessamine, noticing how thin Sampson appeared as he stood before the husky officer.

"Quite an unfortunate accident," Harding said.

"Yessir, that it was. Miss Dade, she's been real nice about it, though. I mean, me nearly killing her cousin and all." Sampson lowered his gaze to the floor.

Jessamine couldn't stand the tension anymore. Her heart was on the verge of exploding, and there was a thin film of perspiration on her face. She put her wrist to her forehead once more and swayed against the major, her hip connecting with his. "I'm so sorry, Major Harding. It's just that I'm so...so distressed. I truly do need to lie down."

"Of course you do." He swept her into his arms. "Shall I take you to your room, Miss Dade?"

Upstairs? Where Lee was? Jessamine was almost too panicky to speak. She looked at Sampson, whose eyes were nearly bulging out of his head. "The sofa in the parlor will be fine, Major," she said with a sigh. "If you wouldn't mind."

The officer strode to the parlor, using a glossy boot to push aside the half-closed door, nearly crushing her against

his brass buttons. "You're light as a child, Miss Dade," he murmured as he put her down on the sofa.

She'd probably just lost fifteen pounds out of sheer terror, Jessamine thought.

Major Harding got down on one knee beside her. "Is there someone here to take care of you?" he asked, his eyes caressing her face. "Perhaps you need to eat a little supper."

"I have servants who look after me," she said.

"I hope so. I intend to return tomorrow to make sure you are well." He stood up and turned to leave, then turned back.

Jessamine put her hand to her forehead again. Major Harding just stood there—all coppery hair and brass and shiny boots—gazing at her with his robin's egg blue eyes. What the devil did the man want?

He cleared his throat and gave a quick twist to his mustache. "Pardon my saying so, Miss Dade, but you need a husband," the major declared before turning briskly on his heel and walking out.

"Major's gone," said Sampson, coming into the parlor a moment later, Maisie right behind him.

"I want to talk to you, Sampson," Jessamine hissed.

"You get in line, Miss Jess," said Maisie. "What you go and do a fool thing like that for, boy?" She cuffed him on the shoulder.

"Maisie's right, Sampson. You shouldn't have done that. It just implicates you more deeply in this whole confounded mess."

"We was listening from the top of the stairs, Miss Jess. I wasn't sure you were gonna come up with an answer for the major," said Sampson. "Anyway, we're all up to our ears in this any way you look at it."

"You in over yore head," said Maisie, cuffing him again.

"Well, it was very brave, even though it was foolish. I thank you, Sampson," said Jessamine.

"That major got eyes for you, Miss Jess," Maisie said. "He be back."

"I'm afraid you're right, Maisie. Lord help us."

She'd been too tired to get undressed, so Jessamine had merely taken off her underskirts before climbing into her bed. She fell asleep instantly, then woke at one in the morning, starving. Down in the kitchen, she found Nathan Anderson sitting at the table, eating a piece of cold spinach pie.

"Sit, please," Jessamine said when he began to get up. "I believe I'll join you, Mr. Anderson."

The boy swallowed his mouthful of spinach. "I wish you'd call me Nathan, ma'am."

"Very well. But only if you'll call me by my Christian name."

His cheeks colored. "I'll try, ma'am."

Jessamine laughed as she walked into the cold cellar, calling back over her shoulder. "I'm probably not much older than you, Nathan. Don't be 'ma'aming' me so much."

"No, ma'am. I mean Miss Jessamine. It's a pretty name. Who was it gave it to you?"

"My mother," she said, emerging from the cellar with a crock of applesauce. "She named me the morning of the day she died. I was but three days old. Who named you, Nathan?"

"My mama. I haven't seen her in over two years. Not since I joined up with the captain."

"Two years," said Jessamine as she ladled applesauce into two bowls. "Lee's been doing this for two years?"

"Oh, more than that, ma'am—Miss Jessamine. Probably closer to three years for the captain. 'Course, he wasn't always in Missouri," said Nathan, forking in another piece of pie.

"Where was he?" Jessamine asked.

"General Buford's had the captain operating all over."

"Operating?" she asked, licking applesauce off her finger.

"Well, organizing, you might say, ma'am—Miss Jessamine. The captain gets sent all over to put together patrols of irregulars, like he did with me and some of the boys I was with in Alabama. We were just hiding in barns and such, taking potshots whenever we could, no particular plan in mind. Pretty much wasting ourselves. Captain Kincannon, he organized us, gave us maps, even saw to it we all had guns and plenty of ammunition. When the captain left, I went with him."

"Where?" asked Jessamine.

"Lordy, we been all over. Mississippi, Georgia, Alabama, Tennessee. Missouri, of course. That was our first real raid up here, the other night at Foley." Nathan put down his fork. "Didn't turn out so well for the captain, I guess, though we did make short work of that bluebelly camp."

Jessamine carried the crock back to the cold cellar. "Sounds like you hold him in high regard, Nathan," she called.

"Who? The captain, ma'am? Well, I wouldn't tell this to just anybody, but he's been like a daddy to me. I never did have one of those." He lowered his eyes when Jessamine came back to the table.

"In what way, Nathan?" she asked, setting a bowl of applesauce atop his empty plate.

"He looks out for me," said Nathan, reddening at the turn in the conversation. "When did you meet him, Miss Jessamine?"

"What?" Jessamine had a hard time imagining the Lee Kincannon she knew in New Orleans as a dyed-in-the-wool

rebel. It was even harder to picture him playing father to a boy. Still, she recalled how gentle his hands had been when he'd sewn her bodice together. And, he had said himself that he "blew with the wind."

"Is that too personal a question, ma'am?"

Jessamine ate a spoonful of applesauce. "It was right before the war in New Orleans. We met at a ball."

Nathan smiled crookedly. "Kind of like Cinderella and the prince," he said.

Jessamine smiled to herself, remembering that night. "Well, not quite."

Jessamine was lost in memory again the next morning when Eamon Dobbs came into the dining room, hat in hand. "Maisie said I'd find you in here, Miss Dade."

Jessamine looked up from her untouched egg. "What is it, Mr. Dobbs?" The mere sight of the man irritated her.

"You give them soldiers permission to pitch camp on Riverbend property, Miss Dade? 'Cause if you did, the judge's gonna have both our hides. Their horses are bringin' most of the east field to ruin."

"What?"

"I said there's half a dozen Yanks—"

Jessamine banged her fist on the dining room table. "I heard what you said, Mr. Dobbs."

He twisted his hat. "Well, if you want 'em out of there, you're gonna have to tell 'em yourself. I ain't tangling with the army. No siree."

"They're welcome to stay," she said flatly. "And you, Mr. Dobbs, are welcome to go now."

"Ain't no work, what with the hemp so wet. I'm just gonna go into town."

"Fine. Goodbye."

Jessamine speared her egg dead center, and watched the yolk as it oozed to the edge of her plate. Damn him! Damn him! Major Harding knew. Somehow he knew, and he was just sitting out there waiting. Like a big damn marmalade cat.

Chapter Four

"Don't know why they calls 'em 'patients,' since that's what sick folks has the least of," Maisie grumbled as she carried a big tray into the kitchen.

"What's he doing now?" Jessamine was stirring a pot of boiling rags atop the stove. The rising steam had flushed her face and curled little wisps of hair on her forehead.

"He want to know whose voice that was he heard downstairs last night," said Maisie. "He mighty suspicious, Miss Jess. And he ain't gonna stay in that bed much longer, neither."

"Well, I don't know what I can do about it, Maisie," Jessamine snapped. She bent her head over the steaming pot. She felt like diving in.

As Lee's strength increased, her own seemed to diminish. In the past two days, she had slept a total of perhaps six hours. She'd hear Lee, think he was in distress, and run across the hall, only to find him sleeping soundly. Or she'd hear horses. Or strange voices.

Major Harding and his men were still camped in the east field. She didn't dare ask them to leave. And she still couldn't figure out if Thomas Harding was courting her or interrogating her. His visits were frequent and unpredictable. Jessamine had feigned so many headaches she truly had one now.

"If I just didn't have to keep being so infernally sweet to that man," she said, stirring the boiling pot once more.

"Who you talkin' about, child?"

"Major Harding."

"He sweet to you?"

Jessamine groaned. "Sweet and sticky as jam."

"He's tryin' to catch two birds in the same net," said Maisie. "That major, he wants the cap'n bad, but he wants you worse. He 'bout glows when he lays eyes on you."

Nathan poked his head in the door from the hallway. "'Scuse me, Miss Jessamine. The captain asked, could you come upstairs."

"Here." Maisie picked up a tall glass of milk from the tray she had just brought down. "You take this up and see if you can't get him to drink it." She pressed the glass into Jessamine's hand.

"You must think I have magical powers, Maisie," she said.

"I just think the cap'n listen to you better'n he listen to me."

Jessamine sighed. "I'll do what I can. I'm not going to pour it down his throat if he says no."

"You lose your temper, Miss Jess, and you'll be pourin' it over his head."

"Now there's a thought," she said. "Wasn't that Cleopatra's beauty secret?"

Maisie chuckled. "That's one thing Mr. Lee don't need more of."

Lee was propped up in bed, trying to load a pistol one-handed. "Damnation!" he said as Jessamine swept majestically into the room.

"Oh, for mercy's sake, Lee. You're going to shoot your leg off. Give me that." She put the glass of milk on the bedside table, and wrested the gun from his hand.

He regarded her coolly. "You know much about fire-arms, Jessie?"

"Practically nothing," she said. "Why?"

"Well, darlin', your finger is on the trigger there and you're about to blow my manhood away."

Jessamine squeezed her eyes closed, pointed the gun away, then gingerly placed it on the floor.

"Come here." Lee patted the bed beside him. "Sit down, Jessie."

"I've brought you a glass of milk, Lee. Maisie wants you to drink it."

He scowled. "You tell Maisie I haven't drunk milk since I was weaned, and I don't intend to start again now. Sit, Jessamine."

She perched on the edge of the bed, her back stiff, facing away from him.

"Tell me about Major Harding," Lee said.

Jessamine whirled around. "Who told you?"

"It doesn't matter who told me. I'm asking you now to tell me about him. What does he know? What does he want?"

Jessamine didn't know why she wanted to make him angry, but she did. She was tired, her nerves were stretched taut as banjo strings, she had dark circles under her eyes, and Lee Kincannon was sitting there, handsome as the devil himself. What was worse, now that he was better he was trying to boss everyone around. She wouldn't be bossed. Not at Riverbend. Not anywhere.

"What does he want?" she said, repeating his question. "Well, me, I suppose."

Lee laughed. "You!"

Jessamine glared at him. "He's courting me. Does that surprise you so?"

"Well, no, I—"

"Fine, then," she said, cutting him off. "If you want to know about him, he's got reddish hair and blue eyes and a freckle or two on his nose. I believe he is twenty-three years old, but I could be off a year either way. His father owns a newspaper in Lima, Ohio, where Thomas joined the Third Ohio Fusiliers three years ago, and—"

"That's enough, Jessie. Hand me one of those cheroots, will you?" He gestured to the bedside table.

"I'll not have you smoking in bed, Lee Kincannon," she said.

He sat up straight, glowering. "In that case, help me over to the chair, and I'll do my smoking there."

"You know you're not supposed to get up yet. Oh, here, damn you. Take your smelly old cigar. Only don't get ashes on my sheets." She handed him one of the thin cheroots, then struck a match and held it until the tobacco caught.

Lee blew out a thin stream of smoke, picked a fleck of tobacco off his lower lip. Then he leaned his head back on the pillow. Of course the Yankee major was courting her. The little minx was probably having the time of her life with a Yankee in her parlor and a rebel in her bed. But he had no right to be jealous, Lee reminded himself. He had no right at all. And his quarrel with the major was not about a woman. "This is not some schoolgirl's game, Jessie," he said quietly.

"I am not some schoolgirl," she replied indignantly, crossing her arms over her chest. "And Major Harding doesn't think so, either."

"He doesn't, does he? All right, then. We'll do this your way, little girl." Lee sighed and took another long pull on the cigar, then blew a ring of smoke and watched it drift up to the ceiling. "Yes, Miss Jessamine, I am in the harsh grip of that green-eyed monster commonly known as jealousy. I am jealous of a man with two good arms to hold your ripe little body so tight against him he can feel your heart beat-

ing inside him. I am jealous of a man who is able to saunter up to your front door to court you when the best I can do at present is lie here in this godforsaken bed and wait for your pretty face to appear in the doorway." He pulled hard on the cigar, exhaling harshly. "Does that give you some notion of my current state of mind, Miss Jessamine?"

"That explains a great deal," she said, trying to sound cool while her blood bubbled at the boiling point.

"I'm glad to hear that," Lee said. "And now that I have explained myself, let me proceed to explain something else to you. Even if I weren't jealous, I'd be inquiring about your Major Harding, because he is my enemy. My enemy, Jessamine. Do you understand that?"

"He isn't what you think, Lee," she said. "He's not a monster."

He rolled his eyes impatiently. "The major has red hair and freckles on his nose! And the major would shoot me dead as soon as look at me, because my men killed his men. Just as I'd shoot him if I got the opportunity."

"You wouldn't!" she said, truly astonished. She'd spent so much time contemplating how to protect Lee from Major Harding, it had never crossed her mind that the major might need some protection from Lee.

"I would. Jessie, this is a war we're fighting. It wasn't cupid who shot me, darlin'. It was—"

He stopped abruptly as the sudden and distinct sound of horses' hooves came from the open window.

"Go look, Jessamine. Be quick." Lee gave her a shove with his leg, propelling her toward the window.

"Oh, my God," she whispered, closing the drapes tight against her back. "It's Major Harding, and he's got five or six soldiers with him." *Think,* she told herself. *Think.* She felt as if she were in a vise, with Lee on one side and Major Harding on the other. "I'm going downstairs," she announced. "I'm sure I can persuade the major..."

Lee plunged his cigar into the glass of milk. "Pick up that gun, Jessamine, and give it to me," he demanded. "Where's Nathan?"

"I'll speak to the major, Lee. Please don't—"

"The gun," he shouted.

As she handed it to him, Nathan burst into the room, his blond hair mussed from sleep, his shirt half-buttoned and still untucked. "Patrol's here, Captain," he said breathlessly. "What do you want me to do?"

For a moment there was just the sound of gravel spattering beneath hooves and the sound of the clock over the mantel ticking relentlessly. Jessamine stood mute as Lee's dark eyes met hers. She saw warmth turn to hard, cold purpose.

"We're taking Miss Jessamine hostage, Nathan. You do what you have to to keep her quiet," he ordered.

"Yes, sir."

Nathan's arms immediately surrounded her, one at her waist, the other around her shoulders with his hand covering her mouth. "I'm sorry, Miss Jessamine," he breathed against her ear.

She struggled, but Nathan only tightened his hold.

"Get her down here beside me on the bed," said Lee. "Be quick."

Nathan sat, pulling the struggling Jessamine with him, both of them listing hard against Lee's bandaged shoulder.

"Christ, Jessie, hold still," he gritted out. "We're not going to hurt you. Just hold still." He stuck the barrel of his pistol in her ribs.

Jessamine froze, her eyes widening at Lee in disbelief.

"Just stay that way," he whispered menacingly as the pounding began on the front door.

It reverberated in her heart. With Nathan's hand partially covering her nose, she could barely breathe. Jessa-

mine glanced at Lee. His whole attention was focused on the closed bedroom door. His eyes were hard and glittering.

Maisie's voice floated up the stairs, her words indistinct but her tone clearly angry and fearful. Then her voice grew louder, punctuated by the major's. Footsteps rushed in the upstairs hall.

The bedroom door opened, slamming back against the wall. No one appeared.

"Come on in, Major," called Lee.

Major Harding stepped into the doorway, his pistol drawn. Except for a slight twitch of his mustache, his expression barely altered when he saw the scene before him.

"As you can see," said Lee, "we have a rather delicate situation here. You're acquainted with Miss Jessamine Dade, I believe."

The major nodded cautiously.

"Miss Dade has a gun stuck in her ribs, Major, angled up toward her heart. Nathan, lean over a bit so the man can get an unobstructed view."

Nathan pulled Jessamine several inches to the right, the pressure from the gun never easing as she moved.

"How's that?" Lee asked coolly, as if he were rolling out a bolt of calico for inspection. "Can you see all right?"

"I see it," he said, blue eyes hardening to ice. He shifted his gaze to Jessamine's face. "Don't worry, Miss Jessamine. I won't let this bastard hurt you."

She could feel Lee's whole body tighten. She heard his long, deliberate intake of breath, his slow exhalation before he spoke.

"I was counting on you feeling that way, Major. Let me tell you what I want to do. I'll be needing a wagon and someone to drive it. There's a young man named Sampson. I wouldn't doubt if he's out there somewhere in the hall right now. You have him hitch up a wagon and have it waiting outside the front door."

Without a word, Major Harding backed out the door. Low voices gave way to the sound of rushing footsteps, and then he reappeared.

"Your wagon will be outside as soon as the boy can get it hitched," he said.

"Thank you, Major," said Lee. "Now, if you would just close the door and give us a bit of privacy, I would appreciate it."

Major Harding stood stock-still in the doorway. "Miss Jessamine, you stay calm. You'll not be harmed. I swear to you."

"The door, sir," said Lee.

Once it was closed, he leaned into Jessamine, his lips brushing her ear. "Jessie, you do exactly what I tell you if you want me to live past noon today, you hear?"

She nodded behind Nathan's stifling hand.

"All right, Nathan. You can let her go."

After she gulped in a few unhampered breaths, Jessamine stood up. She was as furious as she was frightened. "How dare you—"

Lee aimed the gun right at her heart. "Be still," he hissed. "I don't have time for your righteous indignation. And I apologize in advance for your discomfort, and for what I'm about to do." He flicked his eyes toward Nathan. "I want Miss Jessamine muted, Nathan. You'll find some linen strips in that drawer there. Silence her, but don't hurt her."

Nathan sprang into action while Jessamine stared at Lee with cold fury. She knew his life was in danger, but how dare he threaten her, how dare he truss her up like some scrawny chicken when she could probably bring this whole blasted confrontation to an end with just a few words. "How dare—"

A wadded rag stifled her speech. Then Nathan wound a long linen strip around her, immobilizing her lips. He tied

it tight. "Just for a little while, Miss Jess," he said as he grasped her wrists.

Lee had been watching, his expression stony, but as Nathan wrested Jessamine's wrists behind her back, his eyes flickered. "Not too tight," he said.

Jessamine's violet eyes said, "Thank you" and "Damn you" at the same time.

"What now, Captain?" asked Nathan.

"Now you can help me up, Nathan. And pray to God I stay that way. How far is it to the front door?"

"Not too far," said Nathan as he put Lee's good arm around his neck, then heaved him up and off the side of the bed. "But there's a steep flight of stairs. Then more steps once you're outside."

Lee stood gripping the bedpost. He still wore the same blood-spattered grey trousers he'd been wearing when he arrived. He looked down at his bare feet. "Hell," he muttered.

Jessamine walked to the wardrobe and gestured inside, where Nathan found Lee's boots.

Lee put his gun on the bed and pressed his hand against the side of her face. "That's my girl, Jessie," he said softly. "Nobody wants to face ol' Lucifer without his boots on." He stroked her hair.

While Lee guided his feet into the tall boots with his good arm, Nathan broke a leg off a tall fern stand and brought it to him.

"This oughta do for a walking stick, Captain."

"Should do fine," he said. "Now if we can just get some of this wrapping off me, I'll be able to balance."

He picked up the small pair of shears Jessamine had used to change the dressing on his shoulder and began to snip at the bandages that secured his arm and hand.

"Wagon's coming," Nathan called from the window.

He ripped the last bandage off. His right arm was pale, the skin puckered and moist, the dark hair matted down. He flexed his elbow, then his wrist, wincing as he moved joints that hadn't been used for several days.

"Well, it'll do for ballast, if nothing else," he said. With his good hand, he reached for Jessamine and pulled her close. The touch of his lips against her cheek was warm, lingering. "You behave now, Jessamine, you hear. Don't go and get us all killed."

She felt tears rising within her, and bit on the rag to push them down. It didn't have to be this way. If only she could speak. If only she could tell Lee that he was risking far too much and she couldn't bear to see him hunted this way.

Lee picked up the gun from the bed. "Nathan, don't go too fast, you hear. I believe Miss Jessamine will cooperate, but you get a good grip on her all the same."

"Here we go again, Miss Jessamine," said Nathan, his arms binding her as before.

"I do believe we're ready," murmured Lee. Then he called out, "Major, if the wagon's all set, so are we."

Major Harding opened the door and surveyed the three people before him. Lee was standing slightly behind Nathan and Jessamine, his gun wedged into her side.

The major's brass buttons expanded on his chest. His hand was poised on the hilt of his sword. His voice was low and thick. "If you harm her in any way, I swear to God I'll hunt you down and kill you with my own two hands."

"That's fair enough," said Lee. "And now, if you'll step out of our way, Major..."

Jessamine had fallen asleep, her head resting against Lee's thigh, but when the lulling motion of the wagon stopped, she sat up.

The sun was setting, its last light caught high in the cottonwood leaves above them.

"Where are we, Sampson?" she asked as he came around to the back of the wagon.

"Hopkins' Point. 'Bout twelve miles from Riverbend."

"As the crow flies," Nathan said with a laugh, jumping down and stretching out his legs.

"Do you think we're safe here?" Jessamine asked.

"Not for long, Miss Jess."

"Why'd you stop here, Sampson?" asked Nathan.

"Mr. Charles—Miss Jessamine's late brother—he always keep a boat here. Remember, Miss Jess? Mr. Charles said the fishin' at Hopkins' Point 'bout the best on the whole river."

"I do remember," said Jessamine.

Nathan slapped his knee. "A boat! Hot damn!"

"Only we got to find it," cautioned Sampson.

"We'll find it," Nathan said. "Come on, Sampson. You show me where you last saw it."

As the two trudged off through the brush toward the riverbank, Jessamine looked down at Lee in the dwindling light. His dark eyes were open, and a little grin played at the corners of his mouth.

"I didn't know you were awake," she said.

"Your hair's all tangled, Jessie." He reached up and smoothed back a wisp of raven hair from her cheek, letting his fingers drift softly over her skin.

"I'm not surprised." She sniffed. "And I'm still mad as hell at you, Lee Kincannon." She was ready to return to the point where the rag had first been stuffed in her mouth. "How dare you . . ."

He wound a long strand of her hair around his finger and pulled her gently down toward him. "Is this how you look when you wake in the morning, Jessie, with your hair straying all over the pillow?" he asked softly.

"No. Yes. I'm angry, Lee," she said, a distinct lack of fervor in her voice, and a definite quickening in her heart.

"I know it," Lee said, "And you should be angry, but that's not going to prevent me from kissing you." He twisted her hair another few turns, bringing her lips within inches of his. "Sweet, angry Jessie," he murmured.

He kissed her gently. Or was it Jessamine that kissed him and felt the softness of his lips and the rough whiskers on his chin as they rubbed against her? She wasn't sure. Of anything. Only that she felt again the way she had when they'd waltzed in New Orleans. That she never wanted to leave this man. That somehow she was his.

"Open your eyes, Jessie," he said.

She did, and saw his gentle smile. Jessamine traced it with her fingertip as she rested on her elbow beside him. "Lee?"

"Hmmm?"

"Four years ago. In New Orleans. Why didn't you kiss me?"

He sighed. "Maybe I should have."

Jessamine laughed. "I expect it was because you thought I was too young and inexperienced. But I'm not. Not anymore. Please. Kiss me again." She closed her eyes and pursed her lips.

"Jessamine," Lee said sternly, struggling to sit up.

"What?"

"There's a time for kissing, and there's a time for kissing again. And this isn't it." Lee swung his legs over the side of the wagon and eased himself down. That single kiss had rolled through him like a storm, with a thunderous pulse, and a jolt of lightning in his loins. "And don't go thinking that you're not young and inexperienced," he shouted, "because you are. Especially for somebody like me." He gave the wagon's rear wheel a kick, then winced as the shock ran through his shoulder. "Where the hell did Nathan go?"

Jessamine swung her legs over the tailgate. "Are you asking me, or are you just howling to hear your own voice, Lee?"

"I'm asking you," he growled.

"Oh, well, in that case, Nathan and Sampson went looking for the boat my brother used to keep around here."

"Which way did they go?"

Jessamine pointed toward the river.

"Toss me that walking stick, will you?"

She scooted off the wagon, stick in hand. "I'd like to hit you with this, Lee Kincannon."

He put out his hand. "Just give it to me," he said, and she smacked it into his palm. "Now come here, Jessie, and let me just hold you before I have to leave you."

"Leave me!" she exclaimed, bewildered.

Lee gathered her against him with his good arm, pressing his lips into her hair. "I'll have to take your horse and wagon if they don't find that boat soon," he said. "But Sampson will be with you. And I suspect your Major Harding's not too far away."

"He's not *my* Major Harding."

"Shh. Hold me, Jessie. Put your arms around me like you won't ever let me go."

She clung to him, breathing in his strong male scent, feeling the warmth of his chest against her cheek. He tipped her chin up and gazed down at her.

"Darlin' pansy-eyed Jessie," he whispered as his lips sought hers, tenderly at first, and then with a hunger that made her heart feel as if it were turning over inside her.

There was a thrashing in the brush, and Nathan stumbled into the little clearing. "We found the boat, Captain. Sampson's getting it in the water. Oh—I'm sorry, Captain. Pardon me, Miss Jessamine."

Lee eased Jessamine out of his arms. "That's all right, Nathan. I was just thanking Miss Jessamine for saving our worthless hides. Where's this miraculous boat?"

While Nathan jabbered on about the boat and the current and the lack of moonlight, Jessamine gazed up at Lee.

There was just enough light left to tell that his face had hardened. The soft lips that had just been kissing her were rigid now, his jawline severe. He was going to leave her.

"No, Lee, please..."

He put his fingers to her lips, stilling her. "You wait here, Jessie, and I'll send Sampson back. Lead on, young Nathan."

He couldn't do this, she thought. He couldn't. "Lee," she shouted.

He turned back to look at her.

"What am I going to do without you?" she called.

Lee laughed and pulled the gun out of his belt. "Here, Jessie. Catch," he called as he tossed it to her.

Jessamine caught it at arm's length and kept it there. "That isn't what I meant, Lee," she wailed. "And besides, I don't even know how to use this dratted thing."

"Just flourish it," he called. "It isn't loaded anyway."

Jessamine's mouth dropped open. The weapon that had been jammed in her rib cage half the day was no more than a piece of useless metal.

Lee grinned. "Goodbye, Jessie."

Before she could utter a word, he had disappeared into the trees.

Chapter Five

The cobbled alley behind the Imperial Hotel in Memphis was nearly dark. Light leaked from the kitchen windows, along with the pungent odor of fried beef liver. General Calvin Buford looked over his shoulder when he heard the clip of a double team of horses, and watched the carriage lights pass on River Street before he descended a small flight of stairs to a basement doorway and knocked—three hard, two soft.

"Where is he?" the young Confederate general asked as soon as Alpha Parker opened the door.

Alpha stood back, pushing aside the hoops beneath her crimson skirt, to let him pass. "Where do you think?" she answered dryly, angling her head to indicate a narrow passageway stacked with wooden crates.

"It's all over, Alpha," he said. "General Lee surrendered today."

"We heard," she said, following him down the dank hallway.

"How'd he take it?"

"Lee Kincannon doesn't like to lose," she said. "Anything." Under her breath, Alpha added, "Or anyone."

They entered a sparsely furnished room, where Lee sat at a battered oak table, a half-empty bottle of whiskey and a big dictionary on the table in front of him. His lower face

was covered by a full, dark beard, which split to reveal a feral grin.

"General Buford, sir," he slurred. "You'll pardon me if I don't salute. Or stand."

Calvin Buford sat down opposite him. Alpha put a glass before him and reached for the bottle, but Lee jerked it out of her reach.

"Thank you, Red, but this is a private funeral. You go on to bed."

She glared at him. When she opened her mouth to protest, he rasped, "Get out."

The redhead swung her crimson skirt around and swished out the door, slamming it behind her hard enough to knock a framed watercolor of the *Delta Star* off the wall. The glass shattered on the hard stone floor.

Lee ignored it, reaching across the table to fill his visitor's glass nearly to the brim. He refilled his own, then laid the empty bottle down on the floor. "Another dead soldier," he said. "Here's to dead soldiers, Cal." He raised his glass, stared at it a moment, then drank.

The gray-blond, forty-year-old general sipped his whiskey and quietly contemplated his friend. "What's the dictionary for?" he asked after several minutes of silence.

"This," said Lee, picking it up with his right hand and raising it over his wounded shoulder, once, then ten more times, until his forehead shone with sweat.

"That's more than you could do two months ago," said Cal.

Lee scraped his chair back then and rose unsteadily. "I've got another soldier hidden over here," he said, moving toward a bookcase and reaching behind it for a bottle. "Miss Alpha does not approve," he said as he sat down again and yanked out the cork. "Says it makes me useless in bed."

Cal covered his glass with his hand. "No more for me. I've still got some people I have to see tonight."

"Suit yourself," said Lee.

The young general turned his glass in his hand. "We did our best, Lee. We fought outside the regular army. We hit the Yankees hard in their own backyards and kept hundreds, maybe thousands, of them away from the front lines. If they had listened in Richmond and had let us do more, maybe we could have won. Who knows?"

Lee stared into the dark whiskey, cursing himself again for ever having gotten drawn into such a hopeless cause. But he'd done his best. By God, he'd done everything right. He hadn't lost a single man who rode with him. Not until Nathan. He *had* done his best. He'd gotten them away from the Yanks, hadn't he? Made it look like Jessamine was innocent in the whole affair, and even used a goddamn empty gun to do it all.

After six months, that night still haunted him. They'd been slipping down the Missouri River, young Nathan asleep in the bottom of the boat, Lee mooning like some idiot schoolboy over Jessie's eyes and her lush mouth and how she fitted so perfectly in his arms. He'd even been thinking about going back to Riverbend once the war ended. Back to Jessie.

Nathan had woken up just as they were swinging into the Mississippi. Lee had seen him rub his eyes then grin, as if suddenly realizing their escape was real and not something he'd been dreaming. He'd leapt up then to holler out his boyish joy. And the boat had gone over. The current had been cold and swift, and Lee had felt the stitches ripping in his shoulder as he tried to keep hold of the boy.

"I've got you, Nathan," he'd told him though his grip had been tenuous, slipping.

"Oh, I ain't worried. You've always looked out for me, Captain," the boy had said just before the current churned them and slowly broke Lee's hold.

"I've got you, boy," Lee had kept saying. But he hadn't. He hadn't been able to hold on. His best hadn't been good enough for Nathan.

Cal raised his glass. "To better days ahead," he said.

But Lee's thoughts clung to the past.

"You know," he drawled "when I was ten years old my mama sent me out to play when a 'gentleman caller' came. I was playing soldier in an oak grove about a half mile from town. Using a stick for a rifle." Lee smiled to himself. "Shooting redskins or Brits, I don't recall. I stepped into this little patch of wild strawberries under a great big oak, and the next thing I knew I was hanging by my ankles, way off the ground, just swinging back and forth like the pendulum on a clock."

He tipped the bottle over his empty glass. "Ticktock. Ticktock. There were four boys, older than me, tough bastards, all of 'em. They let me drop, then they trussed me up like a little pig."

"Lee," the general said softly.

Lee raised his hand. "No. There's a point to this, Cal. They picked up some oak wood and built a fire. Then they yanked down my breeches and used burning sticks to carve my initial on me." He stuck his long leg out from the table and pointed. "Right there. Right on the inside of the thigh where the skin is so tender. They burned the letter *B* deep into my flesh. *B* for bastard, 'cause that's what I was."

"That was a long time ago," said the general.

"Long time," Lee echoed. "But here's my point, Cal. I yelled and I cried, and before it was over I killed one of those sons of bitches, then stowed away on a riverboat, rope burned and branded." Lee paused for a moment, sipped his whiskey, then put the glass down thoughtfully. "But I wasn't really hurt, because I had such hopes and such big dreams and plans. I looked to my future then, and saw it all stretched out bright and shiny. And I can't do that now."

His voice thickened. "I can't see past the next ten minutes."

General Buford stood up, walked around the table and put his hand on Lee's shoulder. "It'll pass," he said.

"Will it?" Lee asked sullenly.

After Cal was gone, Lee continued to sit there, alternating between lifting his glass and hoisting the dictionary over his head. Well, hell! He'd been a fool to ever get involved. But he wasn't going to think about it anymore. Just let it all slip away. He was going to drown Nathan again, but this time with good Kentucky bourbon. And Jessie. Jessie! He grinned drunkenly as he pictured her that last night, mad as a wet hen, her violet eyes more like nightshade than pansies. He hoped to hell that brass-bound major would take good care of her. God knew he couldn't do it. Couldn't do much of anything. Not anymore.

Doc Ferguson lowered himself into the straight chair next to Jessamine's. "I've seen a lot of funerals in my day, but I do believe this tops them all. The judge would have been right proud."

Riverbend's front parlor was still crowded with mourners, though many had left to gather elsewhere in celebration of the war's end. The dining room table sagged with hams and smoked turkeys, pickled peaches, put-up beans, cheeses, light breads, dark breads, layer cakes and tarts. Maisie had been forced to move the silver coffee service from the sideboard in order to accommodate dozens of plates and trays and baskets.

"I expect he would have, Doc. Thank you for coming."

He leaned toward her. "You're looking right poorly, my dear. You want me to get you a little glass of sherry?"

"No, thank you, Doc. I'm just weary. I wish all these people would go home. I hardly know half of them."

He snorted. "Take a gander at that female over there. The one with no bosom and the peacock feather in her bonnet."

"I see her," said Jessamine, trying not to laugh. "But I've never seen her before. Who is she, Doc?"

"That's Ida Kemp. Only goes to funerals." He leaned closer. "You keep an eye on your dining room table, Miss Jessamine. I've seen Ida put an entire ham in her skirts. Slips bread in her dress, too. The old bat's flat-chested now, but you just take a look at her when she leaves. She'll have a bosom like yours."

Jessamine laughed.

"That's better," Doc Ferguson said. "It does a person good to laugh. Though I don't suppose there's been much to laugh about at Riverbend of late, what with your brother dying out in Colorado, and then the judge."

Jessamine simply nodded. She really couldn't remember the last time she had laughed.

"Nothing I could have done for the judge," he said. "I suppose you know it was the whiskey did him in, Miss Jessamine. That, and getting the unfortunate news about Louis."

Her father had received a letter in February informing him that his middle son had been knifed in a barroom brawl on Christmas Eve. It had given few details, and had been signed simply, mysteriously, "Charlotte." The judge had taken to his bed shortly thereafter—with a bottle—and hadn't left the house again until he was carried out to the undertaker's wagon yesterday morning.

"I don't think anyone could have helped him, Doc. Louis was just one loss too many," she said.

The doctor nudged her elbow. "Here comes that Clarence Dunlap," he snarled. "I never did care for him."

"Hush, Doc," whispered Jessamine as her father's law partner approached, bowed slightly, then took Jessamine's hand.

"My deepest condolences, Miss Jessamine," he said.

"You were kind to come, Mr. Dunlap. Won't you sit down? You know Doctor Ferguson, don't you?"

Clarence Dunlap's eyes flicked toward the doctor, then returned to Jessamine. "There are some matters we must discuss, Miss Jessamine. As you know, I was your father's attorney."

"Yes, I know," she said, wondering how the judge could have suffered this man, with his bald head and his fringe of yellow hair that looked like a dirty halo.

He cleared his throat. "When do you want the reading, my dear?"

"The reading?" she asked.

"Of the judge's last will and testament," Dunlap said, speaking slowly, articulating each word distinctly and, apparently, with great relish.

"The girl ain't deaf, Dunlap," snapped the doctor.

Jessamine nudged him, stifling a smile. How she wanted to laugh. She was tired of death and all its trappings, weary of wearing black and smiling dutifully, and just plain bored with grief. "Must we do it formally?" she asked him. "Can't you simply tell me what it says, Mr. Dunlap?"

The lawyer coughed. "Well, no," he said. "That isn't the way it's done. There are legalities involved. As the judge's daughter, certainly you must be aware..."

Jessamine held up a hand in surrender. "Forgive me, Mr. Dunlap. I'm not quite myself these days. Of course we'll have a proper reading. Shall we do it tomorrow? Would you like to come out to Riverbend, or shall I come into town?"

"These matters are best handled in an office. Why don't we say eleven o'clock, if that would suit you."

"Eleven it is," said Jessamine, and Clarence Dunlap touched his heels together and then melted back into a group of chatting mourners.

"Pompous old fool," snarled Doc Ferguson. "I believe I'll just tell him I'm too dignified next time he asks me to lance a boil."

The clock on the town hall cupola struck half past eleven as Jessamine returned to the buckboard. She was in the front seat before Sampson could even give her a hand up.

"You owe me a five-dollar gold piece," she snapped.

"Now hold on, Miss Jess," said Sampson, pulling out his pocket watch. "My timepiece says 11:34."

"That old watch of Papa's always did run fast. You heard the town hall clock. I said I'd be out of there in less than half an hour, and I was. You owe me a five-dollar gold piece."

"Fine. Soon as I get one, Miss Jess, you can have it."

Jessamine looked back at the door of Dunlap & Delavan and grimaced. "Here. Give me the reins. I want to get out of town fast, in case that fool Dunlap believes he's forgotten something. My Lord, that man went on and on until I finally just looked out the window and closed my ears." She snapped the reins, sending Daniel off at a brisk clip.

"You angry about somethin', Miss Jess?" asked Sampson.

"Whatever makes you ask that?"

"You seem awful riled up. Is it about the judge's will?"

She ignored him, flicking the reins, her eyes straight ahead, until she couldn't stand her own silence anymore. "It was the will he made out right after my mama died, when he probably hated me the most."

"He didn't hate you, Miss Jess."

"Well, maybe not toward the end. He simply ignored me. I meant about as much to that man as the wallpaper in the vestibule."

"He was lookin' out for you, Miss Jess. The judge told me he was hoping you'd marry Major Harding, have a nice life back in Ohio."

Jessamine gave him a murderous look. She fell silent again and stared distractedly at Daniel's rump.

"So you gonna tell me what the will said?" asked Sampson.

Jessamine rolled her eyes impatiently. "It said he leaves Riverbend to Charles, except if Charles is dead, then he leaves it to Louis, except—" she took a deep, dramatic breath "—if Louis is dead, in which case Caleb gets it, unless . . ."

"Then Riverbend belong to you, Miss Jess. We ain't had no word from Mr. Caleb for over two years now."

"I'm not done yet, Sampson. There's a whole string of widows and orphans to run through. It goes from Caleb back to Charles's widow, then Louis's widow, et cetera, et cetera. Hell! You'd think the judge could've just come right out and said, 'I'll be damned if I'll leave my property to Jessamine,' instead of creating some kind of Chinese puzzle," Jessamine snapped.

They rode silently for a mile before Sampson said, "Then who Riverbend belong to, Miss Jess?"

"Well, Caleb, of course, assuming he's alive. Riverbend, and everything in and on it. Oh, except for my mother's diamond brooch. That's mine." She sneered. "Guess I'll wear it when I'm out cutting hemp next autumn."

"I'm sorry, Miss Jess," Sampson said.

"Well, don't be." She untied the black ribbon of her bonnet with one hand and whisked it off her head. "Lord, I'm so tired of this thing." She tossed it into the bed of the wagon. "I'm tired of everything, Sampson. I may just run off with a traveling band of gypsies."

"That'll be the day, Miss Jess," Sampson said with a laugh. "You leaving Riverbend."

"You're probably right." Jessamine frowned. "I only wish I could think of someplace I'd rather be."

By the time they reached home, Jessamine had come to the conclusion that there was no place else on earth she'd rather be than here at Riverbend. She sighed aloud, then gasped when she saw Maisie standing on the front porch, legs spread like a gladiator's, fists on her ample hips.

"Here. Take the reins, will you, Sampson? Maisie'll have a fit if she sees I've ditched my bonnet." She grabbed it out of the back and was tying a quick bow at her chin just as they pulled up in front.

"I think she saw, Miss Jess. Look like she's in a snit."

Maisie stalked down the front steps. "You best get on in the house, Miss Jess," she called as she walked. "We got us a visitor."

Jessamine's face lit up. "I knew he'd come back," she cried, gathering up her skirt, ready to leap down. But Maisie placed a large restraining hand on her knee.

"Oh, child. It ain't Mr. Lee. I could just bite my tongue for sayin' it that way."

Jessamine simply looked at her, baffled and disappointed.

"Who is it, Mama?" Sampson asked.

"Well—" Maisie snorted, "—it some painted woman who say she Mr. Louis's widow. And she say she done talked to Mr. Dunlap early this morning, and he told her she own Riverbend."

"She what?" yelped Jessamine.

Jessamine sat at one end of the table, fiddling with a spoon, barely listening to the conversation. She wondered if she could throw a knife to the other end of the table—the head of the table—stick Charlotte in the throat, then claim it was an accident. Probably not, but it seemed a pleasant

idea nevertheless. Of course, she'd have to move the silver candelabra first. And get a sharper knife...

She studied Charlotte's face, which was squarish and powdered paler than her natural skin tone. Her forehead was arrayed with a line of perfect blond spit curls. Her mouth was a rouged Cupid's bow. In between the spit curls and the Cupid's bow was Charlotte's nose, which appeared to have been broken at some point in her life. Jessamine silently commended the perpetrator.

"Miss Jessamine."

She turned her head lanquidly to the right, gazed into the sky blue eyes of Major Harding.

"Miss Jessamine, I don't believe you've heard a single word I've said," he exclaimed.

She blinked. She had totally forgotten he was there. She had even forgotten what she was wearing—until she'd glanced down at her low-cut watered-silk gown. Hell! No wonder the major was staring at her chest. Charlotte had conveniently seen to it that all her other dresses were in the wash or wadded up in the mending basket—all part of her plan to make Jessamine more alluring to the major, in the hope of wringing a proposal of marriage out of him.

"Really, Jessamine. You're being quite rude," Charlotte scolded. "The major was asking you about New Orleans. You were there before the war, I believe, or so my husband told me."

Clarence Dunlap, the fourth at the table, cleared his throat and said, "The judge took Miss Jessamine to New Orleans, where she was presented to society at a cotillion."

The attorney was directing his conversation exclusively to Charlotte, so Jessamine's view was restricted to the back of his bald head and half a halo of yellow fringe.

"How nice," said Charlotte. "You know, Clarence, when I was in New Orleans..."

Jessamine was happy to return to the faraway place inside her head while Charlotte monopolized the conversation.

In the three weeks since her arrival at Riverbend, marriage certificate in hand, Charlotte Dade had rearranged the furniture, replaced some, replanted the front walk with white petunias carted in from Jefferson City at considerable expense, and ordered seven outfits from the dressmaker, six hats from the milliner, and four pairs of shoes.

If there was another way to tell Charlotte that the money for her luxuries just wasn't there, Jessamine didn't know what it was. If Charlotte had been a mule, she could have just hit her with a board right between the eyes. But the woman's eternal reply was, "My husband, Louis, was a very wealthy man." For a day or two, Jessamine had thought perhaps there had been another Louis Dade in Colorado, but she'd checked the marriage certificate again, and it was definitely her brother's signature.

They owed more money than Riverbend was going to make this year, and that was after just three weeks of Charlotte's tenure. With the judge's death, they had been late getting the hemp planted, and then the skies had just seemed to dry up. But even if it rained, and even if they were guaranteed a bumper crop, it wasn't going to do much good. The demand for hemp had fallen off drastically during the war, as the South's cotton production had decreased. Jessamine knew they'd have to start corn and wheat next year if Riverbend was to make ends meet.

"You've left us again, Miss Jessamine."

She turned her head to see Major Harding's beatific smile. He loved her. He had told her so before dinner. And she couldn't even look at him without thinking about Lee.

"I hope you're considering my proposal, Miss Jessamine," he whispered. "I'd like to ask Mrs. Dade for your hand this evening."

Jessamine nearly choked. "Ask Charlotte?"

"Were you speaking to me, Jessamine?" Charlotte asked.

"No. Actually, I wasn't, Charlotte. But I shall now. Would you be so kind as to excuse me? I have suddenly developed a withering headache."

"Poor dear," said Major Harding.

Clarence Dunlap cleared his throat.

"Another one?" Charlotte groaned. "You don't mind if I remain here, do you, Jessamine? And if you happen to pass through the kitchen, tell Maisie that I want her to serve the brandied cherries now, in those new crystal footed bowls."

Jessamine pulled the judge's leather grip from under his bed and carried it back to her room. Slamming doors and drawers she went from wardrobe to dresser to the grip on the bed, stuffing clothes into the bag.

"Crystal footed bowls!" she snarled as she pitched her hairbrush into the valise. "We're on our way to the poorhouse and she's buying crystal footed bowls."

"What's all this commotion? Sound like you tearin' the house down, Miss Jess," said Maisie, entering her room. Her hands went immediately to her hips when she saw the leather grip.

"Ha! Why don't you go ask Charlotte about tearing the house down, Maisie?" She slapped a camisole into the suitcase. "Or, better yet, ask her where she wants to sell the hemp this year. Or how the hell she intends to harvest it at all, now that she's fired Eamon Dobbs."

Maisie began taking clothes out of the grip. "Miss Jess, she done fired me seven times in the past week. It don't mean nothin'."

"Put those clothes back," Jessamine shouted.

"Just what you think you doin'?"

She tossed a pair of shoes into the grip. "I'm going to look for Caleb. That's what I'm doing. I've got to get that woman out of this house."

Maisie caught her by the wrist. "Mr. Caleb dead, child. You said so yo'self."

"I did not. I said he *might* be dead."

"No, you didn't. You said—"

Jessamine pulled her wrist away. "I'm not going to argue with you, Maisie. Now you get out of my way."

The big woman stood like a brick wall by the bed, blocking her access to the grip. "No. I ain't lettin' you go."

"I'm going," she said, "with or without that suitcase, Maisie. And no one is going to stop me."

"Where you goin'?" Maisie asked, crossing her arms.

"I told you. To look for Caleb."

"No, I mean where? You figure on walkin' to Atlanta, or what?"

Jessamine stood still in the middle of the room, a silk stocking hanging over one arm. "Well, I'll go...I'll go to St. Louis first, and then I'll..."

"You're goin' to find Mr. Lee, that what you're doin'," Maisie said accusingly.

"I am not."

"Oh, yes, you is, Miss Jess. And you're jus' askin' for trouble, girl. More 'n you can handle. You think Mr. Lee be glad to see you, seein' how he ain't wrote or sent no word since he been gone?" Maisie grabbed Jessamine by the shoulders. "Don't you go throwin' yo'self at that black sheep hotelman. He don't want you, honey. Ain't that clear by now?"

Jessamine fought back her tears and lifted her chin defiantly. "I'm going to find my brother," she said. "If I happen to run into Lee Kincannon along the way, I'll tell him you said hello, Maisie."

Chapter Six

"**D**amnation!" Jessamine muttered. She had to stand on tiptoe to sign the guest register of the Imperial Hotel and, while scratching her name with her arm practically over her head, she had gotten ink on her glove. She already felt shabby in the gray plaid georgette she'd pulled out of the mending basket the night before—with Maisie yammering at her about all the horrors that befell young women who traveled alone. Well, perhaps a splotch of black ink on her glove would be her sole tribulation. Perhaps the worst was over.

The marble surface of the desk felt cool when she touched it, cool and elegant. As elegant as the rest of the lobby, with its fringed velvet upholstery, its Persian rugs, and its tall potted palms.

"I wonder if you could satisfy my curiosity about something," she said to the portly, bespectacled desk clerk. "Does this hotel belong to Mr. Simon Pierce of Chicago?"

For a second, she thought, he looked at her as if she were a horsefly he was just about to whack. Then his proprietary mask returned. "I've never heard of Simon Pierce, miss. The Imperial Hotel is owned by Mr. Lee Kincannon."

Jessamine swallowed her grin. "I was misinformed," she said. "I have another question for you, if you don't mind."

"Certainly, miss."

She carefully unfolded her mother's diamond brooch from a linen handkerchief, placing it on the marble counter. "Would you have any idea where I might sell this?"

He readjusted his spectacles and looked closely at the circular brooch. There was a square-cut diamond in the center, surrounded by smaller emerald-cut stones, all set in a leafy filigree of silver.

"This is quite beautiful," he said, his tone a bit more respectful, as if Jessamine had graduated from horsefly to housefly.

"Thank you," she said. "It belonged to my mother. And her mother before her. I believe it's worth at least a hundred dollars, don't you?" Please, please, please, she prayed, don't say I'd be lucky to get a double eagle for it.

"May I?" the man asked, picking up the brooch and turning it over in the palm of his hand. "Easily, miss. I'd say someone was trying to cheat you if he offered anything less than one hundred dollars."

Jessamine rolled her eyes heavenward. "Thank you," she breathed.

"Well, I'm not an expert," he said, "but there are quite a few diamonds in it. There is a jeweler just down the street, if you'd like a professional opinion."

She folded the pin back in the handkerchief and deposited it in her handbag. "I just might do that. Thank you very much."

"You are quite welcome. Don't forget your key, miss."

"Pardon?"

He pushed the brass-tagged key across the counter. "Your room key, miss. Room 620. Our elevator is right across the lobby. And a boy has already taken your grip upstairs."

Jessamine took the key. "Of course," she said. "Thank you." She walked across the lobby. Lord help me, she thought, an elevator. Her brothers had laughed at her in New Orleans when she had refused to ride in one with them.

Louis had called her "lily-livered." But she couldn't do it. Even now she was breaking out in a cold sweat at the mere thought of it.

Imagine Lee being the proprietor of an elevator, she thought, as she searched for the stairs.

Slightly out of breath from the six flights of narrow stairs, Jessamine whisked off her black bonnet and tossed it across the room. Then she kicked off her slippers, bounced on the bed, and finally just lay there looking at the coved ceiling. It was a lovely room, with deep blue velvet drapes, a blue-and-beige Persian carpet, a tweed wing chair with a matching ottoman, and a big brass bed covered with snow-white linens. Jessamine went to the window and looked out at the city of St. Louis. It was hot, and a pale haze scraped the skyline. The street below her window was teeming with carriages, streetcars and pedestrians. Everyone rushing home for dinner, she imagined. To the east, there was just a glimmer of the Mississippi. Above all the street noise, Jessamine could hear the solid blast of a steamboat whistle.

She looked at herself in the mirror over the Chippendale dresser. A smudge on her cheek. A shine on her nose. Her hair flying loose from its chignon. "Jessamine Dade," she admonished her image, "you look like you just fell off a hay wagon." She unpinned her chignon and bent over, shaking her hair into long raven waves, until she was almost light-headed.

And then there was a vigorous knock on the door.

Jessamine jerked upright, but felt as if her heart hadn't kept pace with the rest of her. Her hair was every which way. But she didn't care. In spite of what Maisie had said, she wasn't throwing herself at Lee. She wasn't. She ran to the door.

"Miss Jessamine Dade?" The stunning redhead extended her manicured hand. "My name is Alpha Parker. I'm on the staff of the hotel. May I come in?"

Jessamine offered her hand listlessly, then stepped back to allow for the sweep of the woman's wide and rustling apple green skirt.

"I hope the room suits you, Miss Dade." Alpha gestured to the window with a heavily ringed hand. "You can almost see the river from here."

"It's lovely," said Jessamine. She didn't know quite how to behave toward a woman whose eyes were rimmed with charcoal, whose lips were red and moist as poppies, whose lily fragrance filled the room. Charlotte Dade's efforts at beauty were strictly amateur compared to this . . . this courtesan.

And she was just standing there now, studying Jessamine from the top of her tumbled hair to the soiled hem of her skirt. Jessamine felt like a slave on the auction block beneath the woman's cool, appraising gaze.

"You do have extraordinary eyes," Alpha said almost to herself.

Jessamine blinked. "I beg your pardon?"

The redhead shook her head slightly, then straightened her shoulders. "I've come, Miss Dade, because Mr. Keller at the front desk informed me that you have a brooch you are interested in selling. Is that correct?"

Her disappointment turned to wary interest now. "Yes, that's correct. Would you like to see it?" Judging from the amount of jewelry already pinned, clasped, and skewered on this woman, Jessamine thought she might have an eager, possibly well-heeled customer. And the Lord knew she needed one, with only six silver dollars in her bag to see her all the way to Georgia and back.

She handed the folded handkerchief to Alpha Parker, who unwrapped it rather casually and then stared at the brooch.

"It's very beautiful," said Alpha. "Are you sure you want to part with it? Mr. Keller said it belonged to your mother, I believe?"

"That's right," said Jessamine, sitting down on the edge of the bed. "Mrs. Parker... It is Mrs., isn't it?" She wasn't sure she had glimpsed a wedding band among all the other rings.

"Yes," said Alpha.

Jessamine folded her hands on her lap. "Well, Mrs. Parker, I do want to part with the brooch. I've sold crops, and I've struck some excellent bargains. I sold a horse once. But I have never sold a piece of jewelry. Now I know how much money I require, so why don't you tell me how much you would be willing to give me." And don't take the first pittance she offers, Jessamine warned herself. Don't.

Alpha Parker smiled. "I'm not very good at bargaining myself, Miss Dade. I'll give you four hundred dollars for it."

Jessamine swallowed. "Now? In cash?"

"In gold, if you like. I can have it for you tomorrow. Why don't we breakfast together, about ten? That will give me time to make arrangements with my bank." She handed the brooch back to Jessamine.

The woman gave it back without a second glance, Jessamine noticed, thinking it rather odd, if Alpha Parker prized it so highly—and to Jessamine, four hundred dollars in gold was high indeed.

"Ten o'clock will be fine," Jessamine said. "I'm planning to book passage on a steamboat tomorrow, but I suppose I could be back from the wharf by ten."

Alpha Parker said nothing. She walked to the window and stood looking east toward the river. Then, with her back still

to Jessamine, she said, "Where are you traveling, if you don't mind my asking?"

"Downriver," Jessamine replied. She had the distinct impression that the woman didn't like her. "Downriver," Jessamine thought, was a polite way of saying "None of your business."

"You're traveling alone?"

"I often do." This painted, lily-scented Aphrodite was beginning to irritate her.

Alpha turned from the window, frowning. "It isn't a good time to be going south, Miss Dade. Most people are trying to come north."

"Nevertheless," said Jessamine.

Twisting an opal ring on her middle finger, Alpha echoed her. "Yes. Nevertheless." She pressed her bright red lips together. "What boat are you going on?" she asked sharply.

"I don't know yet. I haven't..."

Alpha's mouth relaxed, slipping into a pleasant smile. "Well, I'm glad I asked. A woman traveling alone can't take any chances, as I'm sure you know. You'll want to get to your destination as quickly as possible. The faster you travel, the fewer the mishaps along the way. Let me suggest that you book passage on the *Kentucky Belle* to Memphis, and then, if you're going farther, the best and fastest boats out of Memphis are the *City of New Orleans* and the *John K. Lang.*"

"I appreciate the advice, Mrs. Parker." The woman had just solved one of Jessamine's problems. She hadn't had the vaguest notion which boat to take. She had planned to inquire tomorrow morning, down on the levee, and now Mrs. Parker had saved her a good deal of time and effort.

"Would you like me to write the names down for you?"

But Jessamine's appreciation had its limits. If it weren't for her four hundred dollars, Jessamine would have told Alpha Parker she wasn't an idiot or an illiterate hayseed de-

spite the way she looked. "No. The *Kentucky Belle,* the *City of New Orleans* and the *John Something Lang.* Right?"

"Perfect," said Alpha, moving to the door with a great sweep of green skirt. "Well, I'll look forward to seeing you at ten o'clock tomorrow, Miss Dade"

"Thank you, Mrs. Parker." And don't forget the gold, Jessamine added under her breath as she closed the door behind her.

Jessamine fingered the gold cord decorating the leather-bound menu, folded it closed, then flipped it open again. Perhaps it hadn't been such a good idea, Jessamine thought as she looked around the Imperial Hotel's elegant white-and-gold dining room. But she had felt so flush after Mrs. Parker left. And she was so hungry. She hadn't eaten anything that day except the two scones Maisie had slipped into her handbag.

Jessamine ordered a boiled egg and a cup of coffee, which after some calculations she decided came to one twenty-fourth of her current fortune. Good thing Charlotte wasn't here. She probably would have ordered the entire left side of the menu.

The white-jacketed waiter placed her egg before her in a delicate gold-rimmed cup. "Will there be anything else, miss?" he asked.

The eggshell was a tawny color. In its fragile porcelain setting, it looked more like a Christmas ornament than a meal.

Jessamine sighed. "No, thank you. This will be sufficient."

As she tapped off the dome of the shell, she wondered bleakly if women were permitted to gamble on riverboats. And, if so, where she could learn to play cards in a hurry.

Jessamine ate a spoonful of the egg. The dining room was filling up. All the women in the room were elegantly dressed

in pale summer frocks and stylish hats with feathers and delicate bows. Suddenly Jessamine felt shabby and forlorn. If a man like Lee Kincannon walked in the room right now, it was a sure bet he wouldn't even notice the skinny girl in the wilted, rat gray dress.

What was she doing here? Jessamine wondered. She should have booked her passage the moment she arrived in St. Louis, then stayed on the boat till it left. She shouldn't have come here. This wasn't her world. She felt so out of place. She wasn't competent here, the way she was at Riverbend. There she felt healthy and smart and strong. Riverbend was where she was at her best.

And, she thought glumly, she'd better quit fooling around with silly dreams about Lee and get on with the business of finding Caleb. Because if she didn't find her brother there would be no Riverbend to go back to.

She should have asked for a room on a lower floor, Jessamine thought as she eyed the staircase on the far side of the lobby. By the time she climbed the six flights, she'd be hungry again. She patted her handbag, stuffed now with cloverleaf rolls, and made her way toward the stairs.

"Miss Jessamine! Oh, thank God I've found you!"

Everyone in the lobby turned, including Jessamine, to see a tall, copper-haired officer striding toward her, brass buttons twinkling, boots gleaming, and a lover's smile beneath his brushy mustache. She wanted to run, but his arms were around her before her feet could move. Major Harding crushed her against his chest, nuzzled his face into her hair.

"Oh, Jessamine, dear, I thought I'd lost you forever."

In some strange way, feeling his warm breath on her hair, and hearing the quiver in his voice was comforting. This man had noticed her in a crowded room. This man would never leave her. He would stand between Jessamine and the

devil, if need be. Perhaps he already had, she thought, remembering her abduction from Riverbend.

"I'm so glad to see you, Thomas," she said. And she meant it, she thought. Surprise of surprises, she meant it.

"Naturally, I don't intend to remain in the army forever. But it does provide a rare opportunity to see the country," the major said, spearing a square of roast beef with his fork.

Jessamine watched as he chewed it twenty-three times. She had begun to count. Twenty-three. Never twenty, or twenty-four, but always twenty-three. She had finished her own dinner ten minutes before, and was eyeing the dessert cart while Major Harding droned on about the army, the merits of the westward expansion and the appalling lack of bravery, in his considered opinion, of both the Cheyenne and the Sioux.

"By the way, your sister-in-law asked me to deliver a message to you."

She raised an eyebrow. "Oh?"

"Mrs. Dade wondered if you would order her some crystal. I've written the pattern down. We could do that tomorrow, if you like."

Jessamine smiled wanly. The only thing she was going to order Charlotte was out of her house. Out of the corner of her eye, Jessamine saw Alpha Parker enter the dining room from the kitchen. She was wearing yellow silk shantung now, ruched and flounced and flowing. This was the type of woman, Jessamine thought bleakly, to decorate the arm of a man like Lee Kincannon. She passed congenially from table to table. When she arrived at theirs, Major Harding stood up.

"Good evening, Miss Dade," Alpha said, looking from Jessamine to her companion.

"Mrs. Parker, may I present Major Thomas Harding," said Jessamine.

"Major." Alpha offered him an elegant jeweled hand, and the major bent appropriately. "What a pleasure it is to meet you," she said. She turned to Jessamine again, her green eyes glittering. "What a handsome young man, Miss Dade. Does he belong to you?"

She had never thought of the major as handsome. And he certainly didn't belong to her, but before she could speak, Major Harding said, "Miss Dade is my betrothed."

Jessamine's eyes widened, but not as wide as Alpha Parker's smile.

"What happy news!" the redhead exclaimed. "I'm going to send a bottle of champagne to your table. Do you prefer dry or very dry, Major?"

"Your preference, ma'am. Won't you join us?"

"I wouldn't think of it," cooed Alpha. "You two lovebirds ought to be alone. My heartfelt congratulations to you both."

Her lily fragrance remained behind after she had gone. Jessamine could barely breathe. She tossed her napkin on the table.

"Major Harding, I am not your betrothed," she snapped. "I was happy to see you this evening, but if you've interpreted that happiness as an acceptance of your proposal, then you are mistaken, sir." Jessamine dropped her hands helplessly in her lap as the maître d' presented them with two crystal goblets and a bottle of champagne in a silver bucket.

"Best wishes," he said as he poured the bubbly liquid into their glasses.

"Thank you," said Major Harding. He raised his glass to Jessamine. "I will persist, Miss Jessamine. And you will say yes."

She drank her champagne glumly, wondering if he was right.

* * *

They were in the lobby, which was nearly deserted now. The major had insisted on seeing Jessamine to her room. He wasn't drunk, exactly, just disgustingly rosy and cheerful.

"I don't use elevators, Major," she said stiffly.

"You must try everything at least once, Miss Jessamine," he said, pressing her forward toward the iron grille of the elevator and the toothy grin of its uniformed operator.

"I have tried them, and I don't like them," she said.

He placed his hands on her shoulders, gazing down at her face. "Why, you're frightened, aren't you, my dear?" His voice was warm and thick with concern. "I can feel your little shoulders trembling."

It was anger, actually, but she was indeed frightened of these contraptions. She didn't know why, exactly. Perhaps it was the enclosed space, the fear of being trapped.

He clamped his arm around her like iron. "Come on. I'll protect you." Major Harding propelled her into the elevator. The iron grille clanged closed. "Sixth floor, if you please," said the major.

The little car jolted upward with a raucous squeak of chains and pulleys. Jessamine was wild. She thought her heart was going to explode. Sweat broke out on the palms of her hands. There was a hideous buzzing in her ears. She was certain she was about to faint or vomit when the floor joggled and the operator pulled back the grille.

"Sixth floor," he said.

"There. You see. You have climbed six flights without so much as moving a muscle or batting an eye," the major said.

Her knees buckled, and Major Harding caught her just in time, lifting Jessamine and cradling her against his chest. "Poor darling," he whispered. "I should never have allowed you to drink so much champagne."

Outside her door, the major set her delicately on her feet. "Give me your key, Miss Jessamine. I dare not come in, but I'll wait till you throw the bolt inside."

The dinner rolls spilled from her handbag as she fumbled for the key. He bent to pick them up.

"Oh, don't," she said weakly. "Just let them go. I'm so tired, Major."

He picked them up anyway, putting them in his own pockets. "I'll dispose of them outside," he said, taking the key from her hand and unlocking the door.

"Good night, Major," Jessamine said, intentionally keeping her chin down.

He kissed the top of her head. "My shy darling," he whispered. "Good night, Miss Jessamine. Shall I meet you for lunch tomorrow?"

"That would be nice," she said.

His lips pressed against her hair. "What time, my dear?"

"I'll no doubt sleep late after all the champagne. Shall we say two o'clock?"

"I won't sleep a wink," he murmured, his mustache just grazing her temple. "Until tomorrow, dear."

Jessamine bolted the door, then heard the hellish elevator grind. She had every intention of being on a southbound riverboat at two o'clock tomorrow.

Alpha Parker watched from a window in the lobby as the doorman handed the girl up into the hansom cab. She couldn't help but regard Jessamine Dade as anything but a girl, and she didn't know if that was her own age showing, or just Jessamine's goddamn innocent eyes—those incredible pansy eyes Lee kept going on about in his fitful dreams and in his drunken stupors.

Alpha gave a little wave as the carriage pulled out into the boulevard and headed east toward the levee. "Good rid-

dance," she sighed, leaning her forehead against a velvet fold of drape.

She blamed the girl as much as the war for the state Lee was in now. She'd gotten into his blood before the war, in New Orleans. And when Lee had seen her again, she'd gotten into his heart. Not that he ever said so—and especially not when he was sober. But, after almost sixteen years of loving Lee Kincannon, Alpha recognized her first real threat. Well, the war had been beyond her control, but by God she had some say-so where Miss Jessamine Dade was concerned.

At first she'd thought the girl had come to St. Louis only to unload her brooch, so Alpha had offered her far more than it was worth just to get her to go home.

Then, of course, Jessamine had mentioned going south on the river, and Alpha had been convinced the little bitch was hunting Lee. And she had given her the name of every boat but the *Delta Princess*.

But after having seen Jessamine with that eager beaver of a major, Alpha felt much better. At least now she knew there was somebody else who had a vital interest in keeping Lee and Miss Pansy-Eyes apart.

Chapter Seven

The *Kentucky Belle* made an unscheduled stop in New Madrid to pick up a family of nine, and then, a mile north of Ashport, the steamboat's big wheel stopped when the current shifted and nearly hung it up on a sandbar. It was an hour getting under way again and two hours late getting into Memphis. The *John K. Lang* was just pulling out as Jessamine trudged down the gangplank. She stood on the torch-lit levee and watched its huge wheel turning, its smokestacks venting thick white ribbons that hung against the black sky in the humid summer air.

It was two in the morning. Jessamine dropped her suitcase on the cobbled levee and kicked it. Now what was she going to do?

"Help you, missy?"

She turned and saw a small boy in a big cap. His skin was as dark as the night sky. His eyes were bright as the stars.

"I've missed my boat," she moaned, turning woeful eyes on the departing steamer.

"That *John K.* he pull out right on time tonight. Don't, ordinarily."

"Sounds like you're an authority on steamboat schedules," she said, smiling, even though she was miserable. The boy was no bigger than a minute. His pants were tied with a piece of rope, and were still about to fall off his little hips.

"A what?" he asked.

"An authority. Somebody who knows a lot," she explained.

"Oh, yes, ma'am. I knows a lot. 'Specially about steamboats."

"What's your name?" Jessamine asked.

"Moses."

"Well, Moses, since you're the authority around here, maybe you can tell me the quickest way to get to New Orleans."

"That'd be the *Delta Princess*. She be leavin' at sunup."

Jessamine picked up her suitcase. "Where is this *Princess?*" she asked.

His little hand slid into the handle. "You let Moses take that for you, missy. The *Delta Princess* right this way. Come on." He began dragging her heavy bag along the levee.

"Hey, you!" someone shouted. "Hey, you, Moses!"

Jessamine saw a burly man running toward them. Moses dropped her suitcase and took off running, too, but in the opposite direction.

"Wait a minute," Jessamine cried.

"The *Princess* three boats north, missy," Moses yelled as his little arms pumped wildly and his bare feet flew across the cobblestones.

The burly man stopped when he was within several feet of Jessamine. He bent forward, hands on knees, puffing. "You almost lost that grip, lady. That Moses," he rasped, "he's the shiftiest little devil I ever did see."

Jessamine put her hands on her hips. "That little rascal. And I was going to give him a whole nickel just for toting my worthless bag. Well, hell! You don't know when the next boat to New Orleans is, do you?"

"I guess the next southbound steamer is the *Delta Princess*," he said. "She's..."

"Three boats north," Jessamine said, finishing his sentence for him.

"Yes'm. There she is." He pointed. "The pretty boat with the big white wheel."

"Thank you," said Jessamine.

"Carry that bag for you, ma'am?" he asked.

"No, thank you. I can get it just fine. Good evening, sir."

"Evenin', ma'am."

Jessamine lugged her bag along the cobblestones and up the clean white gangplank of the *Delta Princess*. She was a beautiful boat—white from stem to stern, her decks all shiny and clean, her wood railings all gingerbread and filigree— like a big white wedding cake, with the two tall smokestacks standing like a bride and groom. The main salon, on the upper deck, was still brightly lit, and Jessamine could hear piano music and laughter.

She found the purser's office on the main deck, near the salon, and rapped on the door.

"Go away," somebody shouted from inside.

Jessamine knocked harder, and kept knocking until the door was opened by a young man with a pale, perfectly round face and wild, curly hair.

"What?" he whined.

"I'd like to purchase a ticket for New Orleans," she said.

He regarded her through half-closed eyes. "Come back tomorrow, about five-thirty," he said hoarsely. He began to close the door.

Jessamine inserted her foot. "It is tomorrow, sir. I'd like to reserve a stateroom right now. For one. For New Orleans."

Sighing, he held out his hand, palm up. "Five dollars," he said. "What deck?"

She fished through her handbag, put a twenty-dollar gold piece in his hand. "I'll wait for my change, of course," she said. "The deck doesn't matter."

He nodded sleepily and disappeared from the door, returning in a moment with a key and fifteen dollars in greenbacks. He yawned the number of her stateroom as Jessamine counted her change, and then he closed the door in her face.

The fact that main salon was still doing a brisk business in the wee hours of the morning would have gratified Lee Kincannon enormously a few years ago. Now it barely made an impression on him. Most of the poker tables, where Lee sat, were occupied. There were several men at the bar, their backs to the room, each with a foot on the shiny brass rail. Riverboat girls in gaudy dresses moved among the men, laughing, touching, allowing liberties.

"Aw," complained one of them as Lee gave her corseted fanny a shove. "I want to watch you play, Lee."

"Then make yourself useful, Daisy. Go get me another brandy," he said.

He drank a third of it as soon as Daisy set it down. She plopped a hip on the arm of his chair and leaned across him. "You got ashes all over your shirt, baby," she cooed, brushing the white frills that ran vertically down his chest. He elbowed her off the chair.

"Lee!"

"Scat," he hissed.

Old habits were hard to break, he thought, especially the bad ones. New habits, too. He took a deep draft of the brandy and let it burn the back of his throat.

A month ago he'd walked out on Red—or she'd booted him out of the basement of the Imperial Hotel. It depended on your point of view. He'd gotten a shave and a haircut, then taken up residence on his finest boat, the *Delta Princess,* intending to play cards and drift up and down the Mississippi until his legs were either under him again or cut off at the knees.

For the most part, they were just wobbly—from the twist of river currents, from too much brandy, from sitting too long at poker tables.

He won. He lost. He was indifferent.

And his bad dreams continued. Every night he lost young Nathan again in the cold, rushing current, the boy's trusting grin turning to a horrible grimace as the river pulled him under. Every night he woke up in a cold and panicky sweat. He had tried for a while to avoid sleep, but he was beginning to dream now when his eyes were wide open. How the hell was he going to avoid being awake?

"Are you playing cards, Lee, or playing with Daisy?" asked Harry Damon.

Lee snapped out of his fog. He picked up his cards, pulled a cigar from his breast pocket. Daisy, still hovering behind him, struck a match. He sucked in the warm smoke, then pushed a stack of greenbacks into the center of the table. "Deuce," he said, looking across the table at the gray-bearded gambler who had tutored him so many years ago, and who, like Alpha Parker, had remained a fixture in his life long after his wild riverboat days were done.

"If I didn't know you better, Lee, I'd say you were trying hard to lose," said Deuce Barnett. "I'll see your thousand, and raise you two."

"You just play your own hand, old man," growled Lee, anchoring his cigar in the corner of his mouth and counting out twenty hundred-dollar bills. He tossed the money to the center of the green-felt-covered table and laid down his cards. "Two pair," he said. "Tens over fives."

Deuce fanned out a full house. "You're losing your touch, boy," he said, raking the money toward his chest.

The expression on Lee's face remained the same as he leaned back in his chair and lifted his hand to signal the barmaid.

"Thank you, pretty Lucy," he said when the barmaid put another snifter of brandy by his elbow. He flipped her a silver dollar which she dropped down the front of her dress, smiling and arching an eyebrow at Daisy Jones.

The game had been running for about thirty-six hours. It was probably the most honest poker game that had ever been played on the Memphis riverfront, the four gamblers being equal in their ability to cheat. In the past few hours, the stakes had climbed dramatically. Conversation, when there was any at all, was terse.

"Your piano man asleep, Lee?" asked Harry Damon.

"Let's have some music," called Lee. "Go light a fire under that piano man, will you, Daisy? Your deal, Gander."

"Right," said Gander McCoy, his fingers hardly moving as he shuffled.

Lee leaned forward, squinting to keep the cigar smoke out of his eyes, just to focus on the goddamn cards. He fanned out his hand—a pair of treys. His lips slid into a private grin as he noted the lowly pair with which he'd bluffed his way to his first steamboat. God, how high his hopes had been then, how huge his appetite for success. Maybe he'd just bluff his way back to the bottom and start all over again. Or stay there.

He took the cigar out of his mouth, balanced it on the edge of a crystal ashtray, then took a slow sip of brandy as he looked over the rim of his cards at Deuce. The old man was holding three of a kind. Lee knew the look.

He knew everything Deuce knew. Good teachers made good students. Lee had been the best—until he'd found out even his best wasn't good enough.

Out of the corner of his eye, he saw somebody walking along the promenade outside the main salon. Jessamine? Lee blinked and the vision was gone. He looked at his hand again. Looked at Deuce.

"You in or out, boy?" asked Deuce.

"Let's go, Lee," Harry Damon muttered.

The piano player struck the last chord of "Camptown Races." Then, clear as a bell, Lee heard Jessamine's voice. Distant, but clear. Like a riverboat coming round the bend. Like a church bell across town on a hot summer morning. Like a ghost come back again to haunt him. He shook his head to get rid of the apparition.

"Get it up, boy," said Deuce.

Lee pushed his entire bankroll of eight thousand dollars to the center of the table.

Daisy gasped.

"Shit! I'm out," snarled Harry Damon.

Gander McCoy shoved his chair back and threw his cards on the table.

Deuce lit a cigar and gazed at his cards.

Sweat was trickling down his sides now. Lee's heart was a clenched fist in his chest. Nathan's joyous whoop echoed in his head, and he was dizzy with Jessamine's voice.

"How much you want to lose, boy?" asked Deuce softly, sliding a stack of greenbacks next to Lee's, and then a second stack of equal size.

Yeah, thought Lee, old Deuce was the closest thing to a father he had ever known. And maybe the old man had a second sense about him. Maybe Red had talked to him. Or maybe he could just smell how bad he hurt. Resting his cards facedown on the table, he extended a leg and reached into his pocket. He withdrew a brass key on a tag and, using both hands, twisted the key from the circular tag. He put the key back in his pocket and tossed the tag into the center of the table. Engraved on the brass was The Delta Princess.

The old man arched a gray eyebrow. "Is she free and clear?" he asked.

Lee nodded, then turned over his pair of treys.

Deuce revealed his three queens and silently raked in the pot, the cash, and the brass tag.

Without a word, Lee pushed his chair back and walked out.

It was going on one o'clock when Jessamine walked out on the whitewashed promenade. She felt refreshed after a long sleep, a sponge bath, and a big breakfast in her stateroom. Lord, it felt good to be wearing her blue poplin instead of that rat gray dress.

She'd been thinking about Riverbend all morning, wondering what Maisie was doing right now, if Sampson had nailed that loose floor board down on the porch, if it had rained yet, if . . . She had been gone three days, and already she was so lonely she could weep. As if that would accomplish anything, she thought.

Charlotte was probably at the tall secretary in the parlor, licking her finger, poring over the pages of *Godey's Ladies' Book,* sketching little hats and dreaming up new outfits.

Jessamine leaned over the white gingerbread rail, watching the water rush by, concocting arithmetic problems. If Charlotte bought a dress a day, how much hemp would they have to sell to pay her bill at the dressmaker's? If Charlotte got a hat a week, how much corn would they have to plant next spring to pay the milliner? If Charlotte ordered the grand piano she was always raving about, how soon would Riverbend be busted flat?

Her fingers twisted around the rail. Caleb had to be alive. He had to be. She wouldn't let him be dead. But why hadn't he come home? she wondered. What if he hadn't wanted to? What if she found him and he refused to come back? None of her brothers had ever cared about Riverbend the way Jessamine had.

Her mouth tightened. "You're coming home, Caleb Dade, if I have to drag you by the scruff of the neck all the

way from Georgia, or wherever the hell you are,'' she muttered.

She jumped when the boat's whistle sounded three long blasts. The *Delta Princess* was moving toward the western bank, where a small group of people stood on the levee. There was a family of four, the mama shading two little girls with a parasol, a one-legged man with his pant leg pinned, who wrestled with a crutch and a camelback trunk, and three men in frock coats and top hats, their carpetbags leaning against their legs. One of them doffed his hat and made her an exaggerated bow. Jessamine waved back as the moon-faced purser sprinted by her.

She found a deck chair toward the front of the boat, eased herself into it, then closed her eyes in the warm sunshine, listening to the water slapping the levee and the gangplank groaning on its winches.

When she woke, she sighed and stretched her arms high over her head.

"It looks like our little bluebell is blooming, boys."

"I believe you're right, John. She's just reaching up for the sunshine."

"And she's even prettier when she's awake."

Jessamine drew her arms back from their languid stretch and opened her eyes. She had to shade them against the afternoon sun to see the man in a tan frock coat and matching trousers who stood at the foot of her deck chair, looking down at her. It was the same man who had bowed to her from the levee earlier. Up close, he appeared anything but courtly. One of his eyes seemed permanently at half-mast. His mouth was slanted down on one side, an ivory toothpick stuck there as if to point out the distortion. The toothpick bobbed up and down as he spoke. "Are we going to toss a coin for her, or what?" he said.

There was laughter on each side of her.

"You got a three-headed coin, Smitty?"

Stretched out in the deck chair on her left was a thin man with a gold brocade vest and a paisley neck cloth. She turned to her right and looked into a pockmarked face whose finest feature was its yellow grin.

Thin lips closed over the man called Smitty's yellow teeth. "Are you a Mississippi girl, honey?"

The man on her left sneered. "Rebel girls do it for a dime. We got lots of money, sugar. Real money. Not that Confederate crap. We're from New York state."

Jessamine opened her mouth to speak, but nothing came out. She was numb with astonishment, rigid with anger.

"How about a couple of dimes' worth, honey?" said the man with the ivory toothpick. He put his foot on the end of her chair, rested his elbows on his knee as he gazed down at her. "You got yourself a room on this river bucket, or you want to come to ours?"

Jessamine drew back her foot and kicked his leg off her chair. His toothpick went flying as he fell backward against the railing. A white post at his elbow snapped and sailed into the water below.

The other two laughed. "Say, I think she likes you, John," said Smitty.

John got up and brushed off his tan trousers.

"Excuse me, gentlemen," said Jessamine, beginning to get up out of her chair.

The pockmarked Smitty grabbed her wrist. "You're not going anywhere, sister." He flicked his eyes to John. "Is she?"

The ivory toothpick was back in his misshapen mouth now as he walked to the end of Jessamine's chair and kicked away the wooden support. The lower half of the chair jolted to the floor, and Jessamine slid sideways down the incline.

She'd been insulted before. And angry. Now she was also afraid.

John picked her up under her arms. "She's going with me," he said.

"Let me go!" shrieked Jessamine. She kicked backward, striking him in the shin. He cursed roughly as the two men in the deck chairs laughed again. "You need a little help there, Big John?"

"John doesn't need any help with that little bitty rebel girl, do you, John?"

Egged on by his friends, John wrenched Jessamine's arm behind her back.

"*Let me go.*" she said. She kicked back and missed, throwing herself off balance, falling sideways and bringing the man down with her. He landed hard, knocking the breath out of Jessamine. She just lay there, stunned, trying to breathe.

John got up on one knee. "That's better," he said. Reaching down, he got a hand under her skirt and ran it up Jessamine's leg. "You be good to old John and I'll give you a quarter, sweetheart."

Jessamine couldn't breathe, but she could bite. The hand that wasn't up her skirt was pinning her shoulder down. She turned her head and bit hard.

John roared, tore his other hand from her leg, smacked her in the face, then sat back, cursing.

Jessamine struggled to her knees, lurched upward, just as the other two climbed out of their deck chairs. They weren't laughing now. Their faces were pinched and mean. And they were coming at her, slow and careful, like hounds on a shivering rabbit.

"I swear to God, I'll scratch your eyes out if you touch me," Jessamine shrieked. She looked around wildly. Couldn't anyone hear her? Wasn't there anybody nearby, anybody to help her?

"You get her left hand," said the pockmarked Smitty, flicking his eyes to the other one. "I'll get her right. We'll hold her for you, John."

"Watch out for her goddamn teeth," snarled John.

They were coming at her from each side. Jessamine screamed.

Lee sat bolt upright in his bed. He was still dressed. He'd only managed to pull off his boots and undo the buttons on his shirt before falling into a heavy, dreamless sleep.

But this wasn't a dream, a sleeping one or a waking one. He knew he had heard her this time. He knew it.

Damnation! His head throbbed as if someone had been using it as a drum. His shoulder ached. Maybe...

Then Jessamine's scream pierced the air. He was up off the bed and out the door of his stateroom in seconds. He looked over the rail of the top deck just as the rail on the deck below gave way and a raven-haired little girl went sailing into the Mississippi in a tumble of blue skirt and white petticoats.

Without a second thought, Lee jumped in after her.

Chapter Eight

Lee hit the water right behind her, and when he surfaced he reached out and caught Jessamine by the hair just as the current was about to sweep her under the boat. He fought the swirling water with his legs and one arm, with every ounce of strength he could muster, and at the same time heaved Jessamine toward him, locking his arm under her chin, trying to keep her head above water. The big white wheel of the *Delta Princess* thundered down on them, pulling them, sucking them toward it, churning the water white as it passed them. And then a crosscurrent swung them out and away, and Lee pulled on the water like a lifeline, getting them clear at last.

As the rolling waters swept their bodies downriver ahead of the boat, Lee fought to angle them toward the west bank, his legs tangling in Jessamine's skirts and her wet hair nearly blinding him at times.

The river pitched them hard to the west, and then they bobbed and floated in still waters for a moment before Lee began straining toward the shore.

He heaved Jessamine and her waterlogged skirts onto the pebbled bank, stumbling on the slippery wet rocks and riverborne debris, his lungs burning as he took in huge drafts of air.

Sweet Christ, she wasn't breathing. On his knees, he flipped her over onto her stomach. In desperation, knowing newborn babes were slapped into taking their first breath, Lee pounded on her back. "Breathe, Jessie. Breathe, damn you." He pounded again, then turned her over, covered her lifeless mouth with his and gave her his own breath, breathed for her, and kept breathing for her until her stomach convulsed and river water streamed from her mouth and nose. Then she coughed and gagged as Lee's head hung over hers, water dripping from his hair, tears falling from his eyes.

Water lapping softly. The shade of a live oak and the sway of Spanish moss. Somebody tugging at her skirt. Jessamine kicked and clawed. Somebody was holding her wrists, hindering her legs.

"Jessie. Jessie, it's me. Hold still. It's Lee."

All the tension in her body flowed out with a sigh. "Lee."

He pulled her to him, cradling her in his arms, rocking her, crooning to her. "You're fine, Jessie. You're safe, little one. I'm with you now."

Lee! If she had died and gone to heaven, she didn't care. If she had fallen from the deck of the *Delta Princess* and landed in perdition, she didn't mind. Lee was here. She touched his dark, curly hair. She ran her hands over the smooth, broad muscles of his back. He was real. He was here. But how?

She pulled her head back. "And what were you doing with my skirts, Lee Kincannon?"

He grinned. "Seems everybody wants to get into your skirts today, Miss Jessamine."

"Oh, Lee." She hugged him. "Are we in heaven?"

"Either that or Louisiana," he said, getting to his feet and pulling her up. "Take off your skirts, Jessie. It's gonna be dark soon."

Her mouth flew open. "If you think that I . . ."

"Hush," he said. "The mosquitoes around here are likely to be as big as you are. I've managed to live without yellow fever so far, and I'm not planning on getting it tonight. Now take off your damn petticoat so I can make us a tent."

"Oh. Well, all right, then. Let me just look at you first."

"You can look at me all you want later," Lee said, going down on one knee and yanking down her petticoats. He stood up and shook them out, then ripped each of the voluminous garments up the side.

Jessamine watched, still not quite convinced that this dark and thoroughly masculine apparition was real. Why ever did he bother to wear clothes, she wondered, when he looked so good in just a pair of cotton-knit drawers? The muscles of his broad back shifted as he tore each petticoat. A strong cord stood out in his neck. The dark hair on his chest narrowed to a soft, enticing line as it approached his waist.

She could have gazed at him for hours. But when she saw the horrible purplish scar on his shoulder, Jessamine closed her eyes, remembering.

With a handful of torn ruffles, he turned toward her and cocked an eyebrow. "You look about pint-sized without all your feminine frills, Jessie. When are you gonna grow up?"

Her blue skirt fell limply, poking out awkwardly where her corset stays jutted over her hips. "Well, if you haven't noticed, Lee . . ."

"I noticed," he said with a sigh. "Well, this is going to be one tiny little tent. Come on help me find some big sticks."

"Why don't you do that and I'll make us a fire," she said.

"That would be real nice, Jessie. You happen to have a flint on you?"

"Well, no, I . . ."

"No, I didn't think so. And I don't even have one soggy match."

"Damnation!" she said.

"My sentiments exactly," said Lee.

"Well, maybe those big mosquitoes of yours will be carrying lanterns." Jessamine grinned.

He caught her hand. "More likely they'll be carrying axes. Come on, Jessie. Let's build our tent."

"That's not so bad, if I do say so myself," Lee said, stepping back and looking at the shelter.

Jessamine sniffed. "Looks like rags hanging on a clothesline. How are you going to fit in there?" She took in the hard length of him, from his wide shoulders down his corded legs to his bare toes.

He picked up his shirt and shook it out. "I can squinch up when the occasion demands it." He put his shirt on, then picked up his black breeches and stabbed his legs into them. As he buttoned up the shirt, Jessamine's eyes roamed over him in a leisurely fashion.

"You like watchin' me get dressed, Jessie?" he asked softly, his dark eyes riveting hers as he proceeded to tuck his shirt in and do up the buttons of his fly.

"What?" she said, as disconcerted by his question as by his smoldering gaze.

"Why is it women like to watch men dress when men take such pleasure in the very opposite?" he mused.

Jessamine felt her cheeks burning. "I'm sure I don't know," she said. The sun was nearly down, but she felt as if the temperature had just increased by ten degrees.

She was thankful when Lee sauntered to the riverbank. Rolling up his pant legs, he strolled out till he was ankle deep, then splashed water on his face, drank a little, swished some in his mouth and spit it out. When her blush cooled, Jessamine followed did the same, one-handed, with her skirt hiked up to the middle of her calves.

Lee gave her a hand to help her over the rocky bank, despite the fact that she still had her slippers on and he was barefoot.

"As soon as that sun goes down, it's going to get very dark, very fast." He cautiously lifted one end of the triangular tent. "Ease on in there, Jessie, and leave a little room for me."

"Oh, Lord," she murmured as she bent over, then got down on all fours to crawl under the fabric. As she stretched out on the cool, mossy ground, Lee slid in behind her.

"Turn on your right side, Jessie," he said.

She did, and he edged closer. She could feel his warm breath on the back of her neck. All she could hear was the *chirr* of insects.

"Now what?" Jessamine whispered.

"Now nothing." He sighed. "This well may be one of the longest nights of both our lives."

Jessamine closed her eyes. Three days away from Riverbend, and she was feeling like a character in a book, dandled by fate, pitching headlong from a riverboat, only to wind up safe in the arms of— Her stomach growled, appallingly loud. Lee sighed again, this time with discomfort. She felt him turn on his back.

"What are you doing now?" she asked.

"I'm taking off my pants."

She didn't say a word, but her silence was eloquent.

Lee chuckled. "Don't worry, little girl."

She wasn't worried, exactly, but her heart had begun a brisk tattoo against her chest.

"I need a pillow," he grunted, trying to get his long legs out of his pants without disturbing the tent. "There. Would you prefer the left leg or the right, Miss Jessamine?"

"I always use left-legged pillows on riverbanks," she said.

"Here. Lift your head." He shoved the folded pant leg beneath her. "How's that?"

"Much better. Thank you."

Lee shifted around again and then lay quietly. It was already dark, and the night song of the insects had begun. "What were you doin' on my boat?" he drawled.

Jessamine looked over her shoulder. "Your boat?"

"Oh, hell!" he muttered. "I forgot."

"Forgot what?"

"I lost her last night in a poker game."

Jessamine started to turn around. "You what?"

Lee put a hand on her hip to keep her in place. "Settle down, Jessie. Anyway, I asked you first. What were you doing on the *Delta Princess?*"

"I'm going to look for Caleb," she said.

"Caleb?"

"My brother. He was captured at Shiloh in '62 and sent to Coulterville Prison in Georgia."

"I thought your brother was killed fighting for the Confederacy," he said.

"That was Charles," Jessamine said.

"Judas Priest! You people in Missouri never did know what you were doing! Yanks, rebs, half of you playing both ends against the middle." He sighed in exasperation. "How's your precious Riverbend, Jessie?"

"Awful. That's why I'm going off to find Caleb. Papa died . . ."

"The judge? I'm sorry to hear that," he said, patting her hip where his hand still rested.

"Well, don't be too sorry. He left Riverbend to everybody in the world but me. Then Louis's widow arrived last month, took the place over, and is now proceeding to carry it straight to hell in one of her many very fashionable handbaskets."

"So Miss Jessamine's on a mission of mercy for Riverbend."

"More or less," she said. "How'd you lose the *Delta Princess,* Lee? I thought you were supposed to be a card-sharp or a cardshark, or whatever it is that means you always win."

"Nobody always wins, Jessie," Lee said thoughtfully. On the other hand, he added to himself, nobody always loses, either.

They lay quietly for a while.

"What was that?" Jessamine asked when there was a stirring in the heavy woods behind them.

"Armadillo, maybe."

"A what?"

"Armadillo. A little critter with armor plate on his back." Jessamine shivered.

After a few minutes she whispered, "Lee?"

"What?"

"I have to... I mean, well, I need to..."

"Sneak on out in the bushes, Jessie. Just don't pull the tent down when you get out."

"It's dark out there," she said.

"You want me to come with you?"

"No," she said sharply. "Well, part of the way. Would you?"

Once outside the tent, Lee slapped a mosquito on his neck. He took Jessamine's hand and strode into the trees.

"You wait right here," she said, inching away from him into the darkness. "Don't leave me."

Lee slapped at another mosquito. "Just go," he said.

A minute later, from not too far away, Jessamine called to him. "Lee? Are you still right there?"

"I'm still right here."

"Well, could you sing or something?"

"Damn it to hell, Jessie...."

"Please?"

He went through two full renditions of "Dixie" before she was back.

Sometime in the middle of the night, Lee woke to discover his hand curved around Jessamine's firm breast and his lips pressed to the nape of her neck. When he moved his hand away, she stirred in her sleep and turned into him, her face less than an inch from his, her soft breath fluttering on his lips.

It was the first night in eight months he hadn't drunk himself to sleep, but he felt drunk now, intoxicated by the sweetness of her, the warmth of her. He closed the distance between their lips, just touching her soft mouth. He felt like moaning, but instead it was Jessamine who moaned in her sleep and moved closer to him, her mouth opening, her tongue wet and warm and inviting. Lee deepened his kiss, his tongue meeting hers with longing. When she stirred again, pressing her hips into him, he pulled away as if her lips had scalded him.

"What? What is it?" she murmured, on the verge of waking.

"Here. Turn over, Jessie," he rasped, elbowing himself up and using one hand to flip her over on her side. She drew her knees up and fell back to sleep.

Lee turned so that their backs were touching. He closed his eyes, but he barely slept. Everything had changed somehow, and yet nothing had changed. His pansy-eyed Jessamine was still as beguiling as she was innocent. And he was still beguiled, and about as far from innocent as a man could get.

Jessamine was wading out of the river, water streaming off her face, when Lee crawled backward out of the tent, caught his foot in a flounce and brought the whole thing

down on top of him. He lurched to his feet in a flurry of white ruffles.

"You look like a debutante," she called from the river-bank.

Lee growled, cursed, and wrenched the damp fabric off his arms and legs.

"It's a beautiful morning, Lee. What time do you suppose it is, about seven or half after?" She approached him, fingers combing through her long raven hair, the tops of her breasts perched above her corset, her waist nipped in, the ruffles on her pantaloons jouncing just above her shapely ankles.

Lee's dry mouth grew drier still. "Seven. Eight. I don't know, Jessamine. What do I look like, a sundial?" he snapped.

"No, you look like a man who woke up surly," she said, turning to pick up her dress and slip it over her head.

Her little backside twitched as she shoved her arms into the sleeves and shimmied the skirt down over her hips.

Surly, hell! It was all he could do not to throw her down on the mossy ground and take her right that minute. A bead of sweat dripped between Lee's eyes. We've got to get out of these woods, he thought. "I'm sorry, Jessie," he said. "I didn't get a lot of sleep last night. I need my sleep." Among other things, he added to himself.

"Apology accepted," she said brightly. "Look at this place, Lee. Isn't it beautiful, with the moss hanging off the trees and that little bit of fog hovering over the river?"

"Uh-huh. Are you ready to go?"

"Now?"

"Jessie, the sooner we get back to civilization, the happier I'm going to be." He handed her some of the torn petticoats. "Here. Carry the south wall of the tent, will you?" Lee trudged off into the trees, trailing a white ruffle behind him.

Jessamine hopped from one foot to the other, slipping into her shoes, then raced after him. Good gracious, she thought. You'd think the devil himself was after that man, the way he trampled through the trees.

It wasn't easy keeping up with Lee, even barefoot. The bugs were awful, and his mood got worse as the day dragged on. He had wrapped part of Jessamine's petticoat around his neck to protect it from the pesky flies and mosquitoes and dispensed with whatever politeness he had awakened with. By the time the sun was overhead, he was storming through the woods, letting branches slap back at her, refusing to stop to rest.

Jessamine was about ready to sit down and just let him trudge back to find her when he stopped and sniffed the air.

"Do you smell that, Jessie?" he asked.

She sniffed. "Wood smoke."

"Civilization," he said. "Come on."

What they discovered when they came out into a small clearing was a board shack with a rusted tin chimney and a tumbledown front porch. An old hound barked twice and then lay down again, his chin between his paws and his tail thumping.

"Afternoon," Lee called heartily to the man chopping wood at the side of the building.

The man put down his ax and shaded his eyes. Apparently judging them harmless, he broke into a toothless grin and called out, "Afternoon to you, mister. You and the missus." He loped toward them, wiping his hand on his trouser leg, then extending it to Lee. "Afternoon, mister," he said. "Name's Sam Bird. Ain't had no company in over a year." He turned his gaping smile on Jessamine. "Greetings to you, missus."

"How do you do?" she said.

"'Bout how far away are we from a steamboat stop, Mr. Bird?" Lee drawled.

"Well, shoot. The *Crescent City* stops right down here at Tulahachee. If anybody's on the levee, you know. Otherwise she just toots and goes on."

"'Bout what time would you say she stopped?" Lee asked.

"Late afternoon," he said. "Every day but Sunday. She comes up from New Orleans, then heads right back down. She oughta be tootin' in 'bout two hours or so, I reckon."

"Is there a road to Tulahachee?" asked Lee.

Sam Bird shook his head. "Used to be, but they stopped usin' it 'bout a dozen years ago, so it's all grown over now. What you gotta do now is head on south a mile or so through that scrub, and then veer east. Couple houses down there. I guess people live in 'em. I never see 'em."

Lee extended his hand. "Much obliged, Mr. Bird. Come on, Jessie." He grabbed her hand and pulled her after him as he headed for the thick scrub on the other side of the clearing.

"Won't y'all stay and have a bite with me?" Sam Bird called.

Without slowing, Lee yelled over his shoulder, "Much obliged, but we'd best hurry if we're going to catch the *Crescent City.*"

"Goodbye, Mr. Bird," Jessamine called.

"Y'all come back now, you hear. Say, I forgot to ask if you had any news of the war."

"It's over," shouted Lee as he led Jessamine back into the dense foliage.

As Lee dragged her into the thicket, Jessamine could hear Sam Bird's voice calling, "Well, now, ain't that good news. I guess my boys will be comin' home any day now."

She wondered how long it would take him to discover that if his boys weren't there by now, they probably wouldn't be coming home again. Ever. A chill inched along her spine

then, and Jessamine pulled her hand from Lee's and just stood there, staring, seeing nothing.

"Jessie?" Lee asked softly, his thumb grazing her stricken face. "What's wrong, darlin'?"

Jessamine blinked. Caleb wasn't dead. That was all there was to it. She wouldn't let him be dead. "Nothing's wrong," she said, forcing her lips into a twitch of a smile. "Caleb's not dead," she said firmly. "And I'm going to find him, Lee, and bring him home, if it's the last thing I ever do."

He circled his arms around her and drew her small body against his. "All right, Jessie," he murmured. "All right." Let her hope, he told himself. Let her dream a while longer. If Caleb Dade had been a prisoner at Coulterville, chances were, hopes and dreams would be all Jessie had. Not many men had made it out of that hellhole alive.

Jessamine's chin lifted, and Lee found himself drowning in the violet mists of her eyes, floundering in currents stronger and more lethal than any the Mississippi could conjure up. He'd survived those brutal river currents twice now, but he wasn't at all sure he would be able to survive the magnetic pull of Jessie's gaze.

Lee was stretched out on the gravel bar with his forearm over his eyes when Jessamine stomped out of the woods, burrs on the hem of her skirt, sweat stains on the front of her dress.

"Whew," she said, flopping down beside him. "It must be a hundred degrees." She undid the top buttons of her dress and fanned the fabric over her chest.

"Pretty Jessie," said Lee softly.

He was looking at her from under his forearm, giving her one of his cagey grins. Jessamine wondered if she'd ever understand this man, warm one minute, cool the next. Today, for instance, when she had been so distressed over Caleb, Lee had comforted her. For a moment she had even

thought he was going to kiss her. Instead, he had charged off through the woods again, yelling that she had best get a move on or they'd miss the boat. He seemed to want to get back to New Orleans awfully bad, and she couldn't help but wonder what the attraction was.

She sniffed, undoing another button. "Oh, you're going to be nice to me now that we're almost back in the civilized world."

"I apologize," he said.

"I'm not going to be so quick to forgive you this time. You've got a nasty streak in you, Lee. Has anybody ever told you that?"

"Just one or two people," he said, "but they were nastier than me, so their opinion doesn't count."

"Huh," she sniffed, picking cockleburs off her skirt and tossing them his way.

"You don't happen to have any money sewn in your hem, do you, Jessie?" he asked.

"Oh, Lord!"

"What?"

"I had four hundred dollars in gold in my handbag. I completely forgot about it. Guess it's scattered all over the delta by now. Damnation!"

He leaned up on an elbow. "Where'd you get four hundred dollars in gold, Jessamine Dade?"

"I sold my mother's diamond brooch in St. Louis. To someone you probably know." She eyed him now.

"Oh. Who's that?"

"Alpha Parker."

Yup. He knew her all right. His eyes just about popped out of his head, and his whiskery jaw fell nearly to his knees. To Jessamine, it was a good indication that Lee knew Mrs. Parker very well indeed.

"Have you known her long?" she asked casually.

Lee barely heard her. He was trying to figure out what Red thought she was doing, giving Jessamine four hundred dollars, when the last words out of her mouth had been "And don't you ever again call out that girl's name in my bed, you son of a bitch." Whatever it was, Lee knew there would be hell to pay somewhere down the road, to Red or Jessie, or to both of them.

"Did you hear me, Lee?"

"Sorry, Jessie. What did you say?"

"Never mind. Since I don't have any gold sewn in my skirt, how are we going to pay our passage on the *Crescent City?*" Better yet, she thought, how are you going to get to Georgia now, Miss Had-It-And-Lost-It?

He scratched a mosquito bite on his ankle. "That shouldn't be any problem," he said.

She gave him a dubious look. Out of the corner of her eye, she caught a glimpse of a red-and-white steamboat coming up the river. "There it is!" she cried.

"Do me a favor, Jessie, will you? Just go along with whatever I say, all right? I mean when we get on the boat. Will you do that?"

"I'm not—"

"Do you want to get to New Orleans or not? If you do, you'll just have to quit being so blasted stubborn for a while and do what I say. Can you do that, Jessamine?"

Her lower lip slid out. "Maybe. Maybe not."

He stood up and began waving his arm over his head. "You best not maybe us right back into a tent in the woods, Jessie. I'm warning you, you hear?"

Her reply was drowned out by the *Crescent City*'s sonorous whistle blast.

Chapter Nine

As the steamboat approached, Jessamine combed through her hair with her fingers and began to button up the bodice of her dress.

"Don't," said Lee.

She shot him a defiant look and did up another button.

"Don't," repeated Lee, walking toward her. "That makes you look like a little blue buttoned-up schoolteacher."

"Don't you tell me 'don't,' Lee Kincannon. We're getting on a steamboat. I'm not going to look like some floozy."

He towered over her, nearly blocking out the sun. "That's exactly what you're going to look like, Jessie," he said, ripping off her top button. He did the same with the next three while Jessamine gaped in stunned silence. He studied the effect, ripped one more button off, then folded the halves of blue fabric back to expose the top of her corset. "That should do very nicely," he said, shoving the loose buttons in his pants pocket.

Jessamine was so mad she couldn't even speak. Of all the— She looked down. Her breasts swelled over the lace top of her corset. Well, hell! She couldn't shove them back down. There was no place to hide the damn things.

"I'm not getting on that boat, Lee."

The *Crescent City* had moved slowly to the west bank of the river, and was now approaching the levee. Its whistle blasted once more.

"Suit yourself, Jessamine," he said from the edge of the levee.

Well, this was a pretty picture, she thought. All she wanted to do was get to New Orleans, and here she was stamping her foot and refusing to go. Damn that man! He got her so riled up she kept saying no when she wanted to say yes. She looked down at her cleavage again and rolled her eyes. Oh, well. There probably wasn't anybody on the boat who hadn't seen a bosom before, and there probably wasn't anybody she'd ever see again. She might as well go with him.

By this time, Lee was helping a deckhand steady the gangplank at the river's edge. Jessamine sauntered toward him. "Well, I suppose I'll go," she said.

Lee grinned, coming toward her in ankle-deep water. He put his arm around her waist and pulled her against his side.

A loud voice boomed from an upper deck. "Lee Kincannon! Thunderation! I never thought I'd see you waving down a woebegone steamer from the Tulahachee levee. And you look like you believe I'll actually let you set foot on my boat, you son of a bitch."

The barrel-chested, gray-bearded captain shook with laughter as he looked down on them.

"Howdy, Captain Witherspoon," drawled Lee amiably, saluting with the hand that wasn't holding Jessamine. "Well, now, I'm not the one who's in such an all-fired hurry to get downriver. I want you to meet Miss Jessie Delight."

Lee hugged her harder against his side—hard enough to make Jessamine think he was actually pinching her.

"Jessie," he said, "say hello to Captain Howard Witherspoon, the meanest son of a bitch on the Mississippi River." He dug his fingers into her ribs.

Jessamine looked up at the captain. "Good afternoon, Captain," she said.

Howard Witherspoon took off his cap. A hank of gold braid came loose and swung from the visor as he gestured with it. "Good afternoon to you, Miss Delight."

Jessamine thought she saw a string of saliva trickle into his shaggy gray beard.

"Miss Jessie is one of those dancers at The LaFayette Ballroom. You been there, Captain Witherspoon? Down on Canal Street?"

The captain's eyes never strayed from Jessamine's cleavage. "I believe I have patronized that particular ballroom," he said, "although I can't say that I remember seeing Miss Delight."

"She looks a mite different with her hair down like this," said Lee.

Howard Witherspoon leered. "And her clothes on."

"Well, that, too," Lee agreed, clasping Jessamine more aggressively as she began to pull away.

The captain plopped his hat back on his head and readjusted the gold braid. "And what are you and Miss Delight doing way the hell up in Tulahachee, if you don't mind my asking?"

Several passengers had come out on the double decks of the little steamboat. They were staring down at Lee and Jessamine while half a dozen deckhands paused to listen to Lee's reply.

Lee proceeded to weave some wild tale of fishing for Miss Delight's favorite northern Louisiana catfish, of lascivious carryings on in a rowboat, the upshot of which was that their rocking boat had overturned, plopping them both into the river. "We never did get to finish." Lee grinned wickedly. "And I can tell you, Captain Witherspoon, Miss Delight wasn't any too happy about that."

Jessamine was mortified when some of the passengers and all of the deckhands applauded. She had never heard such horse manure, but, judging from the expression on his face, Captain Witherspoon believed every last disgusting detail.

"Now, Miss Delight is scheduled to dance at midnight at the Lafayette Ballroom. She's about eaten away with worry that, if she doesn't get back in time to get into all her feathers and such, Mr. Duke McGuire is going to toss her right out on her pretty little fanny."

Howard Witherspoon fingered his beard. "Well, we wouldn't want that to happen, now would we? You just send Miss Delight right on up that gangplank. The *Crescent City* will have you back well before midnight, Miss Delight. I'll swing her around right here and turn a blind eye to any other stops. You just prance right on up here."

At last, thought Jessamine, beginning to step forward. Lee held her tight.

"Only problem is, Captain, Miss Delight won't go without me. Refused to get in a fast coach two hours ago 'cause there wasn't room for me. See, I sort of saved her life back there, when the boat pitched over. I guess she just feels obliged—though I've told her it was nothing. Any man would have carried her soft, wet little body out of the river."

Witherspoon scowled. "I don't want you on my boat, you son of a bitch. You cheated me out of five hundred dollars back when I was captaining the *Silver Moon*. You recall that?"

Lee sighed, all innocence and charm. "I didn't cheat you, Captain. I was dealt those four jacks."

"You were dealing," howled Captain Witherspoon.

"Well—" Lee sighed again, "—if you feel so strongly about it, I guess we'll just have to wait for the next boat. Come on, honey." He whirled Jessamine around and began walking up the levee.

"Wait just a confounded minute," the captain called.

Jessamine felt a ripple of victory in the tight muscles of the arm that clenched her.

While Lee arranged a pair of wood-slat lounge chairs for them on the second deck, Jessamine gazed into the current as the riverboat steamed in a wide swing, turning south, toward New Orleans.

Lee slung his long body onto one of the chairs. "Come rest beside me, Miss Delight," he said.

She gave him a withering look.

"I forgot," Lee said. "You're the one who slept last night, aren't you?" He cocked his arms behind his head, shifted his hips, and closed his eyes. "Wake me when we get to New Orleans."

"It's such a fine, bright afternoon. Maybe I'll take a little stroll around the deck," Jessamine said.

"Sit, Jessie," he commanded, eyes still closed.

"I'm not accustomed to being spoken to like some mangy dog, Mr. Kincannon," she said with a sniff. "If you want me to—"

Lee opened his eyes, rolled them impatiently, and heaved himself up out of the chair. He clamped his arms around her from behind and spoke against her ear. "Jessie, darlin', I haven't slept more than two winks in the past twenty-four hours, and that tends to make me irritable. I haven't had a taste of whiskey in more hours than I am capable of counting right now, and that tends to make me mean. And watching your delectable bosom jiggle for the last forty-five minutes has made my head ache all the way down to my bare toes. Please don't wander around the boat and stir up any trouble. Captain Witherspoon would like nothing better than to pull up at the next levee and boot me off. Jessie, I'm begging you. Sit. Please."

"Well, since you put it that way," she said, her heart flitting inside her rib cage like a wild canary. "I guess I will just stretch out here for a while."

"Thank you." Lee returned to his chair with a sigh.

Jessamine angled herself onto the lounge chair, leaned back, crossed her ankles, and fluffed out her skirt. "It is a lovely afternoon, don't you think, Lee?" She turned her face toward him to discover that he was already asleep.

Drumming her fingers lightly on the arms of her chair, Jessamine watched the riverbank slide by—the live oaks with their veils of Spanish moss, the dappled sycamores, the cottonwoods. It occurred to her that the last time she'd fallen asleep in a deck chair, she'd awakened to the nasty leers of Smitty and company, and she wondered if she dared close her eyes. Then she looked over at Lee and felt safety washing over her like the river itself. She sighed, and soon fell fast asleep.

Something jolted her chair.

"Oh, pardon me, Miss Delight. I thought I'd sit here by you during this quiet stretch in the river. I didn't mean to wake you. I would've been just as glad to sit and watch you sleep." Captain Witherspoon's big, blunt hand patted her thigh. "You go on and close those pretty blue eyes of yours."

"I wouldn't think of it, Captain," Jessamine said. She wouldn't close her eyes if the leering graybeard were thirty feet away, and certainly not with a mere few inches separating them.

He took off his cap and laid it on his barrel of a chest. "It's hard to believe I wouldn't recall a pretty little thing like you. How long have you been at the Lafayette Ballroom?"

"Not long," Jessamine said. Then: "A month or so." She had nothing else to do while Lee slept so soundly. Teasing this old graybeard would at least help pass the time. "I

danced in Tallahassee before that. At least until the city fathers closed the ballroom down.''

He clucked his tongue in sympathy. ''I hope you weren't forced to spend any time in jail,'' he said.

''Two nights, actually,'' she said. ''It was horrible.''

''So I should imagine.''

''And cold. When I was arrested, all I had on were my feathers. The jailkeeper told me he was short on blankets, but I didn't believe him for a minute.'' She blinked her eyes at him.

''Well, I could imagine why he would want to keep you, uh, exposed. . . .''

''Exposed!'' exclaimed Jessamine. ''Why, I was more than exposed. Well, let me see. What was I wearing? There were two peacock feathers stuck in my hair. I remember those. Oh, and a darling little skirt of ostrich feathers. Well, I call it a skirt, but it was truly more like an apron. And last, but hardly least, there were these two fluffy pink plumes I wore over my. . .''

Lee coughed. ''Jessie, I really don't think Captain Witherspoon is interested in your avian splendor.''

''On the contrary,'' said the captain, running a thick finger under his collar. ''I find it fascinating.''

''Why don't you come watch my performance tonight, Captain?'' Jessamine asked, ignoring Lee.

''I intend to, Miss Delight,'' he said. ''And don't you fret about being late. I've had the boys put a little extra fire in the belly of the boat. You'll get there in plenty of time, you pretty little thing.''

''Aren't you just the kindest man?'' she said.

The captain moved his head closer and spoke just above a whisper. ''Tell me, Miss Delight. How did you ever get tangled up with a man like Lee Kincannon? He's a cardsharp, you know. Cheated me right out of my boots, he did.''

"How shocking," Jessamine whispered. "And I was under the impression that he was so gallant."

"You're better off without him, Miss Delight. Take my advice. He's a bounder if ever there was one."

"I appreciate your concern, Captain. Perhaps I shall seek elsewhere for my pleasures. In truth, I find Mr. Kincannon's capacities—how shall I say?—somewhat deficient."

Suddenly, the engine of the steamboat roared and the pilot called out, "Shoal point, Captain!"

"I'd best see to my boat," said the officer, rising from the chair with a sigh and lumbering toward the pilothouse.

"That was quite a performance," said Lee.

Jessamine turned her head languidly in his direction. "Thank you," she said.

"It wasn't a compliment, Jessie. It's no wonder you got in trouble on the *Delta Princess*. Somebody ought to keep you on a real short tether."

"Somebody?" she asked innocently, well aware that only Lee's reassuring presence had allowed her to tease the captain.

"Somebody who has the patience of a saint and the lives of a cat—and carries a whip in his back pocket," he growled.

"Charming," she said.

Lee gazed out at the trees that lined the shore. "We should be in New Orleans in about an hour."

She didn't answer.

"Talk to me, mad Jessie," he teased.

There he goes again, she thought. Running hot and cold in the quick blink of an eye. "I'd rather talk to a post."

"You just were."

Jessamine laughed. "You'd best whisk me off this boat the very minute it docks, Lee Kincannon."

"I'll try, Jessie—" he sighed "—despite the fact that my capacities are so deficient." His dark eyes twinkled as he reached for her hand and brought it to his warm lips.

The kiss licked like fire up her arm, spread a flush over her face, and kindled a fire in the pit of her stomach. Deficient indeed, she thought.

It was like going back in time. The room was exactly as Jessamine remembered it, from the cabbage rose wallpaper to the big walnut wardrobe where she had hidden. This time, though, there was no smoky haze lingering in the air, and Lee—though still darkly handsome—was no longer a stranger.

He had indeed whisked her off the boat, then tossed her up into a carriage, climbed in beside her and told the driver to hotfoot it to the Imperial Hotel. Then he'd left her in the room, returning an hour later, clean shaven and wearing a black frock coat, a high-collared white shirt with a striped cravat, black trousers, and tall black boots. Now he was sitting on the big four-poster bed, patting the place beside him, just as he had done five years before.

Jessamine sat.

"I can't believe I'm fool enough to be doing this again," he said, reaching in his pocket for her buttons and a spool of thread with a needle stuck through it.

She smiled. "Shall I thread that needle for you?"

He was holding it as far away from his body as his arms would allow. "Did I have this much trouble before?" he asked.

Jessamine ran her fingers gently through his hair. "You're getting old, Lee. There's silver in these dark, curly locks."

He licked the thread to stiffen it. "It's bought and paid for, too." This time the thread passed easily through the eye of the needle. "Chin up, Jessie."

She lifted her chin, feeling the warm pressure of the back of his hand against her bare skin. "That feels good," she murmured.

"What does?" Lee asked, squinting, leaning back a little in order to see better.

"Your hand just grazing my skin."

"It's not intentional," he gritted out. "Now hush."

"That's too bad," she said with a sigh. "I like the way it feels."

Lee drove the needle right into his finger. "Damnation!" he howled. "Maybe I should sew one of these on your lip while I'm at it. Now just keep still."

She did, enjoying the crease of his brow, the way the corners of his eyes crinkled when he concentrated, the firm and determined line of his mouth. Jessamine recalled having taken the same pleasure in the same view five years before. And suddenly she remembered very vividly that she had talked a blue streak that night about her obligations at home. Those obligations hadn't lessened in the intervening years; if anything, they had increased. And here she was in New Orleans again, but now it was almost impossible to think of anything but Lee.

"There," he said, breaking the thread and sticking the needle back in the spool. "You may button up like a little schoolmarm now."

She took his hand. "As I recall, that night before the war, it was you who buttoned me up."

He squeezed her hand, then extracted his and stood up. "As I recall, it hurt my teeth to do it."

"And made you perspire," Jessamine added, grinning wickedly.

"Well, you don't want to have a late supper with a man who's sweating like a pig, Jessie." He pulled her to her feet. "Now do those buttons, and we'll go on down to the dining room."

Her grin wilted. "Oh, I look too shabby, Lee. I haven't any petticoats, and my dress is all stained and frayed at the hem. Can't we just..."

He took her in his arms and tilted her chin up. "Jessie, you are a beauty, whether you're wearing a bright, spangled gown or a potato sack. Don't you ever forget that, you hear?" He shook her gently.

"I hear." He was holding her so tightly against him that she could feel his taut abdomen, the long muscles of his thighs, the hard strength between them.

"Open your eyes, Jessie."

"What?" she breathed.

His voice was like dark velvet. "I said open your eyes, little one. I'm taking you to supper, not to bed."

Her eyes snapped open. "Lee, I didn't..."

"Yes, you did," he said, letting go of her. "Now come on."

The dining room was similar to the one in his St. Louis hotel—all white and gold and shimmering candlelight. It was eleven o'clock, and a dozen diners were still lingering over coffee, brandy and cigars.

Lee ordered an extraordinary meal of vichyssoise, prawns in drawn butter, capon with oyster dressing, and green beans amandine.

"We're eating like the hotel's on fire," Jessamine said, licking a bit of oyster from the corner of her mouth. "I can't remember the last meal I had."

Lee poured more wine in his glass.

"Oh, I remember," she said. "I ate breakfast on the *Delta Princess,* right before those awful men... Well, I don't want to remember that."

Lee chewed thoughtfully for a moment. "We need to discuss this little expedition of yours, Jessie."

"I don't want to discuss anything but food. Do you have one of those wonderful dessert carts, Lee?"

Lee pushed his plate away and asked the waiter to bring him a brandy. When it came, he lit a cigar. "Oh, I almost forgot," he said, reaching into his pants pocket. "I want you to take these." He put five twenty-dollar gold pieces by her wineglass.

"What's that?" she asked, only glancing at the coins as she buttered her second roll.

"Jessie, you might enjoy the feel of that dress after all this time, but I'm getting mighty tired of looking at it. There's a dress shop just down the street. They'll fix you up. Just tell them . . ."

"Lee Kincannon sent me?" she said archly, feeling more raggedy than ever. It was pretty clear Lee thought she looked awful in spite of his speech earlier about spangles and potato sacks.

"They know me."

"I'll just bet they do." She bit into the roll, chewed it as if she wished it was a chunk of his flesh.

He shifted uncomfortably in his chair, picked up his brandy and swirled it before taking a healthy swallow.

"Pardon me, Mr. Lee," said a wiry black man as he approached the table. "Somebody askin' for you in the kitchen."

"Fayette, can't you just tell him . . ."

"Well, now, that's the problem, Mr. Lee. It one of those folks jus' won't take no for an answer."

Lee sighed. "Why don't you roll that dessert cart over here for Miss Dade while I'm gone?" To Jessamine he said, "Don't eat so much you bust all those buttons off, little one. I'll be right back." He took his brandy snifter with him into the kitchen.

As she ate a petit four, Jessamine looked around the elegant room. She felt like a guinea hen that had wandered into

the front parlor by mistake. It was foolish to think a man like Lee would be attracted to her. He had already told her he considered her too young and inexperienced. Now he had politely let her know he found her shabby, as well. He may have risked his life to save her from drowning, but that wasn't because he wanted her. She had risked her neck hiding him at Riverbend. And heaven knew he hadn't spent one moment longer with her than he'd had to out there in the woods. She'd never seen anyone so anxious to get back to civilization—or whatever it was he wanted to get back to.

She sighed as she fingered the five gold coins on the table. There wasn't much point in buying a dress. What Lee thought of her wasn't as important as getting to Georgia, finding her brother and taking him home. But with her handbag and her own four hundred dollars gone, she didn't know how she was going to do it. Unless... She dropped the coins one by one into her corset. Once she found Caleb and things got back to normal at Riverbend, she'd pay Lee back.

Jessamine turned to the dessert cart again, picked up a strawberry torte on a little paper doily, then dropped it when she saw Major Harding striding into the dining room from the lobby, his sword clicking against chair legs as he approached her.

She slunk down in her chair. What in the world was happening? This was New Orleans. He wasn't supposed to be here. He was supposed to be...someplace else, anyplace else. How in the world had he found her? And oh, Lord, Lee was in the kitchen and coming back any second.

She swung her panic-stricken gaze to the kitchen just as the door swung open, giving Jessamine a quick but very clear view of Lee Kincannon holding a very familiar redhead in his arms—and kissing the living daylights out of her!

"Miss Jessamine!" said Major Harding sternly as he approached her from behind.

She slapped her napkin on the table, then shoved back her chair directly into his path. "Major, I was about to enjoy a midnight promenade. Would you care to accompany me?"

"Well, I..."

She marched toward the lobby and heard the click of the major's sword as he followed.

Chapter Ten

The night was warm and humid. The streetlights flickered, creating small, distinct pools of golden light. Major Harding took her hand and put it through his arm as they strolled.

They didn't walk well together, Jessamine thought. The major's arm was too stiff. He was either too tall or not tall enough—she couldn't decide—and their adjacent hips kept bumping awkwardly.

He wasn't Lee. That was the trouble. And right now Lee was undoubtedly with Alpha Parker, doing more than kissing the daylights out of her. Little wonder he had refused to kiss her before they went down to supper, Jessamine thought. He'd been saving it all for that courtesan.

"Explain something else to me, Major," she said.

"Won't you please use my Christian name, Miss Jessamine? I think it's time. And I would so like to hear my name on your lips."

"Thomas," she said. It felt wrong on her tongue. Like a mealy apple.

"Yes, Jessamine. What would you like me to explain?"

"I understand why you followed me here. Not that I approve, mind you, but I understand. But I don't know why, after she told you where I had gone, Mrs. Parker came along, too."

"I believe I told you. Mrs. Parker said she had business to attend to here."

"What kind of business?" Jessamine asked, taking a kick at a crumpled handbill on the sidewalk, while visions of that torrid kitchen embrace swirled in her head.

"I didn't inquire," he said.

"You have a distinct lack of curiosity, Thomas."

He stopped, bringing her to a halt. "No," he said, looking down at her, his expression utterly sober. "I was worried about you, Jessamine. Worried sick, if you must know. There was no room in my thoughts for Mrs. Parker."

"You needn't worry about me," she said, taking a step forward. The major didn't budge.

"I intend to take you back to Missouri tomorrow, Jessamine. Back to Riverbend. And then, the good Lord willing, you'll return with me to Ohio, or perhaps we'll go west, to an army post."

There was enough light to see the coppery cast of his mustache above the firm set of his lips. His blue eyes had an intense, smoky hue. "Poor Thomas. You really do love me, don't you?" she said softly.

"How can you doubt it, my dear?" He bent to kiss her. Delicately. Discreetly. His mustache scratched her nose.

"I don't suppose anyone has ever referred to you as a bounder, have they, Thomas?" she asked as they began to walk again. "Or a son of a bitch?"

"Not to my knowledge." he said, with a small chuffing noise in his throat.

Jessamine sighed. She wondered if her feelings for Lee had something to do with the fact that he was a bounder, a sinfully handsome and unavailable son of a bitch. She couldn't have him, therefore she wanted him. On the other hand, here was Thomas—the upright, responsible, utterly devoted Major Harding. Jessamine had him and didn't particularly want him. She might be better off, she thought,

if she gave up both of them and restricted her mental efforts to her search for Caleb. These men were doing nothing but getting in her way. She sighed again.

"Tired?" he asked, patting her hand where it lay across his arm.

"No. I'd like to walk some more, if you don't mind." Jessamine felt she'd rather keep walking than return to the Imperial Hotel, where somewhere, in one of those rooms, in one of those big four-poster beds, Lee held the beautiful Alpha Parker in his arms.

Alpha's red hair shawled over the silken bodice of her nightdress as she stood in the doorway of Lee's room in their suite on the top floor of the hotel.

"You're not going to sleep in that chair, are you, Lee? You look exhausted. Why don't I turn down your bed for you? Or come over to my bed and I'll rub your back." Her hands twitched. She wanted to touch him, yet she dreaded the way his muscles would freeze at her fingertips.

"Go on to bed, Red," he said wearily, without even turning around. He'd been sitting there staring out the window for half an hour. "I'll be there later. I may just go back downstairs in a while. I'm running out of cigars."

"There's a brand-new box in the top drawer of the secretary. I brought them down on the boat today." In sixteen years, she thought, she'd never once let him run out of cigars. He should have married her for that alone.

"Thank you." The glass decanter clinked against his snifter. The pouring brandy made a small lapping noise.

Alpha leaned against the door frame, twisting a lock of her hair. "I'm sorry I was the bearer of bad news, Lee. I thought you should know about her plans to marry the Yankee, that's all."

"Don't, Red."

"Don't what?" Alpha bit her lower lip.

"Don't tell me you're sorry. Best not start lying after all these years. It doesn't become you." His voice was flat, dispirited. "Just go to bed."

He heard the rustle of her nightdress, waited a little while longer, then went down to the fourth floor again and knocked on Jessamine's door. If she was inside, she didn't answer.

What are you gonna do, boy?, Lee asked himself. Go all the way downstairs and get the extra key? That's what a sane man would do. Or maybe put your good shoulder to the door and crack it out of its frame? The gesture of an angry man. But at the moment he was neither sane nor angry. Only desolate and confused.

Hell, what could he say to her anyway? Felicitations, Jessie. Best wishes to you and your major. Thank you, Jessie, and bless you for a few hours of aggravation, sheer delight, and sweet, sweet hope.

Jessamine woke early, dressed quickly—easy enough for a woman without petticoats or a hairbrush—and left the hotel by a rear door. She was thinking only of Riverbend now, of her search for her brother. She was on her way to Georgia, and no one was going to stop her. Not the major. Certainly not Lee.

She knocked at the door of the big Greek Revival house in the Garden District.

It opened a few inches. "Who's there?"

She could see half of a round black face, one big dark suspicious eye. She assumed it was feminine. "Is Mrs. LaPaix in?" she asked.

"Who's wantin' to see her?"

"My name is Jessamine Dade. Emerald LaPaix is my aunt. Is she in?"

"Miz LaPaix still in her wrapper."

"Oh, please, I must see her," Jessamine pleaded.

A lilting voice came from somewhere inside. "Who is it, Delia?"

Jessamine pushed the door. "Aunt Emmie!" she called. "It's Jessamine."

Her aunt appeared in the foyer, looking like an angel in a pink gauze wrapper. "Oh, Aunt Emmie. I'm so glad you're home."

"Jessamine, dear!" the woman squealed. "Step back, Delia. For goodness sake, this is my little niece from Missouri. Don't keep her standing on the street, you silly woman." She opened her arms. "Come hug me, child."

The last time Jessamine had seen her Aunt Emerald LaPaix, the woman had waved a lace hankie in her face and called her a wild and unrepentant child. Having just come down from a smoky room on the arm of Lee Kincannon, Jessamine had indeed felt wild and unrepentant. Now she was ready to go down on her knees to this frilly pink woman and beg for her assistance.

Instead, Jessamine went into her arms. Emerald LaPaix kissed the air above Jessamine's cheek, then took her by the arm. "Come into the dining room, Jessamine. Your uncle Jack is just finishing his breakfast. He'll be so pleased to see you." She chattered as she propelled Jessamine across the foyer and into a large room whose only distinguishing feature was the absence of paintings on the walls.

It was dim, even with the drapes pulled back by fat silk braids. A big magnolia grew in the side yard pressing its glossy leaves against the windowpanes. Jessamine's eyes kept returning to the great square outlines on the vacant walls.

Emerald LaPaix stopped talking long enough to take a breath, then said, "And don't even look at the walls, my dear. We were forced to sell practically everything. I can't tell you how tired I am of looking at those big empty places.

Jack, look who I've got with me. It's little Jessamine. Marie and Levander's child.''

Her uncle Jack looked up from the head of the table, where two candles were lit, dripping wax over tarnished silver candlesticks. He looked old, and as empty as the spaces on the walls around him.

"Well, Jessamine," he said, rising slowly from his seat at the polished cherry table. "How nice to see you. And how like my dear sister you look now that you've grown up."

"Hello, Uncle Jack," she said.

"Is your father with you? And your brothers?" There was some hesitation in his voice, as if he expected bad news.

Jessamine felt her knees begin to turn to jelly. To have to recount all the deaths, all the troubles and woes of Riverbend, suddenly seemed too much for her. She paled.

"Oh, dear," said Aunt Emmie. "Do sit down. Let me get you some water. Delia! Oh, where is that woman? She's gotten so uppity ever since she's started considering herself an employee rather than a slave. Delia!" Aunt Emmie disappeared in a flutter of pink.

"I gather you've suffered losses, Jessamine. Such a terrible thing, the war. We lost our Philip, you know. And our little Ruthellen, too, although she passed away from a fever."

"I'm so sorry, Uncle Jack. I didn't know."

"Your Aunt Emmie behaves as if everything were the same. She still fusses and primps." He smiled wistfully. "Still writes letters to Philip—sends them in care of the Confederate command in Richmond. God only knows where they go. They're never returned. Unless Delia destroys them before Emmie can see. I don't know."

His distress was so palpable, Jessamine didn't bother to mention her own losses. Instead, she told him about her search for Caleb.

"He's alive, Uncle Jack. I feel it in my bones. Only nobody wants me to go find him. And all I need is a little help."

"We have no money left, Jessamine. I'm sorry...."

"Oh, no. I don't need money," she exclaimed. "I just need help. Advice. Encouragement." She put her chin in her hand and sighed woefully. "A hairbrush and a petticoat wouldn't hurt, either."

"My advice, I'm afraid, would not be what you're looking for. I'd tell you not to go, Jessamine. The South's on her knees. There's not much left. Except sadness. Unsavory characters are coming down from the North to snatch up the remains. It isn't the way it used to be. And you're such a delicate little thing. No telling what kind of trouble there could be." He gazed down the table at her. "But you do bear an astonishing resemblance to your mother, Jessamine. Once when we were children playing hide-and-seek, Marie hid for seven hours, till well after dark. We called and called. Stubborn little creature just wouldn't come out until somebody found her."

Jessamine smiled. She had heard that story before, and it always made her feel a special bond with this woman who had died when her daughter was just three days old. Before she'd ever heard the tale, Jessamine had done exactly that at Riverbend—hidden from her brothers in a crab apple tree, and stayed there even after they had given up the game. And Maisie had paddled her thoroughly, too, when she finally climbed down.

"Since you seem so determined," her uncle continued, "I will encourage you. Have you made arrangements? How are you going? By land or sea?"

"I don't know," she said. "I really only thought about getting to New Orleans. That was the easy part, I guess."

"Emmie and I used to go to Savannah by boat. We took the steamer *Belle Fleur* around the Florida Keys. But from

what I've heard and read about General Sherman's invasion, I don't think you'd want to go that way. Georgia's burned to the ground between Atlanta and the coast. The conditions around Savannah could be similar. You might do better going in from the west. Seems to me there's still a train running from Mobile to Montgomery. Then you'd only have to travel about a hundred miles east to that prison. You did say Coulterville, didn't you?''

"That's where we last heard from Caleb.''

He nodded. "You can do it. I'm not saying it's going to be easy, or pleasant, for that matter. Not much pleasantness left in the South these days. But you can do it. Your mama always was a stubborn little critter. You inherited her eyes, Jessamine, and her determined heart, too, I suppose.''

"Maybe so. I truly appreciate your help, Uncle Jack.''

He waved a hand in dismissal. "Wish I could send you with a carriage and driver. Five years ago I could have. What else was it you said you needed? Something about a hairbrush?''

"I lost my luggage on the riverboat coming down here. Everything I own is on my back. But I was just teasing about the hairbrush,'' she said.

"Nonsense. I think we can fix you up.'' He rose from his chair and walked around the table to take her hand. "You just come with me.''

At the foot of the great staircase, with its worn carpet, he called out, "Emmie, I'm taking Jessamine up to Ruthellen's room.''

When they reached the door upstairs, Aunt Emmie appeared like an apparition in the upstairs hall.

"You musn't,'' she said, her fingers picking at the ruffles on her bodice. "I forbid it.''

Uncle Jack sighed. "Emmie, this warm, breathing girl is going to Georgia to look for her brother. She requires a

hairbrush, a petticoat, and sundry other items. Ruthellen won't mind one little bit. She was always a generous child."

Emerald LaPaix stood mute. Her pink gauze wrapper was as still as the carved drapery on a statue. Jessamine wondered if her aunt was going to cry, or scream, or faint dead away. Instead, she fluttered to life again—a smile lifting up the creased corners of her mouth, her hands taking off like startled sparrows.

"You're entirely right, Jack. Ruthellen is a generous girl. She won't mind, I'm sure. Only you must return everything clean, Jessamine, and mended. Ruthellen is finicky about her petticoats."

"All right. All right. Hold your horses. Keep your pants on," Alpha muttered sleepily as she fumbled with her silk wrapper, decided she was in Lee's room rather than her own, and so turned right from the bed in order to get to the door. She had drawn the drapes closed earlier and slid into his bed, against his broad, warm back.

"Damn it to hell! Who's beating on our door at this time of day? Ouch!" She tripped over Lee's boots, kicked them aside and went to the door.

"Who is it?" she said, her head tilted against a walnut panel, her eyes still only partway open.

"It's Major Harding, Mrs. Parker."

Alpha's eyes closed, and she yawned. "What time is it?"

"Shortly before noon," he said. "May I come in? I need your assistance."

She opened the door a fraction. "What?"

"She's gone again, Mrs. Parker. Jessamine. I've had them open her room. She left a note."

"Saying?"

The major pressed his lips together tightly. "It was private, Mrs. Parker. I thought perhaps you..."

Alpha pulled open the door. "Major, how can I help you if you won't tell me anything?" Her voice climbed to a higher register. "What did the note say?"

He doffed his hat as he came through the door. His mustache seemed to droop, and his entire face appeared crumpled. "The note said 'Goodbye, Thomas. Go home.'"

"That's all? Just 'goodbye, go home'?"

"I believe her meaning is abundantly clear," he said, taking another step into the sitting room.

Alpha blocked him with her hip and her shoulder as she stole a glance at Lee's room, wishing she had closed the door when she left it.

"That's about as clear as mud, Major Harding," she whispered. "You have a lot to learn about women."

He looked down at the tips of his glossy boots. "I am beginning to think I know nothing. Jessamine says one thing and does another. Hello means goodbye. Am I to assume goodbye means hello? That 'go home' means 'pursue me'?"

"Well, of course it does. Women never say what they mean. And you can bet those shiny brass buttons of yours that her note was meant only to arouse your interest further. The girl's just running you a merry chase. But she wants to be caught. You must persist."

"How?" he asked bleakly. "I don't know where to turn. She's left the hotel and I don't know if she has family here, or friends. I don't know if she's here in New Orleans, or if she's already on her way to her brother in Georgia. And by what means? Carriage? Ship? This is a big country, Mrs. Parker."

"Not that big," Alpha snapped.

"And Jessamine's such a little girl, so utterly defenseless."

Alpha gazed heavenward, then patted the major's arm. "There, there, Major Harding. You go back down to the lobby and wait for me. And then we'll put our heads to-

gether and try to resolve this problem." This goddamn mess, she said to herself.

Finally, a long half hour later, the door closed softly on the swish of Alpha's skirt. Lee waited till she was gone. No sense in getting her all stirred up and delaying him even more.

He dressed quickly, threw a few things in a leather valise, took whatever money was stashed in the cherry-wood secretary, his gun, and the cigars, and shut the door behind him.

Goodbye means hello, his Aunt Matilda's ass! "Goodbye, Thomas" meant "Goodbye, Thomas." And Jessamine did have family in New Orleans. And Lee remembered exactly where they lived.

Jessamine tossed her suitcase from the carriage, threw a coin to the driver and jumped down. Aunt Emmie's suitcase in one hand, the other holding Ruthellen's wide-brimmed straw hat on her head, she rushed down the pier.

"Is that the *Orion?* She hasn't left, has she?" Jessamine asked breathlessly as she pointed to the triple-masted side-wheeler sitting low in the water a quarter mile from the pier. The boat was rocking on the Gulf waves, her white sails rising.

There were six men standing there, all of whom turned to look at the tiny female in the delft blue traveling suit and the huge straw hat.

"Oh, no, ma'am," said a young man wearing heavy gray work pants and a chambray shirt. "The Yanks have loaded her down with artillery. Cannons and such. She's riding so low she can't come in to the pier."

Jessamine frowned. "How do I get out there? Swim?"

A tall man, made even taller by his top hat, laughed. "I was planning to walk on the water, myself," he said. "What about you, Smitty?"

The man she remembered as Smitty dropped his carpet-bag and turned full face to Jessamine, each of his pock-marks visible, his yellow teeth prominent in his ugly sneer. "I'll go whichever way the little lady goes," he said, his eyes boring into hers.

Jessamine's heart began to pound. She stepped closer to the young man in the chambray shirt. "Is there another boat to Mobile?" she asked, trying to sound casual.

"Not till Sunday," the young man said.

Two days, she thought. That was too long. Two days meant she'd have to slink around and avoid Major Hard-ing, sharing the city with Lee and his red-haired lover; and passing the time in that big, sad house in the Garden Dis-trict, with its empty squares on the wall and Aunt Emmie making plans for Ruthellen. Another two days meant an-other two dresses for Charlotte, and more debt for River-bend.

"Are there any other ladies sailing today?" she asked, hoping to find strength in numbers.

"I don't believe so, ma'am," said the young man.

"No *ladies* at all," sneered Smitty. "Just cats with claws and sharp little teeth."

Jessamine's spine turned to ice.

The young man pointed toward the ship. "Tender's coming back now. If y'all want to get your gear together, we'll be ready to go pretty soon."

A wagon pulled up to the pier, discharging a dozen Union soldiers. Jessamine took one look at their blue uni-forms and made up her mind. She wasn't going to let the major drag her home. If she pitched overboard into the Gulf of Mexico, so be it. She was going on the *Orion*.

She waited, a safe distance from Smitty and his compa-triots, while the soldiers carted box after box to the end of the pier. The tender banged against the side while the young

man in the chambray shirt scurried around, catching ropes and lashing them to the huge rusty cleats.

They loaded the boxes first, and then the soldiers climbed down into the pitching tender.

"Gentlemen," said the young man, helping one after the other into the boat. Smitty looked skittish. He slipped on the edge of the pier, while Jessamine heartily wished he'd go headfirst into the Gulf. Unfortunately, he didn't.

"Ma'am," said the young man, holding out his hand to her.

"Oh, Lord!" Jessamine cringed as she gave him her suitcase, then tried to manage her skirts, her hat and the pitching tender, all at the same time. All the while, Smitty was leering and the soldiers were watching and the clatter of a fast carriage sounded from the street above the pier.

She thudded unceremoniously onto the seat beside Smitty, who flashed his yellow teeth at her and said, "Sit closer, rebel girl. My friends and I are going to show you a real good time."

The young man began to unlash the ropes. He had the last rope in his fingertips when somebody called out, "Hold it!"

Jessamine looked back up at the pier and saw Lee, valise in hand, cigar jammed in his teeth. Her heart somersaulted.

As the young man turned around, the last rope slipped from his hand and the tender slid away from the pier.

"Well, hell," said Lee, throwing his cigar down. He heaved his valise into the boat, cursed again, then launched himself into the air.

Chapter Eleven

It wasn't a soft landing, and it wasn't particularly graceful. Lee's feet skidded out from under him and his right hand whacked the side of the tender as he tried to control his fall. Still, the soldiers cheered, and the man in the top hat applauded.

Jessamine could only gape. She thought for a moment she had gone as crazy as Aunt Emmie.

Lee got up, his legs spread wide for balance, and made his way to the plank she shared with Smitty. One look at Lee's black expression, and Smitty moved aside. Lee sat down beside Jessamine, his lips pinched together, his right hand tucked under his arm.

"Did you hurt your hand?" she asked him. "Let me see."

"Jessie," he gritted out, "just be still."

"But I . . ."

He gave her a killing look.

Jessamine watched the horizon. This was no apparition. Only the genuine article could be so ill-tempered and rude. And so wonderful, she thought. And wasn't she glad he was here.

The tender slammed into the side of the *Orion* and the soldiers began handing boxes to one another up the rope ladder. The smaller boat bobbed up as the big steamer sank down in the water, and they thunked against one another for

a full fifteen minutes before the passengers were permitted to board.

A sailor held out a callused hand. "Ma'am."

Jessamine stood up, then sat right down again when the tender rolled.

Lee lifted her by the elbows and passed her along to the sailor. "Just hang on tight, Jessie," he said. "I'll be right behind you."

She swallowed hard. "What if I fall?" she asked, eyeing the waves bashing the side of the boat.

"Swim," said Lee. "Up you go." He put his hands around her waist and lifted her partway up the rope ladder.

She had a hard time getting her feet where they were supposed to go, with her skirts in the way and the wide brim of her straw hat bent in half against the ropes. "My hat," she wailed.

Lee had started to climb below her. "Pitch it if it's in your way," he yelled.

"I can't. It's Ruthellen's." Lord, she thought, she *was* as crazy as Aunt Emmie. She tugged on the bow at her chin, but before she could take it off, the wind carried the hat away. "Now my hair's in my eyes!"

"Christ, Jessie!" Lee gave her rump a shove with his shoulder.

"Don't do that!"

"Will you climb, for God's sake? I'm stuck here like a prawn in a net."

It was a struggle, but Jessamine made it to the top. Well, almost to the top. Lee gave her one last shove and clambered over the rail beside her.

"You didn't have to do that," she snarled, trying to subdue her windblown hair and her thrashing skirt.

Lee wedged his injured hand in his armpit again. "I didn't want to sail all the way to Mobile hanging on that ladder,

Jessie. You're more trouble than a blind cat up a tree, woman.''

She lifted her chin into his dark face. "I don't remember asking you to come along, Lee Kincannon."

"Jessie, I don't need an engraved invitation to go to Mobile, Alabama."

She sniffed. "I'm sure you'd never get one, either."

Lee looked down at her, started to grin, then seemed to change his mind. "I'll be in the salon," he said, "if you care to join me." He walked away.

Maybe she would. Maybe she wouldn't. Maybe she'd just go re-pin her hair before she went to find him.

Her cabin was small. Small enough for her to bang against each wall as she tried to stand before a handkerchief-sized mirror to do her hair. She dropped a hairpin and watched it slide under the door, then slide back.

Her palms were wet as she grasped the rail to climb to the second deck, where the salon was. Jessamine staggered in and saw Lee sitting back in a captain's chair, pulling on a cigar, sipping a whiskey and serenely watching the waves.

"This is terrible," she said, slipping into a chair beside him. "Is it going to be like this all the way to Mobile?"

"A storm's blowing up. I expect it'll get a bit rougher once we're farther out." He shifted in his chair toward her. "You're looking a bit green around the gills, Jessie. Here. Take a sip."

She held the glass and watched the whiskey slosh from one side to the other. When she sipped, it dribbled down her chin.

Lee gave her his handkerchief, and she dabbed at the whiskey.

"Do you have to blow that smoke right in my face, Lee?"

"I wasn't," he said. "There's a draft."

"There's no air at all," she snapped, fanning herself with her hand.

Lee eyed her. "If you're going to be sick, Jessie, tell me and I'll get you out of here."

She gave him a look of pure disdain that withered in an instant. "I'm going to be very, very sick."

Lee pressed the cool cloth to her forehead, smoothing back the damp, dark wisps of hair.

Jessamine opened her eyes a fraction. "I didn't know anybody could be so ill. My ribs ache from hanging over the rail."

"Shh. Try to close your eyes and sleep, Jessie."

She moaned. "I'm going to die."

"You're just seasick. You're not going to die. I promise you."

"But I want to. I truly do."

Lee smiled down on her. "And you were going to go on this wild-goose chase all by yourself. What would you be doing now, all alone?"

"I'd be dying, just like I am anyway." She tried to turn on her side in the small bed, then reeled back. "Oh, Lord, Lee, what if I get sick again?"

He reached out with his foot and tapped a bucket. "Just lean over the side. Same as out on the deck."

Jessamine took in a big, quivering breath. "I want Maisie."

"Shh." He put his finger against her lips. "Maisie couldn't do anything more for you than I'm doing right now."

"You are being sweet to me," she said, her eyes widening a bit.

"Hush," he said softly, stroking her hair.

"How did you find me?"

"I paid a call on your aunt and uncle." He chuckled. "Your aunt Emerald is a little daft, Jessie."

"I wonder if insanity runs in the family," she mused morosely.

"I'm sure it does. Most of it right in your own little veins. Now close your eyes." He pressed his fingertips gently over her eyelids.

"If you've come to cart me back home, you can just forget about it," she said, as forcefully as she could manage. "I'm going to Georgia. I have to. Otherwise..."

"Shh." Lee stilled her with a finger on her lips. "Otherwise the walls of your precious Riverbend will all come tumbling down," he murmured, as if he were telling her a fairy tale. "I never saw a little girl so determined to do things her own way. But you can't do this alone."

"I'm going, Lee, and you can't stop me."

"I realize that, Jessie," he said softly. "So I guess I'll just have to go along, won't I?"

She blinked and tried to raise her head. "You'd do that for me?"

"Well, let's just say I'm indebted to you and Riverbend for saving my life. I feel obliged to help you."

Her sudden happiness soured. She had thought for a moment that he was coming because of her, because he loved her. But Lee was merely working off a debt he felt he owed. Her stomach churned as much with bitter disappointment as with the pitching of the boat.

"Could you move that bucket a little closer?" she asked bleakly, leaning over the side of the bed. "You won't leave me, will you, Lee? I truly am dying."

"I'm not going to leave you, Jessie," he said, lifting her hair and placing the cool cloth on the back of her neck. "I'm not sure I could leave you even if I wanted to, little girl," he added to himself.

Jessamine awoke in a big, soft bed, stretched languidly, then yelped, because her ribs and stomach muscles ached.

She vaguely remembered Lee slinging her over his shoulder and carring her off the steamship and lugging her up what had seemed like seventeen flights of stairs. She had wanted just to crawl into bed with her dress on, but he had shrugged her out of it, tucked her in and turned out the lamp.

She sat up, testing the weather in her head and stomach. It was fair to middling. When she stood, the floor was solid under her feet. Actually, she felt pretty good—considering. Her suitcase lay on a chair, so she opened it and got out her hairbrush and began working on the tangled mess on her head.

She was bent over in her corset and pantaloons, her hair nearly touching the floor, when Lee walked in.

"Didn't your mama teach you to knock, Lee Kincannon?" she asked, only half in jest.

Lee leaned against the doorframe. "I barely had a mama, Jessie. Now that's the prettiest sight, you with your hair all slung out like a black silk banner."

She continued to brush. "You're liable to walk in on me and see something you shouldn't."

"Don't forget, Jessie, I've seen the contents of your stomach. You probably don't have a lot of surprises left."

"I wouldn't count on that if I were you," she said.

"Well, speaking of stomachs, you'd best get dressed quick if you want breakfast before our train leaves."

She tossed her head back, and her raven hair went flying. "I'll meet you downstairs in ten minutes."

Lee grinned. "I'll see you in twenty, then. I always double it when a woman estimates time and halve it when she estimates money."

Jessamine sniffed. "We'll just have to work on your mathematics. Now get out of here."

When she sashayed into the dining room wearing yards of peach moiré and ecru lace, Lee took out his pocket watch.

"By God, I don't believe it," he said as he stood to hold her chair. "You're a miracle, Miss Jessamine."

"Surprise, surprise, Lee," she said, slipping into the seat.

Lee returned to his chair, and his gaze moved immediately to the dipping neckline of her dress.

Jessamine sat up straighter. "You needn't ogle. I know this isn't proper for early morning or for traveling, but it's comfortable, and it's hardly wrinkled after being jammed in that valise."

"I was admiring you, Miss Jessamine, not criticizing you. And I've ordered you fried eggs, sausages and grits." He watched her reach aggressively for a biscuit. "I hope that's going to be sufficient."

"Ordinarily I eat like a sparrow," she said, biting a hunk out of the biscuit. "I don't know why I'm such a vulture when I'm with you."

A waiter placed their plates before them.

"Oh, that looks wonderful," Jessamine said. "I don't know what to eat first."

"Well, just jump in with both feet, Jessie. But do it fast. We want to catch that train."

The Mobile-to-Montgomery train was dark green, with Gulf & Alabama Railroad lettered in gold across the top of both its passenger cars. Its big black locomotive was already belching a column of white steam as Jessamine and Lee took the rear seat of the last car, facing the front. Four Union soldiers—a sergeant, two corporals and a private—were already seated up front, and as the other passengers straggled on board, Lee sat with his arms crossed, his hat tilted forward, as if he were napping.

"Oh, Lord, there's that horrid man again," Jessamine whispered when she saw the pockmarked Smitty walk down the aisle. When he saw Jessamine, he winked lewdly and pursed his lips in an exaggerated kiss.

Jessamine's blood ran cold. "If I had a pistol," she spit out, "I'd shoot him right between his beady little eyes."

"Who?" asked Lee, tipping his hat back slightly. "Where?"

"Well, don't look now. He's watching. That plug-ugly man in the brown frock coat and gold cravat."

"Carpetbagger," Lee snarled.

"A what?"

"A carpetbagger. Down from the North to pluck the South like a dead chicken. Was he one of the thugs on the *Delta Princess?*"

Jessamine shivered and nodded. "It must be awful," she said, a disturbing note in her voice, "to have a man like that be your first time, against your will. I always imagined . . ." Her voice trailed off.

Lee turned toward her, his dark eyes soft as he gazed into her violet eyes, his deep voice husky. "What did you always imagine, Jessie?"

You, Lee, she yearned to say. Your warm hands touching me, and your whiskey-edged voice whispering in my ear. "Sweetness," she said.

His eyes caresssed her face, lingering on her pink, moist lips. "The firt time's not always so sweet, little one," he murmured. "Sometimes it takes a while. For the sweetness, I mean."

"It won't for me," she said. "It'll be perfect."

He grinned. "You're pretty sure of that, are you?"

"Absolutely certain."

"Do you have any particular partner in mind, Miss Jessamine?"

She blinked and smiled, as if to say, "Wouldn't you like to know?"

With a beleaguered sigh, Lee retreated beneath his hat. "You might want to dampen your expectations a bit, Jes-

sie. There probably aren't too many men who could live up to them."

"We'll see," she said.

Lee was dozing when the train stopped half an hour later in the middle of nowhere. Untended cotton fields ranged out as far as Jessamine could see from the windows on either side.

She nudged him with her elbow. "Lee, the train stopped."

He grunted. "Probably a cow on the track."

She leaned out the window, looking toward the locomotive. Everybody else was leaning out now, too, except for Lee, who returned to sleep.

Jessamine nudged him again. "There's a whole slew of men out there on horseback, Lee. And, oh, Lord, they've got guns. What do you suppose is happening?"

Lee reached in his pocket immediately and withdrew some bills and coins. "Put this down the front of your dress, Jessie. Be quick about it. If you've got any money in your handbag, put that in there too. And make sure it doesn't show. See if you can get some in the hem of your skirt."

By now all the passengers in the car were busy hiding money, pocket watches and other valuables in hats and boots, and under the seats. The four soldiers were tending to their rifles and whispering among themselves.

Jessamine shoved money down her corset as fast as she could. Lee leaned across her to look out the window, where one of the robbers was riding slowly down the side of the train, his gun pointed into each window as he passed.

"Damn." Lee ducked his head back and slid down in his seat. His hat was now covering most of his face.

"What is it?" Jessamine asked frantically, taking a look out the window for herself. The robber was approaching, his horse appearing to tiptoe along the track. Three men followed close behind him.

"He's a mean-looking varmint," she muttered. "Oh, look! He's wearing part of a Confederate uniform. Well, I'm sure they're not soldiers. Or maybe they are, and nobody told them the war is over. Do you think that's possible? Lee? You're not going to sleep at a time like this, are you? For heaven's sake!"

He shifted his hat just enough to skewer her with his dark eyes. "You don't know me, Jessie. You got that? You do not know me."

"Lee, what—?"

Just then the glass on the rear door of the car shattered. Jessamine saw a gloved hand reach in and turn the inside handle. The nasty-looking man she had seen earlier walked in, followed by three others, all of them wearing at least one item of the regular Confederate army uniform.

"If nobody moves, you'll all be eating supper in Montgomery tonight." His voice was a mixture of sociability and menace. "You Yanks up there," he called. "Your officer's up in the first car with a gun to his head. I know he'll be real pleased if you hand your rifles over to us."

He gestured to the men behind him, who walked up the aisle and took the soldiers' guns. "Anybody else care to make a contribution?" asked one of the robbers. "Any other firearms? Gents?"

All the men shook their heads. Lee seemed to be trying to dig himself into the upholstery with his shoulders.

The nasty-looking man joined his men at the front of the car. His hair was a dirty blond. His eyes were the color of his gray tunic, and there was a crescent-shaped scar on his left cheek. He took one of the rifles and rested it on his shoulder, then turned to the gaping passengers.

"Gentlemen," he drawled. Then his gaze shifted to Jessamine, in the back of the car. "And ma'am. My name is Colonel Merit Sinclair of the Alabama Irregulars. We're taking contributions for the widows' and orphans' fund. As

we're passing among you with our hats in our hands, I strongly urge you to give. And I caution you not to withhold anything. Dead men don't need watches, gents. Or rings, ma'am.''

They passed slowly, from seat to seat, their hats moving like collection plates in a Baptist church. Travelers were turning pockets inside out, taking off boots, opening luggage. Jessamine could feel the gold coins growing hot against her abdomen and chest. She prayed they wouldn't make her get up and walk, because she knew she'd jingle like a child's bank.

And what did Lee mean, for heaven's sake, that she wasn't supposed to know him? Here he'd planted all his damn money on her, and now he was supposed to be a perfect stranger!

''Ma'am,'' crooned Merit Sinclair, passing his sweat-stained hat across Lee's lap to Jessamine.

Up close, she could see green flecks in his gray eyes, and the pearly sheen of his scar.

''I have a five-dollar gold piece in the hem of my skirt,'' she said, her voice shaking, ''if I can only find it.'' As she leaned forward to poke through a length of peach-colored fabric, a coin spilled out of her bodice, clattering on the floor.

Jessamine picked it up with trembling fingers. ''Well, look at that. It wasn't in my hem after all. There you are, Colonel,'' she said, dropping it in the hat. ''For the widows and orphans.''

''Thank you kindly, ma'am.'' The hat didn't move. ''I'll take the rest of it now, if you don't mind.''

''The rest?'' she asked, all innocence and big, blinking eyes.

''You just undo a might and then dig down real deep and see what you can come up with,'' he said, ''while I take a contribution from this gentleman here.'' The hat moved di-

rectly in front of Lee, who was still skulking under the brim of his own hat and, as far as Jessamine was concerned, being no help at all.

Lee reached in his pocket, took out his watch, opened it, and checked the time. "It's runnin' real well, Merit. You take good care of it now, you hear." He dropped it in the hat.

Merit Sinclair's jaw hung loose. "Lee? Lee Kincannon?"

The black hat tipped back to disclose Lee's grinning face. "Afternoon, Colonel," he said.

"Well, I'll be horsewhipped and hung out to dry. Boys, look who's riding on our train."

The robbers paused in their hat-passing and looked to the rear of the train.

"Howdy, Captain."

"Afternoon, Captain."

Now it was Jessamine's jaw that was unhinged.

"Lee Kincannon!" said the colonel. "Last I heard you were hiding out in Memphis. What the hell are you doin' in Alabama?"

Lee sighed. "Well, Merit, I was on my way to Montgomery, but now it looks like I'm going with you, doesn't it?" He gestured with a black eyebrow to the Union soldiers, who were staring at him, along with everyone else on the train.

Merit Sinclair leaned closer. "I'm real sorry, Lee. About the Yanks, I mean. Well, hell. We'll be happy to have you with us. Here. Take your watch back." He retrieved Lee's pocket watch from the depths of his hat and dropped it on his lap. "We've even got a horse for you. Young Jimmy Cates— You remember him, don't you? The skinny kid with no eyebrows? He took real sick this morning and we had to leave him behind. He's got a fast dappled gray. Guess it's yours now."

"Show me the way," said Lee, starting to rise from his seat.

"Just one minute." Merit Sinclair focused on Jessamine. "You find all those other coins, ma'am?"

Jessamine gazed helplessly at Lee.

Merit Sinclair regarded him, as well. "This little gal with you, Lee?"

Lee gestured with his thumb. "Who her? Naw."

"Lee Kincannon, how dare you—?" Jessamine wailed before Lee cut her off.

"I met her yesterday on the *Orion*. I guess I've had about enough," he said, giving the colonel a meaningful look and then Jessamine a cold, hard stare. "She doesn't have any money. Only that five-dollar gold piece I gave her for her favors. Let's go."

Sinclair fit his hat, money and all, on his head. He handed the Yankee's confiscated rifle to Lee. "Might as well take this, Captain," he said. Then he yelled, "All right, boys. Let's go. Thank you, gentlemen. Ma'am, thank you."

Lee stood up, rifle in hand. Jessamine stood up, too, and six gold coins clattered onto the floor.

Merit Sinclair turned around. "I thought you said..."

Lee turned one palm up in an innocent gesture. "That's what she told me, Merit. Why don't I just take her outside, give her a good shake and see what falls out?" He grabbed Jessamine's wrist and pulled her into the aisle, then closed his arms around her and hustled her out the back of the train.

She struggled and kicked and hissed at him. "Shake me just once, you son of a bitch, and I'll—"

His voice was a rasp against her ear. "Give me a few coins, Jessie. Just enough to make them happy. I'll meet you at the Plantation Hotel in Montgomery in a day or two. You wait for me, damn it, you hear?"

"You can't just leave me!" she shrieked.

"I have to, Jessie. Those Yankees know who I am now, and they're going to make a prodigious effort to hang me." He put her down on the ground.

"The war's over, Lee," Jessamine said, yanking up the bodice of her dress and stamping her foot.

"Not completely," he said stonily. "Give me those coins."

"I will not." She crossed her arms, and stood—for all that she was wearing peach-colored silk—like a brick wall.

The robbers had mounted now, and Merit Sinclair was leading a riderless dappled gray. "We best be going, Captain," he called.

Jessamine bit her lip as tears brimmed in her violet eyes. "Take me with you."

His jaw hardened. "No, Jessie."

"Please. I can't get back on that train alone. Don't leave me with that...that man...that carpetbagging rapist. Please. I'm begging you, Lee." A tear broke loose from the inner corner of her eye and streaked down the side of her nose.

Something flickered in his eyes then, like a match striking in pitch darkness. He cursed, then put a rough arm around her waist and dragged her toward the waiting horse. "I'm taking her with me, Merit," he called to the colonel. "I want to see what else the little tart has been holding out on me."

Lee nearly threw her onto the saddle, then swung up behind her. "Damn you, Jessie," he said as he dug his heels into the horse.

Chapter Twelve

They rode hard for three or four miles south along the tracks, then turned east through ragged cotton fields. Jessamine gritted her teeth and clutched the saddle horn for dear life, even though Lee's arm was wrapped around her as tight as a band on a bale of cotton. When they reached a forest dense with oak and elm, they slowed their horses to a walk.

Jessamine wasn't thrilled with her predicament; riding with a gang of train robbers wasn't getting her any closer to Georgia and Caleb, but it was preferable to being left behind with that loathsome carpetbagger. She was grateful to Lee for bringing her along, but not so grateful that she could forget his behavior toward her on the train. When their wild gallop ended, she leaned back against his chest. He relaxed his arm a little, but didn't release her. His hand was splayed out on her rib cage, his thumb resting just beneath her breast.

"Am I to play the tart again?" she asked him with an exaggerated sigh.

"Just play dumb, Jessie. That shouldn't be so all-fired hard for you to do."

Better dumb than rude, she thought. What a talent he had for infuriating her. "Well, if I'm so dumb, and you're

traipsing around after me like a pet dog, then what does that
make you?"

"I guess that makes me pretty dumb, too."

She twitched her shoulders in satisfaction.

"A pet dog, Jessie?" he asked.

"That's what I said." Jessamine crossed her arms, realizing too late that her little act of defiance forced her more
closely back against him.

His tongue traced the curve of her ear.

Jessamine's eyes widened. "What are you doing?"

"Your pet dog is licking your pearly little ear, Miss Jessamine," he whispered. "Isn't that what pet dogs do?" And
he proceeded to do it again.

Every nerve in her body lit like dry kindling, beginning at
her ear and crackling all the way to her toes.

"What's this?" Lee asked, his hand pressing harder on
her ribs, his thumb wedged under her breast. "Is that some
little pet bird, Miss Jessamine, or might that be your heart
fluttering in my hand?"

Her mouth had gone too dry for her to speak. She let her
head rest against his shoulder and just swayed with the
rhythm of the horse, feeling Lee's heart pounding against
her back, marveling at how easily he could turn her wrath
to warm desire.

Since their pace was so leisurely, Merit Sinclair let his big
roan lag back.

"When'd you leave Memphis, Lee?" he asked, all sociability now.

Lee straightened himself in the saddle, and Jessamine's
head pitched forward, off his shoulder. His hand tensed
once again on her midriff. "Right after General Lee signed
the treaty at Appomattox," he drawled. "Didn't seem much
need to hide out anymore." Plus, Miss Alpha had broken a
bottle over his head and then planted her dainty foot on his
backside, he added to himself.

"That was what we thought, too. Hell, we thought we could walk down any street at high noon, saying 'how do' and 'good day, Miss Gussie.' Damn Yanks hanged Charlie Stillwater just three weeks ago. You remember him?"

Lee nodded. "Smoked that damn Cuban tobacco in his pipe. I remember him."

"Poor Charlie," said Sinclair. "A patrol rode us down not too far from the Georgia border. They strung him up from a big old shagbark, with a hand-drawn Stars and Bars pinned to his chest. It was pure awful, Lee, I'll tell you. Those Yanks can be vicious devils when they're not under the thumb of a good officer. I miss old Charlie. Even miss that stinking tobacco."

"I expect if we just keep our heads down for a while it'll pass," said Lee.

"Vicious damn blue devils," muttered Sinclair.

Jessamine's blood had turned from hot to cold. Goose bumps riddled her arms at the thought of Lee with a rope around his neck and a homemade Confederate flag on his chest.

"Oh, hell," Sinclair snarled. "Let's change the subject. How's that pretty redheaded woman of yours, Lee?"

On the other hand, Jessamine thought, a rope might do quite nicely.

Lee cleared his throat. "Well, now, Merit, I'm not sure that's polite, seeing I'm with this little lady now."

The colonel caught his meaning and gave Jessamine an appreciative glance. "You're a pretty one, too, miss. Remind me a little of my Maggie, back in Talladega County."

"Thank you, Colonel," said Jessamine modestly. "And you may tell Captain Kincannon I don't mind at all if he'd like to talk about his redheaded woman. How silly of him to think it would bother me."

"How long have you been robbing trains, Merit?" asked Lee, almost before the last word was out of Jessamine's mouth.

"Hell! Ain't it awful, Lee? Being reduced to theft just to make a little money? We're trying to get enough together to go west and buy some cattle. Eldon Taylor's already left. So's Bobby Joe McCandless. Course, I don't suppose you've got to worry about anything like that, with your boats and hotels, you fortunate son of a bitch."

"Not all that fortunate, Merit. The railroads are already killing my riverboat business, and they're going to be building new hotels, bigger and better than mine, now that the war's over. I'm looking at starting all over again, just like you."

Over her shoulder, Jessamine aimed a glare of pure malice at him. "Why, Captain, you and that redheaded woman ought to head on out west to seek your proper share of fame and fortune."

Merit Sinclair gave Lee a sympathetic look. "I believe I'll ride up with Carlton for a while. We'll be getting to our camp in an hour or so, Captain." He kicked the big roan into a trot.

"Lean back, Jessie. Where were we before we were interrupted?"

Jessamine remained rigidly upright. "I believe you were drooling in my left ear and making a fool of yourself."

"Sweet, mad Jessie," he taunted.

"Just leave me alone, Lee."

"Lean back."

She shot her elbow into his rib cage, hard enough to hurt her arm. Lee didn't utter a cry or a word. And he didn't repeat his request for her to lean back.

Jessamine yawned. She'd been lying with one elbow propping her head up, listening to the men reminisce about

their glory days when the war had just begun, taking her own swig from the bottle on every third or fourth pass. But she was sleepy now.

And she was tired of watching Lee with the firelight shining on his hair and glinting in his eyes. He hadn't spoken a word to her since she'd driven her elbow into his ribs. She'd just sort of padded along behind him as he unsaddled his horse, greeted some of the men, helped gather wood for the fire. No, that wasn't entirely true. He had spoken to her when she followed him into a dense thicket, to curtly inform her that he was on his way to relieve himself and to tell her she was certainly welcome to follow if she was so inclined. She had turned from pink to crimson before stalking back to the campsite.

She was lonely for Riverbend, too, and mad at herself that tonight, instead of looking for Caleb, she was looking at Lee, which wasn't going to do a whole hell of a lot to keep her plantation from going under.

He stood above her now, his legs like tree trunks, his hand open and extended. "Come on, Jessie. It's time for bed."

Lee pulled her up, then bent to pick up the blanket she'd been lying on. It had grown dead silent around the fire. Jessamine felt the longing gaze of each of the men as she bade them good-night.

"Night, Miss Jessie," said Merit Sinclair, his gray eyes and his moon-shaped scar almost glowing in the light from the fire.

"Good night, Colonel," she said as Lee led her away to a small stand of pines.

He shook the blanket out and laid it on the ground, then knelt to straighten it. "No tent tonight, Jessie, but I don't think the bugs will bother you too much."

She stood watching his broad shoulders, his calf muscles hard against the fabric of his breeches, his finely shaped

hands smoothing out the dark wool of the blanket. As she knelt down, Lee stood up.

"Sleep tight, Jessie," he said.

She jumped back up. "You're not leaving me, are you?" she asked, trying to sound angry, or frightened, or anything other than disappointed.

"I'll be back in a while."

"Lee!"

"You're not afraid, are you, Jessie? There's nothing to be afraid of around here. Now you just go on and curl up and you'll be asleep in about two minutes." He kissed the top of her head and began to walk away.

Jessamine's lower lip slid out. She hated the notions that were roiling in her head. She hated even more that she couldn't keep still about them. "You're thinking about her, aren't you? You've been thinking about her all afternoon, and all night, too. That's why you won't stay with me, isn't it? Why you can't even bear to be near me."

Lee turned back toward her. "You truly believe that, don't you?" He laughed softly. "My Jessie's as jealous as a little green-eyed cat."

"I'm angry, that's all."

"And jealous," Lee said softly, taking her into his arms. "I like that. And I haven't been thinking about anything but your tender ears and my bruised ribs and some high old times before the war turned sour." His cheek was pressed against her hair. He stroked her back as he spoke.

"Then stay here with me, Lee. I want to fall asleep in your arms."

He leaned back a little, tipped her chin up. "Jessie, I'd like nothing better than to hold you close to me while we both fall asleep. I don't know if you'll be able to understand this, but I'm going back to the fire to sit with six hungry-eyed men who know they can't have you, tonight or any other night—six brave and dirty men, half of whom will

probably be hanged before the summer's over." Lee paused as his throat caught. "I can't keep a noose from around their necks, but I can sit with them tonight, share a bottle with them, and be hungry-eyed myself." He kissed each corner of her mouth.

She did understand, so she feigned a yawn. "I'm probably too sleepy to appreciate it anyway," she said, sinking down on the blanket and curling up on her side. "You go on back. Tell everyone I said good-night, Lee." She crooked her arm under her head, yawned again, and closed her eyes, then listened long into the night to the sounds of quiet talk and laughter around the fire.

Lee woke her just before dawn.

"Shh... I don't want to wake anyone else. We're leaving, Jessie. Fold up that blanket and come on."

She got to her feet, still blind and dumb and stiff with sleep. "Where are we going? How are we going?" she yawned.

"Give me five or six gold pieces," he said. "I'm going to leave them for the horse."

She fumbled with the top of her dress.

"Come on, Jessie. Hurry," Lee rasped, looking over his shoulder to make certain all the men were still asleep.

"I'm doing the best I can, Lee. They're all stuck to me down here," she said, one hand down the front of her dress. "Here. Here's two." She handed him two twenty-dollar coins, then reached into her corset again. "Here's three more," she said.

"That'll have to do. Wait here." Lee walked back to the burned-out campfire and put the coins on the ground beside it. Then he took Jessamine by the hand and whispered, "Come on."

They walked about half a mile, Lee carrying the saddle and a rifle, Jessamine leading the horse. A little after sunrise, Lee saddled the horse and strapped the rifle in place.

"Let's go to Georgia, Jessie," he said, hoisting her up, then getting on behind her and urging the big horse on its way.

Jessamine fell asleep against his shoulder, and when she woke they were riding down a little stream, the horse picking its way carefully among the rocks and fallen tree limbs. She guessed it was about ten o'clock.

"Are you awake?" Lee whispered softly.

"Just barely. What a beautiful place this is, Lee. Are we in Georgia yet?"

"Nope. It'll take us a good day, day and a half. That's assuming there are no mishaps." He sighed. "And somehow, Jessie, I can't imagine you going twenty-four hours without one of those."

She sniffed. "I don't feel like arguing with you this morning. Just look at the pretty flowers all along there. Are flowers edible, Lee?"

"I don't think so, Jessie."

"I'm ravenous. My stomach is growling like a tiger in a circus cage."

"Is that what that noise was? I thought you were snoring."

She started to dig her elbow in his ribs, then had second thoughts about it and merely clucked her tongue. She sighed. "I've lost another suitcase. Can you imagine that? I've been gone from Riverbend one week, and I've managed to lose everything I've got—twice. I certainly hope Caleb appreciates this."

"Tell me about Caleb," Lee said, shifting a little in the saddle to stretch his back.

"He is probably the sweetest of all my brothers—the sweetest of the four of us, for that matter. His eyes are the

same color as mine. His hair, too. We both take after our mama. Caleb is five—no—six years older than I am, so that makes him nearly twenty-eight now. That's hard to imagine," she said.

"It's hard to imagine you're almost twenty-two when you still look..."

"You're not going to ramble on about my youth and inexperience now, are you, Lee?" she asked tartly.

He laughed. "No, I wasn't. In fact, after this past week, I'd say you're a very experienced woman."

"Well...more or less," she said.

"More or less," he echoed softly.

"Caleb has a kind of innocence about him. He can't abide slavery. That's why he joined the Union army. I remember when we were little he'd always be whispering to our people, encouraging them to run away. And he never had any money, because he was always giving it to Maisie or Sampson or one of the others as payment for their services. Papa was always furious with him." She laughed. "And poor Caleb was always so shy. There was a girl from a few miles up the river who adored him and kept chasing after him. Caleb spent about as much time in haylofts as my other brothers did—only Caleb was hiding from girls, while Charles and Louis were kissing them."

"When did you last hear from him?" Lee asked.

"Over two years ago. We didn't hear from Caleb, exactly. We had a letter from a man named Henry Alexander, who said he'd been captured with Caleb at Shiloh and was looking out for him at Coulterville."

"Don't get your hopes up too high, Jessie. A lot of men died in those prisons. Andersonville, Coulterville, and the rest."

"I just have a feeling, Lee. I know Caleb's alive."

Lee pulled on the reins of the horse. "Now that's what I've been looking for," he said.

"What?"

"Over there." Lee pointed to a gentle green slope by the stream bed. "See 'em?"

"Oh, my Lord!" she squealed. "Strawberries!"

Licking her fingers, Jessamine lay back in the middle of the strawberry patch, arms flopping at her sides. "I never want to see another strawberry," she said. "I think I ate five quarts."

Lee was stretched out, leaning on one elbow, smoking a fat cigar he'd lifted from Merit Sinclair. "You're going to get berry stains all over the back of your dress," he cautioned.

She shook her head. "I ate them all. There's not a berry left within a six-foot radius of me."

"Here's one you overlooked," he said, pulling it from a vine. "Open up, Jessie." He leaned over and fed her the sweet, overripe berry.

She chewed it slowly with her eyes closed, almost purring at the taste. Juice trickled from the corners of her mouth. Then she sighed. "Now I never want to see another strawberry—unless you've found another just like that one. Or maybe..." She opened her eyes, falling speechless when she realized how close Lee's face was to hers.

"Or maybe what, Jessie?" he murmured as he kissed a corner of her mouth.

"Maybe..." she whispered as his tongue touched the juicy crevice, then softly traced her lower lip to the other corner.

"You taste like strawberries, Jessie," Lee said, his breath warm on her mouth. "Sweet, sweet berries." His lips closed softly over hers.

Jessamine heard herself murmuring at the feel of his rough chin, his strong arms gathering her against him, his moist tongue sliding over her lips, then her chin and her throat, before returning to her lips again. Her heart felt as

if it were swelling with joy and she had to remind herself to breathe.

"Let me taste you, Jessie," he whispered. Lee moaned softly as his tongue breached the barrier of her teeth to meet her tongue in a tender greeting.

Her fingers traced the hard muscles of his back through the fine cotton of his shirt. She could feel the strong beating of his heart in the veins of his solid neck. Jessamine wanted to kiss him forever, but his mouth left hers to rain kisses on her chin, her neck, her collarbone, her cleavage, and she twined her fingers through his thick, dark hair.

His lips were warm as they roved over her skin, his fingertips gentle as they caressed the fabric of her dress, the lace top of her corset, the curves of her flesh. Desire shimmered through her.

"Jessie," he said hoarsely, as his hand freed her breast from her corset and his mouth closed over its pink center.

"Oh, yes," she whispered. "This is the way I've always imagined it would be. So sweet. Please love me, Lee."

Lee froze as if a cold wind had just blown through him. He lifted his head and looked into Jessamine's glazed eyes. Then he cursed, and stood up so fast that Jessamine plopped back down among the berry vines, astonished and out of breath.

"What did I do wrong?" she gasped.

"Nothing," he snapped, throwing her a black look. "Kissing's over, Jessie. Get yourself back together there, and let's be off." He picked up his hat and jacket, found the cigar he had tossed away just before feeding Jessamine the strawberry and walked to the bur oak beside the stream where the dappled gray was tied.

With her heart sinking to a normal pace and her wind back, Jessamine punched her skirt out of the way and stood up. Her hair was half-undone, and her bosom exposed above the lace neckline of her dress. Her corset was all out

of kilter, one whalebone stay biting into her hip and another poking at her breast. There were berry stains on her skirt. She rolled her eyes. "Good Lord, I look like I've been shot and left to die here," she wailed.

Tugging on her neckline, she managed to settle everything in its proper place. She stuffed her stray hair back into her chignon, stiffened her shoulders and stalked to the stream.

Lee was seeing to the saddle, tightening cinches and strapping the rifle in place. He ignored Jessamine as she took her shoes off, hiked up her skirt and stomped out into the stream, muttering all the while.

She went after the spots on her dress with some water. "Looks like a damn tornado picked me up and set me down in Alabama. And look at Ruthellen's dress. If this is what kissing you is going to be like, Lee Kincannon, then you can just forget about it. I know I intend to. Never again. No, sir." Jessamine was angling for a berry stain toward the back of her skirt when her foot slid on a slime-covered tree limb. She tried to regain her balance and wound up landing with a splash in the middle of the stream. "Damn it," she howled.

Lee didn't feel much like grinning, but he couldn't stop his lips from sliding sideways. He gave the horse a pat on its solid gray rump, then walked to Jessamine.

"Don't you come near me, Lee Kincannon. This is all your fault." With the flat of her hand, she splashed water at him.

"Come on, Jessie," he said, his throat still dry. He wanted to pick her up, but that would mean he'd have to touch her, and he wasn't sure he could stand it, or withstand it, or stop once he got his hands on her again.

He wanted her more than he'd ever wanted a woman in his life. He'd wanted her so badly up there in the strawberry patch, he'd almost forgotten it was the wrong time and

the wrong place. Jessie and all her great expectations! He wouldn't take her like some wild country girl on the bank of a stream, hard and fast, then put her on a horse and let her ride forty miles wondering what all the shouting was about.

For all her pluck and endurance, Jessie was still a little girl playing hide-and-seek. She had no notion of what might be riding down on them right this minute, now that he had added robbery to his list of other crimes, most committed in the name of the Confederacy and in wartime but all crimes nevertheless.

With a little luck—and if the horse could hold out—they'd have plenty of opportunities for a quick roll in the hay or a fast poke in a berry patch. But for Jessie's first time, Lee wanted clean sheets, and leisure enough to lead her to the sweetness her heart imagined.

She was pulling coins and currency out of her dress now. "And take your damn money. I'm tired of it scratching and poking me," she said, tossing a fistful of greenbacks at him. They landed on the water and began drifting away with the current.

Lee splashed after them. "For crissake, Jessie, how do you think we're going to get to Georgia without two cents to rub together?"

She threw a gold coin at him.

Lee caught it. "That's it," he said. He jammed the wet bills and the coin in his pocket, then hauled her up under her arms. Jessamine kicked and screamed.

It was like trying to land a mad catfish wearing a big, wet dress. Then Lee's foot slipped on the stream bottom, and they both went down, Jessamine right in his lap.

"Jessie, you're going to make me an old man before my time."

Chapter Thirteen

It took most of the day, with a hot Alabama sun beating down on them, but by the time they reached the little town of Calverton, their clothes were dry. Lee left Jessamine and the horse in the shade of a big mulberry tree and walked, hat dipping over his eyes, black coat hooked over his shoulder with a finger, into town. One look around the town square reminded him it was Sunday. There was a single carriage beside the redbrick courthouse, with a black man sleeping in the driver's seat and a black horse nodding over the iron hitching post. In front of the courthouse, on a tall flagpole, a new and vivid Stars and Stripes snapped crisply in the breeze.

It occurred to Lee that the war and its aftermath were a flagmaker's dream. He'd seen enough red-white-and-blue flags in the past few years to last him his whole life. How many men had gotten rich, he wondered, selling flags for windows, flags for balconies, flags for coffins. Next time he'd sew flags. Let somebody else do the fighting. But now, on a sleepy Sunday in Calverton, Alabama, this particular Union flag made him very uneasy.

The chances were good that news about the train robbery had been telegraphed to every town and Union garrison in this part of the state. And that fool Merit not only hadn't

had sense enough to wear a mask, he'd announced his name right out. And Lee's name, too.

But for the past hour and a half Jessie had been going on—at great length—about mattresses and pillows and food. He'd promised her a hot meal and a bed, and that was what he was searching for. If they kept their heads down and didn't attract any undue attention, Lee figured they'd be all right.

He walked into the little hotel, bumped shoulders with a blue-uniformed corporal, mumbled an apology, and then walked right back out.

Damnation! He was probably a bigger fool than Merit, thinking he could get away with this. If he had any sense at all, he'd slink back to the stream. But the horse was exhausted, he was exhausted, and Jessie was yearning for a bed.

She might be better off now if he left her, Lee thought. But then he thought again about young Nathan, about losing him in the cold, swift currents because he couldn't hang on tight enough, couldn't get a grip and keep it. Well, he had a grip on Jessie now and, by God, he was going to keep it. There weren't enough soldiers in the whole goddamn Federal army to force him to let go.

When he returned, Jessamine was sprawled under the mulberry tree, licking her finger and rubbing at a spot on her skirt. The gray was pulling up wood sorrel beside her.

At the sight of him, she scrabbled to her feet and ran into his arms. "You were gone so long," she said. "I was worried."

Lee hugged her to him and closed his eyes briefly, reveling in the feel of her slight body, wishing this was the time and the place to love her, knowing all too well it wasn't. Then he let his gaze wander down the peach-colored silk of her skirt. "Jessie, Jessie," he said, "now you've got mul-

berry juice all mixed in with the strawberries. What am I going to do with you?''

''Now you just be still, Jessie, and let me do the talking,'' he said as they walked to the door of the white clapboard house on the edge of town.

Lee took off his hat when a white-haired woman opened the door. ''Afternoon, ma'am,'' he drawled.

''Oh, my,'' she said at the sight of him, then, ''Oh!'' when she realized Jessamine was just behind his shoulder.

''I understand you take in boarders, ma'am,'' said Lee.

''I'm afraid I only have one very small room,'' said the woman, looking more closely at Lee's shadowy jaw, and from there to Jessamine's flyaway hair and limp peach dress.

''That's perfect,'' exclaimed Jessamine as she pulled the screen door out of the woman's hand. Her voice was a lilting mixture of cheer and surprise and relief, and she moved steadily into the house as she spoke. ''We'll take it. My husband and I are just exhausted from riding all day. The axle broke on our carriage, first thing this morning. We'd hardly been on the road an hour. I asked him to make certain that old buggy was up to the trip. But did he do it?'' Well established in the front parlor now, she gave the elderly woman a conspiratorial look, as if to say, ''Well, I'm stuck with this fool.''

There wasn't a doubt in Lee's mind that the woman believed they were husband and wife.

''You poor little thing,'' the woman said, glancing at Lee, then dropping her gaze to Jessamine's skirt. ''Oh, my.''

''Strawberries,'' said Jessamine. ''And mulberries. That's all we've eaten today.''

''Well, my name is Mrs. Tremaine and I would be pleased to have you both in my home and at my table, Mrs....''

''Dade,'' said Jessamine.

"Dade," echoed Lee quickly, extending his hand between Jessamine and Mrs. Tremaine. "Levander Dade. And this is my charming wife, Jessamine."

"I'm so pleased to meet you," said Mrs. Tremaine, her face coloring as Lee took her hand. When he let go, she fingered the pink cameo brooch she wore at the throat of her black dress. "Well, as I said, it's a small room, but if you'd like to get your luggage, I'll show you on up to it."

Jessamine sighed dramatically, hooked her arm through Mrs. Tremaine's, and sauntered toward the stairs. "He wouldn't bring it. Our luggage, I mean. Said he had quite enough with me on his hands, thank you very much. I believe I'll punish him by wearing this ratty old dress for the next three weeks." She looked at the staircase as if it had just appeared out of nowhere. "Well, here we are. You needn't bother walking up all those stairs, Mrs. Tremaine. Just tell us which room, and we'll go on up by ourselves."

"The one on the right," she said, seemingly almost breathless from just listening to Jessamine's harangue.

"Thank you so much. Aren't you sweet? And would you mind telling me what time's dinner?" Jessamine started up the stairs, then paused. "Oh, and Mrs. Tremaine, would it be too much trouble to arrange for Mr. Dade to take a bath? Long as we're going to be sleeping in the same room and all." Sighing as if she bore the burdens of the world—the worst of which was her husband—on her frail shoulders, she walked up the stairs.

Jessamine whirled through the door of the carriage barn behind the boardinghouse, then twirled in her borrowed pink-and-white-striped gown. "Look what Mrs. Tremaine found for me, Lee. She's got a whole trunk full of clothes she can't wear anymore now that she's a widow. It's a little out-of-date, but it's better than wearing berry juice." She twirled again and came to a halt beside the metal washtub

in which Lee was sitting, his long legs hung over the side, his elbows stuck out and a cigar in his teeth.

"You look like a peppermint stick, Jessie," he said, continuing to soap his chest and neck and underarms.

She hadn't hesitated a moment coming into the barn, even though she'd known Lee was taking a bath. They'd spent so much time together that it hadn't even occurred to her that she might be embarrassed. But suddenly there he was, in all his soapy, hairy splendor, and her face was growing hotter and redder by the second.

"Oh," she said. "Well, I'll just let you finish up." She started to turn for the door, but Lee reached out a soapy hand to snag her wrist.

"As long as you're here, Mrs. Dade, you might as well wash your filthy husband's back," he said, still clamping down on the cigar. "Here." He slapped a wet washrag into her hand and leaned forward.

"I never said you were filthy," she said, pushing up the long sleeves of her dress.

"That's true. You merely implied you didn't much relish the idea of sleeping with a pig." His teeth showed, white and gleaming, around the cigar.

She started scrubbing his back, hard. "Oh, hush, Lee. It worked, didn't it? We got a room. I got a whole new wardrobe, and you got a nice hot bath. Not to mention the dinner that Mrs. Tremaine has her girl working on in the kitchen. You should smell the house. It's wonderful."

"Jessie, it's a wonder you don't weigh two hundred pounds."

Jessamine studied the smooth, hard muscles of his back as she worked it over with the washrag. There was a scar that ran horizontally from his shoulder blade to disappear beneath his arm. She traced it with the washrag. "This isn't from when you were at Riverbend, is it, Lee?" She had already seen that scar.

"That's an old one," he said.

"And look here. You've got another one just like it on this side. I don't remember seeing those before, but then maybe I never looked at your back. They look terrible, Lee. What are they? Where'd you get them?"

"Natchez," he said. "When I was a boy. They're rope burns."

"Rope burns," she exclaimed, looking more closely at both white stripes, thinking she could see the impression of twisted hemp. "You mean somebody tied you up?"

He pulled on the cigar and sent a stream of smoke toward the peaked roof of the barn. "Tied, gagged, and branded. Just like a little calf."

The judge had always kept a few head of cattle at Riverbend, and Jessamine remembered well what it was like when they were branded—the smell of the seared flesh, the way the animals wailed. She closed her eyes, stopped scrubbing his back and began stroking it. "How awful for you, Lee. Who did this to you?" She spoke as if it had taken place the day before.

"Some boys who wanted to remind me of my heritage," he said.

"I don't understand," said Jessamine.

Maybe it was time, Lee thought, to tear at least one veil of innocence from her eyes. Time to let her know he was no pillar of society. No gallant white knight. He doused the cigar in the bathwater, then pitched it onto the floor. "Come here, Jessie. Come around here where I can see you." He reached back for her hand and led her around the side of the tub, then kissed her hand and held it. "My mama was a whore, Jessie. She made her living on her back, and she never did particularly love me or treat me with any tenderness, but she kept me fed and clothed. She even scrubbed me raw, like you were doing a little while ago."

Jessamine took the washrag with her free hand and began smoothing it over his soapy chest.

He leaned back and closed his eyes. "That feels good, Jessie," he said.

"Good," Jessamine said softly. "What was your mama's name, Lee?"

"Elizabeth. But everybody called her Liz, or Lizzie."

"That's a pretty name," murmured Jessamine.

"She wasn't an especially pretty woman. She had dark eyes, like mine. Dark circles under them, I remember. She didn't smile much, but then I guess she didn't have much to smile about." His eyes still closed, he lifted his chin as Jessamine brought the cloth up to his neck.

"Is she still alive?" she asked.

Lee shook his head. "I never saw her again after I left Natchez. Right after that little rope incident. I went back to see her once. I was fifteen, I guess, sixteen. I knocked on the door of our house. House, hell! It was a cockeyed, unpainted shanty with newspaper for window glass. I've been in better privies. Anyway, I knocked on the door, and a toothless blonde with a black eye told me she was gone. 'Lizzie's gone and don't want to be found.' I can still hear her saying it." He sighed, a muscle clenching in his cheek. "So I didn't try. I heard she died of a fever. I don't know for sure."

"And your daddy?" she asked softly. "Did you know him?"

His eyes opened. They were hard. "I knew him. I wish I hadn't."

Jessamine washed him gently. "Well, Lee Kincannon," she murmured, "in spite of all their shortcomings, they did combine to make a fine and beautiful man."

Ham and beans and boiled potatoes sat cooling on the table as they waited for Mrs. Tremaine's other boarder. The

widow had done up her white hair and put on a fashionable black gown. She kept jumping up from her chair to look out the window for the missing guest. Each time she did, Jessamine snitched a bean.

"Well, finally," the widow said with a sigh when the screen door opened.

Someone called, "My apologies, Mrs. Tremaine," from the vicinity of the hat rack, and then a blue-uniformed captain hurried to take the empty seat at the foot of the table. He was out of breath. A hank of brown hair fell across his forehead. "I do apologize, ma'am," he said. He looked at Jessamine and then at Lee. "I see you have acquired sudden guests."

"This nice couple just arrived this afternoon. Mr. and Mrs. Dade, may I present Captain Jacob Van Dorn of the...what was it, Captain?"

"The Third New York Infantry, Mrs. Tremaine," he said, flicking a smile to Jessamine to indicate that he'd said it many times before.

"Yes, well, these are the Dades of...I can't remember if you told me or not, Mrs. Dade."

"No, I don't believe I did," said Jessamine, casting a look of controlled panic at Lee.

"My wife and I have been living in St. Louis for the past few years," Lee said. "We've come back to Alabama to visit relatives."

"Are you a native of St. Louis, Mrs. Dade? I'd ask your husband, but I hear right off he's a Southerner."

"Yes, I am, Captain," she said. "Mrs. Tremaine, would you like me to start passing those beans?" Jessamine's hand was trembling as she picked up the bowl, served herself, then handed it to the captain on her left.

"Where are you from, Mr. Dade?" he asked as he spooned the green beans onto his plate.

"Vicksburg," said Lee.

"Mississippi?" asked the captain.

"That's right." Lee took the bowl from him.

"Oh, Vicksburg…" Mrs. Tremaine sighed. "That's where they had to endure that horrible siege, isn't it? I do hope you don't have family there, Mr. Dade."

"Not anymore, ma'am. They're all dead."

Jessamine slapped a piece of ham on her plate. "Lovely weather down here this time of year, don't you think, Captain?" She passed the ham along. "Or are you not accustomed to the heat?"

"I'm not, Mrs. Dade, and that's a fact. I'm from upstate New York, where it rarely gets this warm." Captain Van Dorn turned to Lee as he passed the ham platter. "Did you take part in the war, Mr. Dade?"

"No, sir. I manufacture flags and footwear in Saint Louis. The army decided I'd be more useful making boots than carrying a rifle. The flags are just a temporary endeavor. Quite lucrative, however."

"He does make lovely boots," said Jessamine. "And shoes. Mrs. Tremaine, you should see the dainty little slippers Mr. Dade gave me only last week, before we left on our journey. Black satin, with the most delicate bows." She turned to the captain again. "Is there a Mrs. Van Dorn, Captain?"

"No, ma'am," he said politely, before turning once more to Lee. "I couldn't help but notice your horse out by the barn, Mr. Dade. Handsome animal. Have you had him long?"

Lee chewed thoughtfully on a piece of ham before answering. "He belongs to my wife's second cousin. He allowed us the use of his horse and carriage this morning to complete our journey. The horse, as it turned out, held up better than the carriage."

"I've always been partial to dappled grays," Van Dorn said, spearing a chunk of potato. "I never saw one that

failed to have a gentle disposition. Fast animals, too, ordinarily."

And so the meal continued, with Jessamine struggling to change the subject and Captain Van Dorn being polite and persistent in his interrogation of Lee. Lee ate sparingly, and Jessamine put her fork down before her plate was clean.

"Why don't we all go into the parlor for coffee?" Mrs. Tremaine asked.

"Allow me, Mrs. Tremaine," said the captain, pulling out her chair for her. "I'd like to explain to you why I was so late for your wonderful Sunday dinner. We had a telegram from our commander in Montgomery. Seems a train was robbed, not too far from Tunnel Springs."

"Oh, my," said Mrs. Tremaine as she took his arm and led him toward the front parlor. "Coming, Mr. Dade?" the widow asked.

Jessamine and Lee exchanged glances. He gestured toward the stairs, and on cue, Jessamine developed another "Yankee headache." Lee, obedient husband that he was, followed her up to their room.

"Well, does he know or doesn't he?" she whispered when the door was closed.

"Damned if I know, Jessie. He's a subtle bastard, that's for sure." Lee reached under the bed and brought out the rifle, checked the breech twice before leaning it near the door.

Jessamine gazed longingly at the bed. "Oh, and here I was looking forward to a mattress and a pillow. Well, I don't have anything to pack, so let's go." She started toward the window, and had one leg up on the sill before Lee stopped her.

"Slow down." He wrapped his arm around her waist and moved her with his hip. "We're not going to leave. We'll just wait and see what happens."

"But that's foolish, Lee, when we could be miles down the road in no time at all. You saw how that Yankee was staring at you all through dinner."

"He might just be the type of soldier who's suspicious of any man with a Mississippi accent. Anyway, what's foolish, Jessie," he added sternly, "is going miles down the road and getting caught. If it happens here, so be it. At least I know you'll be safe in this house if they take me away. Out on the road, you'd be all alone if something happened. Or almost alone. Just you and a Union patrol."

She looked at him with disbelief. "You're just going to sit here?"

Lee stretched out on the bed, adjusted the pillow under his head. "No, Jessie. I'm going to lie here."

"Well, go by yourself then, Lee. That horse will get even farther down the road without me on him." She sat down on the bed beside him, hands upturned in her lap. "I know I've been pouting and sniveling about your leaving me, but this time I want you to go. I can get to Georgia by myself. It's what I planned all along. I'll meet you there. Please. Go. Get away from here."

He pulled her down to lie beside him. "Shhh. Just be still and close your eyes for a while, Mrs. Dade. It's going to be another long night."

At seven o'clock, Jessamine saw Captain Van Dorn walk into the carriage barn. "He's going to take a look at the horse, Lee," she whispered from her perch on the windowsill.

"Calm down, Jessie. There are probably a hundred dappled grays in Alabama."

Not long after that she heard Captain Van Dorn's footsteps coming up the stairs, and then the click of his bedroom door as it closed. She nudged Lee.

"I heard it," he said.

"He can always climb out the window. Don't you think we should be doing something?"

When he didn't answer, Jessamine went to the window again. "It's getting dark," she said, looking out at the big white oak in the side yard. "Do you want me to light the lamp?"

"Best have it dark," he said. "The moon will be light enough."

She roamed around the room, straightening a doily on top of the dresser, dusting the top of a picture frame with her finger, checking the oil in the lamp. "I'm not good at waiting. I can't stand this."

"Don't ever gamble, Jessie," he said from the bed.

"Why?"

"You'd make a lousy cardplayer."

"I don't know how to play anything but cribbage, and I'm no good at that," she said.

"You lack patience."

She looked at him, lying there, his arms crossed over his chest, one boot crossed over the other at the ankle, seemingly relaxed and without a care in the world. "Is that what this is, Lee? Gambling?"

He merely looked at her, his eyes dark and dispassionate.

"Well, there's too much at stake," she wailed.

Jessamine flung herself into the rocking chair and chewed on a fingernail for a while as the light changed in their room, daylight going to dark, a rising moon turning everything from gold to silver.

She had no patience when Lee's freedom, perhaps his very life, were at stake. If he was too damn stubborn to leave without her, then it was going to have to be Jessamine who left—in the knowledge that he would come after her.

But how was she ever going to get out the window quietly in this pink-and-white tent of a dress?

"What are you doing, Jessie?" Lee asked a while later, eyes half-closed, voice low and rife with suspicion.

"Well, I'm so warm. Don't you think it's awfully hot in here? And I hate to get this dress all wrinkled, just lazing around this room." All this as she was unbuttoning the pink-and-white dress, her back to the bed, but her reflection silvered again and again in the arched, moonlit triple mirror over the dresser.

"Open the window wider," Lee suggested.

She already had, to ease her passage later. "I did. I'm still too warm." She lifted the dress and its sweeping skirt over her head, folded it carefully, and laid it over the arms of the rocker.

"Better?" he asked, watching her through narrowed eyes.

"Some. But I'm still uncomfortable." She twisted to unhook the crinoline at her waist, pushed it down in a heap, and stepped out of it, wearing only her ruffled pantaloons and white lace corset.

"Surely you're cooler now, Miss Jessamine," he said.

"Much," she said with satisfaction, thinking all she'd have to do now was shove the dress out the window, then climb down after it. She hoped the widow Tremaine hadn't let the trellis or the drainpipe fall into disrepair. And she hoped that if she yawned enough, Lee would fall asleep.

Jessamine stretched out on the bed beside him, yawning, punching the pillow, shifting her hips to find a comfortable position. She dug her bottom into the mattress with a sigh.

Lee leaned up on one elbow. "Are you trying to seduce me, Mrs. Dade?"

"Perish the thought, Mr. Dade," she said, yawning again.

His eyes roved over her moonlit face, and the lace top of her corset. "Good," he said, "because I've already been through that particular wringer today, and once is enough." His finger drifted down the inner curve of her arm.

Jessamine yawned again, trying to ignore the little sparks his lightest touch set off inside her. "I'm not doing anything but lying here trying to go to sleep, Lee."

"I wish that were all you were doing, Jessie," he said roughly as he dropped his shoulders back onto the bed.

She turned on her side, planted her fanny firmly against his hip. "Good night," she said.

Chapter Fourteen

Jessamine stroked the soft nose of the dappled gray, whispering to calm him, before she put the bit in his teeth and the bridle over his head. She'd decided to take care of the horse before she put her dress on. He was tall, probably twenty hands, and she didn't want to be tripping over her hem while she was trying to saddle him. She had considered going bareback, but she wasn't sure she could stay on if she had to ride fast.

He took the bit well enough, but raised his head as she was bridling him, nearly lifting her feet off the floor of the barn. "Hold still," she hissed.

The big horse stood quietly then, with the reins drooping to the floor. As she walked to the rail for the saddle, she thought she heard a noise outside the door. She stood still, held her breath. The animal snuffled and stamped. It was just a dog or a possum, she thought, turning to hoist the saddle off the rail. Lord, it was heavy.

She toted it over to the horse. "Now just hold still while I get this thing on you," she said to him as she planted her hands on each side of the saddle. She swung it up. The horse whinnied again and sidestepped, and the heavy saddle slid down his side.

Jessamine tried three times with the same results. She wasn't strong enough or tall enough. She cursed, louder

than she had intended, then went to find a box or a pail, anything to stand on so that she'd have a bit of leverage.

Saddle in hand, she stepped up on the overturned pail. "This time we're going to do it," she said to the horse as she heaved the saddle up. The pail tipped, and Jessamine went down, the saddle on top of her, the horse nervously stamping his foot not far from her head.

A pair of strong arms wrapped under her arms and dragged her away. "Damn it to hell, Jessie. You've been bashing that poor animal in the side with that saddle for half an hour," Lee snarled, dropping her and going to calm the horse.

She got to her feet, brushing hay and dirt from her pantaloons. "And I suppose you've just been standing there watching me do it," she snapped. "I'm trying to save your hide, Lee Kincannon. I'm leaving, and if you know what's good for you, you'll come with me."

He smoothed the horse's forelock and flank. "You took me in with your little flimflam, Jessie." Lee grinned. "Nobody's done that since I was seventeen. After you first went out the window, I thought maybe I'd drag you back by your hair and say we'd had a lovers' quarrel. But I decided it would only draw more attention to us. Then I figured I'd sneak in the captain's room and truss him up long enough to give both of us time to get away. So that's what I did."

"You tied up Captain Van Dorn?" she asked, eyes wide.

Lee continued to stroke the big horse. "No, I sneaked in his room. Only the captain wasn't there."

She was wild-eyed now. "And you're just standing here petting that animal when he's gone to get his troops?"

"Well, I thought I'd best check around the house before I got all panicky," Lee said.

"And?" she demanded.

"And I found the captain." His grin widened. "In the widow's room. They were re-creating the South's surrender, so to speak."

"They weren't!"

"They were."

"And then what happened?"

"Then the three of us all sat on the widow's bed and discussed our various reputations, and it was agreed that we would all benefit greatly from a solemn vow of silence." He picked up the saddle and eased it over the back of the horse.

Jessamine just stood with her hands on her hips, flabbergasted.

Lee looked over his shoulder at her. "We can go back in the house, if you want, Jessie."

"Back in there? With all that . . . all that 'surrendering' going on? I'd rather die first."

"That's what I thought," Lee said, continuing to tighten the cinch.

Two days and one horse later, Lee and Jessamine crossed the Chattahoochee River near Gunter. They had ridden as much as possible through dense woods or along the quiet streams. For the most part there were no incidents.

Jessamine had tangled with a blacksmith in Claymore who'd tried to trade her a lame Morgan for the gray. She'd wound up with a tick-infested bay. "You do it next time," she'd snapped at Lee when he'd expressed his displeasure.

"Next time! Hell, Jessie, I'm going to be real lucky if I survive this time," he'd shouted back.

"Welcome to Georgia," said Lee as he led the horse he had named Jessie's Folly off the rickety ferry that had taken them across the river. "And if I remember right, I know a place where we can get a good meal and sleep in a big, soft bed."

* * *

"I'm not going in there, Lee."

Jessamine had been standing in the street with the horse while Lee knocked on the door of the big yellow-brick house. The door was red, and the woman who opened it was wearing a red dress, and so were all the other females, each one prettier than the last, who couldn't rush to the entrance fast enough to kiss, hug, hold, and squeeze Lee. And wasn't he just loving every minute of it, she thought, gritting her teeth.

"Come on, Jessie. There's fried chicken for supper. I can smell it. Take a sniff. I bet you can smell it from here."

"I'm not going in," she said. "You know what that place is, don't you?"

Lee unstrapped his rifle. "Yes, I do. It's the headquarters of the Georgia Irregulars, an ammunition repository, a hospital—and a whorehouse. Now come on." He grasped her elbow and headed her toward the red door, but Jessamine planted her feet on the sidewalk.

"I can't, Lee. I wouldn't know what to say or how to behave with...with...and I look so shabby, and those girls are all so...so..."

His jaw tightened. "Those girls are just girls. And any one of them would be more than delighted to trade faces with you, pretty Jessie. Now I'm going in there for some fried chicken and a bath and a good long nap. You can come with me, or you can stay out here with the horses. I'll pitch you a drumstick out the window."

She followed him, muttering about hairbrushes, pink-and-white-striped circus dresses and confounded drumsticks.

Ten minutes later, Jessamine felt warm and welcome and thrilled to be gazing at a plate of fried chicken, peas, carrots and mashed potatoes with cream gravy.

"How's the chicken, Jessie?" Lee asked, licking his fingers and winking at her from across the table.

"Just let her eat, Lee. Poor thing looks half starved to death," said Myra Coffee—unofficial Georgia Irregular, nurse, and madam. Her lampblacked hair was piled high on her head and studded with pearls. Her ample breasts threatened to spill from the front of her red dress at any moment, and her long red fingernails flew incessantly around the table, serving, pouring, salting, touching.

There were twelve of them at the big dining room table, nine young ladies, in addition to Jessamine, Lee, and Myra. The house was closed for business during the huge noon meal. From the conversation, Jessamine gathered it was the only time they were all together without interruption.

The dining room was splendid with bright floral paper on the walls, a crystal chandelier and sconces, and fine French furniture. Jessamine looked at the paintings on the walls and thought about her aunt Emmie and uncle Jack in New Orleans. Apparently war was good for Myra's business, or at least it hadn't taken a visible toll on it. And the chicken was wonderful.

Lee had finished his meal and was regaling them all with the story of the widow Tremaine and Captain Van Dorn. They seemed to find it much more hilarious than shocking.

Jessamine picked the last bit of meat off a drumstick and put it on her plate. "I don't think I ever want to see another chicken," she said with a sigh as she wiped her mouth. "I must have consumed an entire barnyard."

"We have cherry upside-down cake for dessert," said Josie, the girl on her left. "Don't you have room for one little piece?"

"Well, maybe just a little one," said Jessamine.

"Make it a little slice about that big," said Lee, measuring a healthy portion with his fingers. "I don't know where you put it all, Jessie."

She sniffed. "I've only eaten three meals in the last four days, Lee Kincannon."

"She could use a little meat on her bones," protested Mary Ruth, who had a sufficiency of meat on hers.

"Stop picking on her, Lee," said Doretta.

Lee took the cigar that Myra offered him, held it to the match she struck, and exhaled. "I wouldn't think of it, Miss Doretta," he said, then smiled at Jessamine. "You've acquired a few admirers, Jessie."

Myra, swirling around the table, stopped behind Jessamine's chair and rested her hands on her shoulders. "And we're going to take good care of her while she's here, too. And you see that you're on your best behavior, Lee. If you catch my drift."

All eyes turned on Lee as if he were a rooster that had sneaked into a henhouse.

After lunch, the girls took Jessamine upstairs and helped her undress, then tucked her into a big brass bed and pulled the drapes. She fell asleep instantly.

Jessamine dressed in the sumptuous blue velvet wrapper that someone had draped over the foot of her bed. Downstairs, she heard laughter in the front parlor, so she peeked in. Doretta was sitting at the piano, leafing through some sheet music. Another girl sat beside her on the piano bench. Josie was carrying a tray full of empty glasses and full ashtrays. Myra and Lee were on the settee, deep in conversation.

"Oh, look, here she is now," said Josie. "We didn't know whether to wake you for dinner or not."

"Jessie wouldn't sleep through a meal, would you?" said Lee, standing up and going to take her hand. He kissed it. "You slept seven hours," he said as he led her over to the settee. "I missed you."

"You look refreshed, Jessie," said Myra. "Sleep does wonders for a body, doesn't it?"

"Did you take a nap?" Jessamine asked Lee, who didn't look quite so refreshed.

"I took a bath and fell asleep in the tub."

Doretta giggled. "He almost drowned."

Myra stood up. "We have something special planned just for the two of you. Come along. Josie, you get on with your picking-up in here. And Doretta, you need to practice that last tune again."

Once in the dining room, Myra closed the sliding doors, saying, "This way you won't be disturbed by any comings and goings out in the vestibule."

The table was elegantly laid with fine china and heavy silver. One by one, Myra put out the candles in the chandelier with a long candle snuffer so that the only light came from the candles on the table and the sconces on the wall.

Jessamine looked at Lee, who stood looking at her with a warm smile on his face.

"This is lovely," Jessamine said. "Myra, you shouldn't have gone to so much bother."

Myra fussed around the table, moving silverware and smoothing the table cloth. "We wanted to do something nice for you, Jessie. For both of you. Lee did us a big favor once, a few years ago."

"Oh, hell, Myra . . ." said Lee.

"Well, you did," she insisted.

"What was it?" Jessamine asked.

"The Yankees stole a wagon full of Irish whiskey we had coming from Savannah. Lee and a couple of his boys stole it back."

"And got good and drunk before we ever returned it to you." Lee bowed. "One of the Confederacy's more gallant hours."

Jessamine laughed. "No wonder the Yankees want you so bad," she said.

Lee pulled out the chair at the foot of the table. "Miss Jessamine," he said.

"Why, thank you, sir." She slid into the seat.

As Lee took his seat at the head of the table, Myra rang a small silver bell. Mary Ruth appeared from the kitchen carrying a platter of cold sliced chicken and cucumbers. Another girl followed her with green beans and pickled peaches. A third had a bottle of wine, which she poured into each of their goblets.

"Well, now," said Myra, after their plates were heaped. "We'll just leave you two to enjoy this." She put the bell at Lee's elbow. "You give a little tinkle to this if you need anything, you hear?"

After Myra sashayed through the kitchen door, Lee raised his wineglass to Jessamine. "Here's to you, Jessie," he said. Then he raised an eyebrow. "And to think you didn't even want to come in here."

She sipped her wine. "Well, I was wrong. I admit it. And I will never again question anything you tell me to do."

"Not anything?" he asked.

"Absolutely nothing." She speared a piece of cucumber and popped it in her mouth. "Ask me anything, and I'll do it."

"Come here and kiss me before you fill your face," he said.

She wiped her mouth with the linen napkin, took another sip of wine, stood and pushed her chair back. "You think I can't walk away from a full plate of food, Lee Kincannon," she said, coming toward him down the long table. "You think I'm nothing but a glutton."

He angled his chair out. "No, I don't. I just want to kiss you. Come here. Sit."

Jessamine adjusted her blue velvet wrapper and sat primly on Lee's lap.

"You've got to look at a person to kiss him, Jessie," Lee said, turning her toward him, her chin in his hand. He grinned. "I'd bet a steamboat and two hotels that you're the first person who's ever blushed in this house."

"I'm not."

Lee's hand slid around the back of her neck. "Kiss me," he said softly, drawing her toward him.

Her lips touched his tentatively, tasting the wine. Then her arms went around his neck, and the kiss deepened. It was Lee who finally pulled away.

"Jessie, Jessie, you make my heart melt and the rest of me wild with wanting you," he whispered as he held her. "We're safe here, and there's a big warm bed upstairs, if you're willing. If you want me, Jessie. Look at me and tell me. Is this what you want, little one?"

She raised her eyes to his. Lee's gaze was dark and burning, but there was also a tenderness there, and perhaps love. She knew she could say no if she wanted to. But she wanted him. Had wanted him for so long she couldn't remember how it felt not to want him. She'd always loved him—from the first minute she'd seen him. She had learned to trust him with her life. Perhaps now she could trust him with her love.

Her violet eyes didn't waver from his gaze. "Yes," she said.

Lee held her close. "You'll have your sweetness, my Jessie. I promise you." He leaned back his head and smiled. "I'll even let you finish your dinner. And then, if I'm not mistaken, the girls have a little surprise planned for you."

She narrowed her eyes. "What kind of surprise?"

"You'll see." He stood her up and swatted her rump. "Now go finish your dinner."

She wasn't all that hungry, Jessamine thought, pushing a crescent of spiced peach across her plate. She looked down

the table at Lee, whose appetite seemed to have picked up. He was on his second helping of everything.

Jessamine set her fork down. "May I have a little more wine, please?"

Lee brought the bottle to her place at the table. He kissed the top of her head, then filled her glass. "Nervous, Jessie?" he asked, returning to his meal.

"Why ever would I be nervous?" She spilled some wine when she lifted the glass.

"Did I fill that glass a bit too much?" he asked, knowing he hadn't, grinning like a fool.

"Why are you doing this to me?"

"I'm just teasing you," he said.

She was furious, and she was scared to death. And there he sat, stuffing chicken into his face, swilling his wine, not caring the least little bit about her feelings. She lowered her head, and a hot tear dropped on her lap.

"Sweet, mad Jessie," Lee said. "If it's any consolation, my hands aren't all that steady, either. I believe it's time for your surprise." He picked up the little silver bell and rang it.

A moment later Myra came through the sliding doors from the vestibule, closing them behind her. "How was your dinner?" she asked, frowning at Jessamine's nearly full plate.

"It was wonderful," said Jessamine, quickly wiping her eyes.

"Wonderful, Miss Myra, but a bit too prolonged, if you know what I mean. Jessie could probably do without my company for a while."

Myra put her hand on Jessamine's shoulder. "Well, you come on with me now, Jessie. Some of the girls are upstairs waiting. We'll leave Lee to a brandy and a smoke, and just go have us a little hen party."

* * *

Jessamine sank to her chin in the hot, scented water that had been waiting for her upstairs. "Oh, this is heaven," she said. "What a wonderful surprise."

"I hope it's not too hot," said Doretta. "I told Josie three kettles ought to be enough, but we weren't sure when you'd be coming up, so Josie poured five or six kettles in."

"It's perfect," sighed Jessamine. "What's that fragrance?"

"That's some bath oil Myra gets from Paris, France," said Mary Ruth, sniffing the steam from the little porcelain tub. "She lets us use it on our birthdays."

Myra returned. "My, doesn't it smell good in here. Mary Ruth, you're wanted downstairs, dear."

Mary Ruth took one last long sniff of the fragrant steam, then said, "Well, good night, Jessie. I hope...I mean, well...just good night."

"Good night, Mary Ruth. And thank you for the most wonderful bath of my life."

Myra held up a hank of Jessamine's dark hair. "Josie, go get me a hairbrush. And some tortoise combs, too, while you're at it." Myra planted her hip on the edge of the tub, plucked at a curl, then gazed solemnly at Jessamine. "I've been trying to think of something I could say to you, Jessie. Being in this business and all, you'd think it would be easy." The black-haired, bosomy Myra sighed in frustration. "Lee told me you never did have a mama, honey, and that you lived with your daddy and a plague of brothers who probably set you wrong on a lot of things."

The madam studied one of her long red nails. "Your Lee is a wild one, no doubt about that. But he's a good man, and he won't hurt you. There's nothing to be scared about, honey."

Jessamine nodded dumbly, then was relieved to see Josie come back with the hairbrush and the combs.

"See what you can do with all that hair," Myra told her.

"You just squeal if I pull too hard, Jessie," Josie said, taking the brush to her long hair. "Is that all right?"

"Yes, it's wonderful," said Jessamine, closing her eyes, savoring each sensation—the warmth and fragrance of the water, the feel of the brush against her scalp, the pull of it on her hair.

By the time Josie had her hair brushed out, then piled up and anchored with Myra's tortoise combs, the bathwater had cooled considerably. Jessamine started shivering.

Doretta held up an huge bath sheet and wrapped it around her as she climbed out of the tub. "When you're dry, Jessie, I've brought my talc for you to use. It was a gift from an admirer last Christmas."

"Thank you, Doretta."

Myra looked at Josie, who reached under her skirt and removed a blue satin garter.

"This is from all of us, Jessie. It's for good luck."

"And this," said Myra, holding up a white cotton night-dress with a ruffled hem and ruffled scoop neckline, "is still brand-new. I always keep one for when one of my girls decides to run off and get married."

Jessamine touched the soft fabric, letting a ruffle glide through her fingers. "It's perfect, Myra. I don't quite know what to say."

"You don't have to say anything, Jessie," Myra told her. "Now let's get you all gussied up for your Lee."

When they were done, the girls in the red dresses stood back to admire their creation. "You look so pretty, Jessie," said Doretta.

"Turn that looking glass around here, Josie. Let Jessie see herself," said Myra as she pressed a wrinkle in the hem ruffle between her fingers.

Josie turned the cheval glass toward her, and Jessamine stood looking at her flushed cheeks, the white simplicity of

the cotton gown, her bare toes just peeking out beneath. "Oh, my," she said.

"Where's that garter?" asked Doretta. "You haven't gone and lost it have you, Josie?"

"Here it is," said Josie, waving the circle of blue silk. "Here, Jessie. You're almost ready now." Josie kissed her on the cheek and stood back while Jessamine slipped the fragile garter up her leg.

"Well, now," said Myra, taking her by the shoulders and turning her toward the door. "Somebody's waiting for you, Jessie, down the hall, second door on the left."

Chapter Fifteen

Jessamine's fingertips drifted along the wall, dipping under the oval frames of portraits of people she didn't know. She stepped on the same petal of the same rose as it repeated in the pattern of the carpet runner under her feet. She dropped her hand at the frame of the first door, and resumed her touch on the other side.

She was trembling as if she had been standing too long out in the cold. And she had, she thought. A whole life spent out in the cold—from the day of her mother's death until Lee and the promise of warmth. And now the fulfillment. When she reached the second door, her fingers sprang from the frame as if they had been burned. Had Myra said the second door? There was one farther along the hall. Oh, why in tarnation hadn't she listened harder, instead of ogling herself in the looking glass? Instead of trying to see herself as Lee would see her, hair swept up and anchored with combs, face rosy and glowing, skin glistening with talc.

Was it the second door or the third? Damnation! She stood there, immobile, dreading opening the wrong one, dying at the thought of interrupting Mary Ruth or someone else, and wishing she were anywhere else in the world but here in this hall, in this house, scared as a rabbit and stupid as a mule.

The door swung open, and there was Lee, tall, sturdy as the oak that framed him, his handsome face grinning down at her, his dark eyes full of pleasure at the sight of her.

"You look just like a bride, Jessie," he said softly.

She lowered her gaze. Her toe traced a rose on the carpet as her cheeks grew hot. She knew she wouldn't be able to take the step or two it would require to get through the door.

"Barefoot and blushing," Lee whispered. "Jessie, you don't know what you're doing to me." He swept her up in his arms and carried her over the threshold, slamming the door with his foot.

The lamp was low. Golden light gleamed on the rails of the big brass bed, whose fresh white linen bore Lee's long impression. A brandy bottle and a snifter stood on the nightstand, along with a spent cigar in a porcelain dish, and a full glass of ruby red wine.

He put her down. "Let me look at you," he said softly, holding her hands and lifting her arms away from her body.

Jessamine noticed now that he was barefoot, too. Her gaze wandered from his toes up the black fabric of his pants, over the place where it molded to his thighs, past his belt, up the soft white cotton of his collarless shirt. The top three buttons were undone, exposing a dark V of hair. His eyes were burning with an intensity she had never seen as they took her in from head to foot.

"Jessie—" he sighed "—you're my most precious gift." He brought her arms around his waist, his own arms clasping her close.

So close that she could feel the strong beat of his heart, the throb in the pulse at his neck, the hardness of him as he pressed against the thin cotton of her gown.

"You're trembling, little one," he said, dropping kisses on her neck.

There was a tremor in her voice when she said, "I'm all right. My bathwater just got a little cold."

Lee took her hand and led her to the bed. When she sat on the edge, he handed her the glass of wine. "A little liquid courage," he said, then picked up the snifter. "I could do with some myself." He drained it in one swallow, and stretched out on the bed, stroking her upper arm, watching her.

The wine was sweet and mellow, warming her throat and twining with the waves of pleasure that shimmered through her from Lee's touch.

"So soft," he murmured, tracing a finger down the length of her arm, then retracing the path up to her shoulder.

She laughed. "Doretta nearly smothered me with talc. The girls were so sweet to me, Lee. And Myra, too. She gave me this gown. And they all gave me this." Jessamine put down her wineglass, then lifted her foot and pointed her toe as she inched up the hem of her gown to reveal the blue satin garter. "For luck," she said, turning to look at Lee, whose eyes were focused just above her knee now, his hand having stilled on her arm.

"Did they . . . did the girls have a little talk with you?"

"Oh, we talked a lot," Jessamine said, angling her leg to see the outer circle of the garter. "Doretta's a serious student of the piano. Did you know that, Lee? And Mary Ruth spent a year in Missouri with her maiden aunt. Not all that far from Riverbend, either."

"No, Jessie. I mean, did you talk about this? About tonight. Did you ask them any questions?"

"Well, no," Jessamine said. She had wanted to, Lord knows, but she hadn't wanted to show her blasted ignorance. Nor did she want to display it to Lee, although she assumed he'd find out for himself soon enough. "Besides, there wasn't anything to ask," she said, stiffening her shoulders a little, picking at the ruffle on her hem.

"So you know all about this, then?" Lee asked, his voice light and teasing.

"Of course I do, Lee," she snapped. "I'm nearly twenty-two years old, for pity's sake. Not twelve, the way you treat me half the time."

"I'm sorry, Jessie," he said. "I had no idea you were so well schooled in the art of loving. In light of that, why don't you just turn around and finish undoing my shirt here?" Lee cocked his arms under his head, his hands clasped behind his neck.

Jessamine didn't move. "Is . . . is that how you want to begin, then?"

"It's as good a way as any," Lee said. "Unless, of course, your knowledge and experience dictate otherwise."

He was grinning at her like a jack-o'-lantern. She couldn't so much see it as feel it on her back. She picked up her wineglass, drained it, and put it back down purposefully. "It is as good a way as any," she said, turning and taking a button in her hand, averting her eyes from his face as she jammed the button through the narrow buttonhole. Why did her fingers insist on shaking like jittery leaves on a cottonwood tree? She'd seen men's bare chests before—seen Lee's, for that matter, and more than once, too. She arrived at the button just above his belt buckle.

Lee was dying, button by button, at the light touch of her trembling fingers on his chest, the stubborn concentration on her face in the soft lamplight, her pink tongue just moistening the corner of her mouth, her lush lower lip clenched between her teeth, the neckline of her white gown dipping in his direction. He tended to be a patient man, but that tendency was thinning to a wire at the moment.

Her hands hovered at his waist.

"As I see it, Jessie, you have two choices here. You can either do it the hard way by tugging my shirttails out, or take the easy way and unbuckle my belt."

Jessamine grabbed a hunk of shirt in each hand and tugged and tugged till the long shirttails came free. Then she undid the last three buttons.

"Cuffs," said Lee, taking his arms from under his head and placing one across her lap.

She fumbled with the first cuff link and dropped it to the floor, cursing roundly. She started to get up and go after it, but Lee caught the back of her gown.

"We'll find it later," he said, extending his other arm.

"There." She placed the second cuff link on the nightstand with a small concluding sigh.

"Correct me if I'm wrong," said Lee, "but I've still got my shirt on, Jessie."

"How do you expect me to do it with you flat on your back like that?"

Lee sat up. "I figured you knew some special trick," he said, letting his arms hang loosely, rolling his head a bit to ease the tension in his neck. He began pulling one arm out of its sleeve. "Let me help you a little."

"I can do it. If this is what I'm supposed to do, then hold still and let me do it." She yanked the shirt down over his back and upper arms, exposing the horrible scar on his shoulder. Jessamine blinked and stared, remembering when Lee had been at Riverbend, how she had wanted him, wanted to touch him, to take away his pain—and how she had nearly lost him. She met his quiet, searching gaze, then leaned to kiss the cruel marks the bullet and the blade had left on him. She kissed his collarbone, strung a necklace of kisses to his chin, his jaw, the corner of his mouth. She pressed her lips softly to his. "Hold me, Lee. Hold me close."

He sighed. "Jessie, honey, I can't. You've pinned my arms behind me with my shirt."

She pulled away, and Lee shucked off his shirt and grabbed her to him before she could get too flustered. He

stroked her hair and whispered, "That scar doesn't hurt anymore. It's just a souvenir."

"I'm glad," she said, nuzzling her face against the warmth of his chest, pressing her cheek against its sculptured muscles. "I'm glad I'm here with you. That we're together like this." She sighed against him. "And I'm glad at least one of us knows what to do next."

He continued stroking her hair, pulling out a pin here, a comb there. "The book I read," Lee drawled, "advises a little kissing right about now." He tilted her face up and covered her mouth with his.

He took her breath away, and with it the last vestiges of her stubbornness and pretense. Jessamine gave herself over to his warm mouth, to his wet, seeking tongue, his knowing hands, bracing her head for the plunder of his kiss.

Lee was lost in the deep and sweet wine caverns of her mouth. He moved, sampling the curve of her cheek, the angle of her nose, the delicate intricacies of her ear, then back to her soft mouth again, now open and inviting.

He leaned her back, lifted her gently onto the bed, kissing her all the while, lying beside her, his fingers drifting up and down her arm.

Jessamine closed her eyes, not wanting sight to distract her from touch. And Lee was touching her, fingers on her collarbone and throat, along the neckline of her gown. His warm hand cupped her breast, and his mouth followed, wetting the thin cotton that covered her.

"Jessie..." he moaned as his hand slid up the back of her, beneath her gown, to stroke the curve of her rump, cup it in his hand and draw her closer. And he moaned again, more hoarsely this time, as he sat her up, bunched the cotton gown in his hands and whisked it off over her head.

He knelt by her ankles, looking only at the blue garter, as he eased it down her calf, over her ankle and heel and off her foot. When he finally looked up at her, Jessamine heard his

aw intake of air, saw his chest quicken and his eyes burn
even hotter than before.

"You're prettier than moonbeams on magnolias, little
Jessie."

She moved—it was the slightest arching of her hips—and
saw the fire in his eyes deepen. She moved again, setting off
the same reaction. Jessamine's lips curved upward, and she
felt her heart swell at the discovery of her power to kindle
such a blaze.

"You're a quick study, Miss Jessamine," Lee drawled.

Next it was his turn to fumble, first with his belt, then
with the buttons of his pants. Finally, he lay beside her,
sliding a hand up her thigh, over her ribs, cupping her breast
and bringing his mouth down to dally and feast. He lav-
ished the same attention on her other breast, Jessamine's
fingers running through his thick hair as she tried to keep
breathing while her heart drummed wildly and every nerve
in her body sang.

His hand traveled down her outer thigh again, then up the
inside, touching her intimately as her breath turned irregular and ragged.

Lee covered her with his hard body, whispering harshly
against her ear. "Jessie, Jessie, you're driving me close to
the edge. I have to take you. Now." He parted her legs with
his thigh, and with a determined thrust, he entered her,
covering her mouth with his to still her cry of pain.

And when he finally sank his head into the crook of her
neck, moist now with his sweat, she stroked him and kissed
his hair. He shifted onto the mattress then, with his arm
across her, his hand idling on her flank.

After several moments, Jessamine asked softly, "Lee, are
you sleeping?"

"No, Jessie. I'm just cooling off a little bit. And I'm lying here realizing I'm not a boy of seventeen anymore."
Realizing, he thought, that the fires she had ignited in him

had flashed out of control and she had yet to know sweet, all-consuming flames.

"You were wonderful," she said.

He leaned up on an elbow, one eyebrow cocked. "Compared to what, Jessie?"

"Well, you just were," she said.

"Uh-huh." He kissed her delicately on her eyelid. "I'm sorry I had to hurt you, Jessie," he whispered, then got up and went to the washstand, returned with a moist rag. He knelt beside her on the bed and began to dab at her thighs. "Open your legs a little bit, honey," Lee said.

"What are you doing?" Jessamine raised up on her elbows and looked down. "Good Lord, I'm bleeding. What did you do to me, Lee?"

"Only what the book said, honey. There. That's got it." He stood up and swabbed himself, then tossed the towel back to the washstand.

Jessamine had put her gown on and flopped back down and was staring at the ceiling. Lee sat beside her. He lit a cigar, then poured a little brandy in his empty snifter.

"Want a sip, Jessie?" he asked.

Her reply was a crisp "No, thank you."

Lee downed the brandy, licked his lips, took a long pull on the cigar. He rubbed his belly, a man well satisfied. "Well, how was it, Jessie? Did I live up to all your expectations?"

"Oh, my, yes," she said, still resolutely studying the ceiling.

"And it was worth waiting for? Matched all your girlish dreams, did it?"

"Absolutely," she said.

"There's only one little problem." Lee sighed. "You know that book I was talking about? Seems every time I read it, I get through with a chapter or two and I lose my place. And then you know what happens?"

"I can't imagine."

"I have to open up that damn book, and start all over again, right from page one." He stubbed out his cigar in the porcelain dish and took her into his arms.

"Isn't once a night enough, Lee?" she asked, resisting, angling her head away from his mouth.

"Sometimes. Why don't we wait awhile, and then you tell me." He pulled her gown off. "Same book, Jessie, only this time we're going to turn the pages a little slower."

And it wasn't long before Lee, with his slow hands on every inch of her and his knowing mouth and languid tongue, turned her indifference to a driving passion that equaled his own.

This time it was Jessamine who was driven to the very edge.

"Tell me now how it is, Jessie," Lee whispered against her ear, as his fingers explored her velvet depths.

Jessamine caught enough of her breath to say, "Wonderful."

"Tell me it meets with your high expectations," he rasped.

She couldn't even speak now, could only look at him, her back arched, her gaze unfocused.

She matched him thrust for thrust, their bodies driving into one another like relentless waves in a storm, and when she could do nothing but mindlessly call out his name, Lee whispered hot at her ear, "There, Jessie. There's your sweetness, darlin', my sweet, sweet, warm Jessie-darlin'."

They stayed in the room two and a half days, leaving only to take an occasional bath together down the hall—with notes left to apologize for all the water on the floor—or to sneak out to the necessary and then rush back. Myra sent their meals up on trays the girls left in the hall. They fed each other grapes and cold chicken, cucumber slices drip-

ping with vinegar and strawberries dipped in thick whippe
cream.

Jessamine learned how to swirl brandy in a snifter, how
to blow smoke rings, how to deal from the bottom of th
deck, and the difference between a straight and a flush. Le
had made her feel beautiful, had praised her with his eyes
had compared her to just about every species of flower soutl
of the Mason-Dixon line. If he hadn't told her that he love
her, Jessamine wasn't going to let that ruin their idyll. An
if his plans for the future only entailed what he was going t
do to her body during the next half hour or so—well, tha
was simply the kind of man he was. She could only take hin
as he was. He was wild, and he was unashamedly himself.

They slept like bent spoons when they did sleep. An
when they were awake, they were talking and touching an
making love.

Toward dawn on Saturday morning, Jessamine dreame
about Riverbend. She saw it in ruins—its tall chimney
broken, the porch rotting and sagging, the shutters hang
ing and banging in the wind. Its barren fields were pitted, a
if a great battle had taken place there. Charles appeare
from behind the crab apple tree. His face haggard. His eye
closed. And then Louis limped out of the ramshackle barn
And Caleb. Caleb just stood in the side yard, crying, his fac
all mottled and wet with tears. "I tried so hard," Jessa
mine told her brothers. "I did the best I could." They shool
their dreamy heads and turned away from her, away from
the sorry sight of Riverbend.

She cried out to them and Lee reached over and smoothe
a hand along her flank, soothing her back to sleep.

Two hours later, Jessamine sat up in bed and announce
that she was leaving for Coulterville to look for Caleb.

Lee walked his lazy fingers up her spine. "I thought you'
given up that notion," he said.

Jessamine looked over her shoulder at him. "You were going to say *'silly* notion,' weren't you?"

Lee rolled his eyes toward the ceiling. "Why do I have the silly notion that our little honeymoon boat has just sailed over a waterfall?"

She threw him a look as black as her violet eyes could manage. "Married people have honeymoons, Lee. Anyway, we can't just stay here forever."

He slid his hand around to cup her warm breast. "It'd be nice though, Jessie, wouldn't it?" he murmured. "Living in a whorehouse, making love all the damn day long." Truly content for the first time in his life, Lee had managed to limit his thoughts to the present. He had no reprehensible past, no uncertain future. He had just what he wanted—Jessie, here and now.

She slipped out of his reach. "Lee Kincannon, we both have better things to do, and you know it."

"*Other* things, Jessie. Nothing is better than this."

She was putting on her borrowed blue wrapper and moving purposefully around the room, picking up lost grapes and tossed towels, talking more to herself than to Lee. "And a dress or two. Wonder if I could get one from Doretta or Josie. They're about my size. Lord! I wonder if they've got anything but red ones. What do you think, Lee?"

"About what, honey?"

"Doretta or Josie?"

"I wouldn't kick either one of 'em out of bed," he said, then prepared to catch her hand when she smacked him playfully. But she didn't.

Jessamine sat on the edge of the bed, hands in her lap. "I have responsibilities, Lee. You've been distracting me from them, from my purpose."

"Well, pardon me all to hell, Miss Jessamine. It was my impression you were enjoying my—how shall I call it?—company."

"It doesn't have anything to do with 'enjoyment,'" she said, rising and pacing around the room again.

"Does it have something to do with marriage?" Lee raised himself up on one elbow, the sheet tangled around him. He sighed dramatically, knowing this conversation was inevitable, but still resisting the intrusion of the future on the perfect present. "Jessie, I'm thirty-six years old. I've never been married, and I—"

Jessamine picked up the hairbrush from the dresser and threw it at him. "I wouldn't marry you if you if you were the last man breathing on this earth, Lee Kincannon." She stomped to the window and stood looking out. "I want to find my brother. I want to take him home. Back to Riverbend."

"Seems like this is where we began, Jessie," Lee said quietly, feeling the past creep into their idyll.

Jessamine felt lost, suddenly, as if the past four years had been a tornado that had picked her up and set her down in a strange place, with a strange man. "I want to go home," she said, raising her chin to the soft Georgia sun outside the window. "You can come with me or you can stay here till you're a hundred and twelve, for all I care."

Lee got up, stiff and grim-faced, and dressed silently while Jessamine furiously stripped the sheets from the bed and shook the pillows out of their cases. She shook one so hard it split at the seams. Goose down spilled out and caught in the morning breeze, swirling around the room. It was like a blizzard.

Lee yanked on his belt buckle. "Christ, Jessie, when you get in a snit, you really are a dangerous woman." He picked a feather off his tongue and spit another out on the floor. "I truly do think insanity runs in your family. Rampant." He stalked out the door and slammed it, setting the feathers off again.

Jessamine stood in the downy snowfall, wanting to cry, but too proud and mad to do it. Didn't he understand how important Riverbend was to her? Didn't he know that if she couldn't have him, then Riverbend was all she had?

Her dream had been so vivid, so horribly real. She had to find Caleb. Now. If she didn't, that terrible dream was going to come true.

Chapter Sixteen

Doretta was playing the piano when Jessamine entered the front parlor. "Damn it to hell," the girl said when her finger slipped from a black key.

Jessamine laughed, and Doretta turned around. "Oh, pardon me, Jessie. I thought I was alone. Say, you look quite elegant in that old dress of mine."

"Why, thank you, Miss Doretta." Jessamine curtsied in the bright red dress, the least revealing of all the ones Doretta or Josie were willing to part with. The billowy sateen skirt featured a Greek-key design of black cord near the hemline. Its scooped neck was corded in black, and the big puffed sleeves were black chiffon.

"How nicely that sets off your hair, Jessie," said Myra as she entered the parlor. She hooked an errant wisp of hair back into Jessamine's chignon.

"Thank you, Myra." Jessamine took her hand. "And thank you for...for everything. I'll never forget all the nice things you and your girls have done for me."

Myra walked her to the settee. "Sit a minute, Jessie." The madam cast a dour glance toward the piano. "I heard that slip on the keyboard, Doretta, by the way. Why don't you practice a little more?"

The soft chords of "Come Where My Love Lies Dreaming" once again filled the parlor.

"Lee tells me you're going to Coulterville today," said Myra. "It's not a pleasant place, Jessie. I was there a month or so ago, visiting an old acquaintance, Colonel Moore. He lost a leg early in the war, and they put him in charge of the prison." Myra sighed. "It wasn't the colonel's fault the conditions got so bad there. Most of the food and all of the medical supplies had to be used for our own boys. I know you can understand that, regardless of your opinions about the war."

Jessamine nodded, not sure what Myra was trying to tell her, and not sure she wanted to hear it.

Myra fussed with her skirt, then picked a thread off Jessamine's. "There aren't too many bluecoats left at Coulterville now. Prisoners, I mean. There's a whole damn garrison of soldiers who came in to take over the place. As for the prisoners, the healthy ones beat it up north right away. The rest kind of straggled out. You need to know, Jessie, if your brother is still there, then he won't be the man he was when he left home. In body or in spirit."

"I'm ready for whatever I find, Myra. I only want to take Caleb home."

"There's something else you need to know. I've tried to talk Lee out of going with you...."

"Myra," Jessamine snapped, "I'm not asking him to go."

The madam fixed Jessamine with a stony gaze. "He's not the kind of man you have to ask," she said. "The mere fact that you're going means he feels he has to. I told him I'd send one of the girls with you, and if he didn't feel right about that, then I'd go myself." Myra sighed. "He's a bull-headed son of a gun."

"You've noticed," said Jessamine glumly.

"That prison's completely in Yankee hands now. There's a Colonel Grove who gives the orders. My friend, Colonel Evan Moore, is supposed to be in charge, but he has about

as much say so as a parrot on a perch. I've told Lee that. If
your brother is there, and since he's a Yank, you won't have
any trouble getting him out. They're glad to have those boys
go home.''

"That's good to know," said Jessamine.

"Your problem is going to be Lee. He's known around
here, Jessie, and he wasn't a regular soldier, so the regular
rules don't apply to him. As far as those Yankees are concerned, Lee Kincannon is a murderer and a thief. And if
they ever get him in that prison, they're going to slam the
door so hard we'll hear it all the way back here in Gunter.''
A tear slid down Myra's cheek, and she wiped it away as if
it were scorching her. "Damn," she said.

"But, Myra, I . . .''

Lee appeared in the door of the parlor, a picnic basket in
his hand. His eyes found Jessamine and regarded her red
dress.

"Myra, I best get Jessie and her pretty red dress out of
here before one of your gentlemen callers tries to escort her
up those stairs," he said, flashing a white grin.

Myra blotted her eyes with a red silk hankie. "You damn
fool," she sniffed.

Jessamine rose from the settee. "You know, Lee, I've
been thinking about Coulterville, and—''

"You've been talking to Myra, Jessie, the mama hen who
thinks her chicks can't get along on their own." He patted
the hamper. "Josie has loaded this thing down with half the
food in the pantry. We're going to spread a blanket under a
big pine tree and have ourselves a regular picnic.''

"I don't think I'll be the least bit hungry," Jessamine
said, glancing at Myra.

"I'll just put this in the surrey anyway, darlin','" Lee said,
"for when we're ten miles down the road and you start
rambling on about roast beef and boiled potatoes and
making up little songs about strawberries.''

Jessamine took in his handsome face, his gleaming grin, the width of his shoulders in the doorway. How she loved him. She laughed with pure joy.

"I'll take good care of him, Myra," she said. "I promise."

As Lee had predicted, Jessamine's stomach began complaining noisily ten miles down the road. He barely had time to spread the blanket under a tree before she dived into the picnic basket.

"Isn't this just the best pound cake you've ever had, Lee?" Jessamine broke off a corner, held it to his lips. "Here. Try another little piece."

"No, thank you, Jessie. I have had enough. I've progressed to other appetites."

"Have you, now?" She raised a wicked eyebrow.

"But I'm not going to kiss you with your mouth all stuffed with pound cake."

She made a great show of chewing and swallowing, then lay back on the blanket, gazing up at him. "You may kiss me now, sir," she said.

On his knees, Lee picked up her skirts and threw them over her head. He pulled down the waistband of her pantaloons and circled her navel with his tongue. "Jessie," he said, "there are crumbs in here from yesterday's lunch."

Her protest was muffled by yards of red satin and white taffeta. She felt her pantaloons being lowered, slowly and with great determination. His warm mouth searched along the inside of her thigh.

"I can't breathe," she moaned, flipping her skirts down and giggling. "Oh, Lee, you should see this. I look like a woman with four legs. Two of them with long black boots on. What are you doing now? Oh, Lord. Oh, Lee."

* * *

It was well past dark when they reached the town of Coulterville. Jessamine drove Myra's surrey to the little hotel on the town square while Lee walked down a side street. She paid a boy to see to the surrey and horse, and walked into the hotel, where she had to convince the clerk that she wasn't what her red dress implied before he would even consider letting her stay there.

Once upstairs and in her room, Jessamine pulled a sheet off the bed and draped it over the windowsill. A few minutes later, a black-booted leg slid over the sill.

"Give me a hand, Jessie, will you? I'm about to break my neck here."

She did, and Lee came sprawling through the window, cursing a dark blue streak. Jessamine looked down. There was no ladder, no drainpipe, no trellis. "How'd you climb up?" she asked.

Lee sucked on a scraped knuckle. "Not up, Jessie. Down."

Jessamine angled her head in the other direction. The roof was two stories beyond her. "Lord, Lee, you could have broken your neck."

"That's what I said, Jessie."

He struck a match and lit the lamp on the chiffonier.

"Did you hurt your hand? Let me see," she said, pulling it away from his mouth, and studying it in the light. "It's only a scrape," she said, kissing it.

Lee was smiling softly. "You're getting to be a mama hen, just like Myra. I wonder if it's the dress."

"I promised her I'd take care of you." She narrowed her eyes. "And you, if you'll recall, have promised me you won't leave this room under any circumstances."

He dipped his head to kiss her. "As I recall, Jessie, what I promised was to stay here if I was properly entertained."

She began to unhook his belt. "How would you suggest I do that?" she asked, her voice low and sultry. "Maybe you should consult that book of yours."

"Page fourteen might be interesting," he murmured, at the tender mercy of her hands.

The prison wasn't at all what Jessamine had expected. Most of her notions about such places were from books by Charles Dickens, whose fictional London prisons were dank and dark institutions. She'd seen the town jail in Newton once or twice, when she'd had to bail out her overseer, Eamon Dobbs, but the military prison at Coulterville was neither dark nor small. After she'd walked the quarter mile from the hotel and stated her purpose to the blue-coated sentry at the gate, she entered a sunny compound with ten or twelve barracks surrounded by a high fence. One building, painted gray, was marked with a sign: Coulterville Military Prison, Colonel Evan H. Moore, Commandant. A Union flag flew from the pole outside the door.

Jessamine entered what appeared to be an office. A young man in civilian clothes rose from a desk and stood smartly.

"Good morning, ma'am. Corporal Timothy Ryan, at your service, ma'am."

"Good morning, Corporal Ryan," Jessamine said. "I've come to inquire about my brother, who was a prisoner here after he was captured at Shiloh."

"Yes, ma'am," he said, reaching across his desk for a gray ledger bound with dark red leather. "And what is the name, ma'am?"

"Lieutenant Caleb Dade of the Fourth Illinois."

His jaw dropped a fraction, and then the corporal put the ledger back down on the desktop. "I won't be needing this," he said. "Your brother is here, ma'am."

Jessamine's hand sprang to her throat, and her knees felt suddenly weak. It had never occurred to her that it would be so easy. She'd thought . . . Well, she didn't know what she'd thought, only that it would be more difficult, more taxing, even impossible. But this . . . now . . .

Corporal Ryan came from around his desk, took her elbow and led her to a chair. "May I get you a glass of water, ma'am?"

"Yes," Jessamine said thinly. "That would be kind of you."

Caleb was here—his presence so obvious that the corporal hadn't even found it necessary to look it up in his ledger. Caleb was here, and he was alive, and everything was going to be good again once she got him home.

"Your water, ma'am."

"Thank you so much."

"Before taking you to see Lieutenant Dade, ma'am, I need to get the colonel's permission. If you'll excuse me a moment."

"Yes, of course," said Jessamine.

It was quite a while before the corporal returned, but Jessamine didn't mind. A wonderful feeling of peace had settled into her heart. She felt patient. She had found Caleb—so easily, after all—and they would be going home. To his home. Riverbend belonged to Caleb now. Goodbye, Charlotte. Goodbye, dressmakers and milliners and cobblers. Goodbye, footed crystal bowls. Goodbye . . .

A tall, lean man in brown pants and a tan shirt came through the door. He had a wooden leg and walked awkwardly with a cane. He was clean-shaven, handsome, with dark curly hair not unlike Lee's. Jessamine could understand why Myra would travel such a distance to be with this man.

"Good morning, Miss Dade. I'm Colonel Evan Moore.
My corporal tells me you've come for your brother."

"How do you do, Colonel? Yes, I have indeed."

He angled himself into a chair at a desk, grimaced as he
hooked his cane over the chair arm. "We'll need to fill in a
few blanks on some papers, Miss Dade." He winked. "The
Yanks don't cotton much to paperwork. Guess that's why
they kept some of us around."

"Yes, I understand."

As he prepared to write, another colonel came through
the door, this one in a smart blue uniform. "Here she is,
Major," he called back over his shoulder.

"Thank you, sir," said Major Harding as he paused in the
doorway, then rushed to Jessamine and lifted her—stupe-
fied—up and into his arms.

"Oh, my dearest," he whispered tremulously. "You're
here. You're safe. I feel that I can at last start breathing
again."

"Thomas!" It was all she could manage to say.

"Oh, Jessamine." He tipped her chin up to give her the
briefest of kisses as his blue eyes devoured her face hun-
grily.

"Major Harding," said Colonel Moore, "I'd like to get
a little information from your fiancée before she sees her
brother."

"Yes, sir," answered Major Harding.

"Naturally, you may accompany her to see Lieutenant
Dade, Major," the Union colonel said.

"Thank you, Colonel Grove, sir," he said, hardly able to
take his eyes off Jessamine, curling his fingers through her
limp hand, squeezing it repeatedly as if to make sure she was
truly real.

Colonel Moore's questions were a matter of vital statis-
tics—full name of the prisoner, date of birth, permanent

residence, and so forth. Jessamine answered automatically, her mind reeling with the consequences of the major's unexpected presence. She pictured Lee as she had left him only an hour or so ago, lying with his hair all mussed, a shadow on his jaw, his long, dark eyelashes just touching his cheek, so beautiful and defenseless in sleep. For a moment, when she had learned that Caleb was here, it had all seemed so easy. Now, heaven help her, she was staggered by the complications.

"You will find your brother changed, Miss Dade," said Colonel Moore, twisting his cane as he spoke. "When he arrived here at Coulterville, he either would not or could not speak. In the three years since then, he has withdrawn completely." He gave a last twist to his cane, then used it to rise from his seat. "I am no longer permitted to enter the prisoners' barracks. Colonel Grove and Major Harding will see you to him. I wish you well." He limped toward the door.

Colonel Grove, with his gray muttonchop sideburns and his neatly pressed blue uniform, also stood. "Let's get on with it, Major," he said.

"Yes, sir," replied Major Harding. "Jessamine." He offered her his arm.

She stood and let him twine her arm through his, then walked out the door, nearly oblivious to her surroundings.

"Thomas, have you seen Caleb? What did the colonel mean when he said he was withdrawn?"

"I've visited with him several times, informing him of your iminent arrival. He doesn't speak, dearest. He merely stares."

"Poor, poor Caleb," she said.

"Perhaps when he sees that his sister has come for him, when he sees your lovely face, he will come out of his trance," said the major. "Whatever happens, dear, I'll help you take him home. We can leave as soon as you wish."

She nodded dumbly. First Caleb. First she had to see Caleb. Then her mind would be clear enough to formulate some kind of plan.

As they walked along, a Union corporal joined them, and the colonel consulted a penciled list of duties for him—there were walks to be swept, windows to be repaired, more lice-infested mattresses to be burned, a pile of greasy rags in the kitchen to be disposed of before they caught fire. Jessamine found she was almost comforted by the sound of his authoritative voice, his list of duties and details, so clear-cut, so easily accomplished. If someone could only tell her what to do—about Caleb, about the major, about Lee.

"This is it, isn't it, Major?" asked Colonel Grove, halting at the door of one of the barracks.

"Yes, sir." Major Harding opened the door for them.

How strange, thought Jessamine. A prison with open doors, and jailers eager to have the inmates go free.

The major took her arm again and walked her slowly up a flight of stairs to a large room where a silent figure was sitting on the only made-up cot in a barracks full of empty ones.

"Caleb!" breathed Jessamine.

He was leaning forward, his elbows on his knees, his chin resting in his hands. Although he was looking at them, he gave no sign of recognition, no indication at all that he was even seeing them.

"Caleb. Oh, my poor Caleb." Jessamine kissed the top of his head, then knelt down before him. "It's Jessamine, Caleb. I've come to take you home. Back to Riverbend."

She looked into his eyes. They were her eyes—violet and round—but they were devoid of any feeling, any sign of life. "Oh, Caleb, what have they done to you? Can you hear me? Do you know me? It's Jessamine. Your sister. Caleb, it's me."

Jessamine's eyes clouded with tears.

Major Harding knelt beside her. "I thought perhaps he would know you, Jessamine. I'm truly sorry."

She reached up to brush the hair off Caleb's forehead. Her hair—raven—but dull and dirty and matted. "Has anyone seen him, Thomas? Has a doctor been here? Is anything being done for him?"

"Nothing was done before the war ended. The conditions were despicable here. To tell you the truth, it's a wonder he's alive at all. But no, I don't believe a doctor has been here." He turned to Colonel Grove. "Am I correct, sir?"

"Yes, Major."

"It doesn't mean he can't be helped, Jessamine," the major urged. "We'll talk to a physician in St. Louis on our way home."

"Yes. All right." She grasped Caleb's hand and squeezed it, then she stood up. "I'm ready to leave now, Thomas. I'd rather that Caleb not see me cry."

Once outside, Jessamine dissolved in his arms, choking on her tears. He stroked her hair, murmuring "There, there, dearest . . . There, there . . ."

Lee was tossing cards at his hat, which lay halfway across the room, when she returned. He pitched the card in his hand without looking, took her in his arms. She wept for the second time in an hour as she described her brother's condition.

"I've seen it happen once or twice," Lee said, wiping her face with a cool washrag. "Seems like the mind can only tolerate so much, and then it just shuts off. Nothing comes in. Nothing goes out."

Jessamine sniffed. "I don't know what to do."

"You'll take him home, Jessie. And then you'll talk to that old geezer of a doctor and see what he has to say. And then you'll go from there."

"You make it sound so simple." It wasn't simple at all. And it wasn't just Caleb. Major Harding had insisted on walking her back to the hotel—the same hotel, as it turned out, where he was staying, for lack of proper quarters at the prison. He had left her in the lobby and gone to make arrangements for a wagon and a team of horses to take them to the coast. They would leave, he told her, shortly after dawn on the morrow.

After seeing Caleb, Jessamine couldn't sort anything out in her head. She just looked at Lee helplessly. "It isn't simple at all," she said.

"Your brother's alive, Jessie. Be grateful for that. And he's free. For all you know, he was tickled to death to see you and just couldn't show it."

"Oh, I hope so, Lee."

He rubbed her back until she fell into a restless sleep. He played solitaire till she awoke.

"What time is it?" Jessamine asked, woozy with sleep.

Lee opened the pocket watch lying on the nightstand. "Five o'clock," he said. "You must be getting hungry."

She was starved, but she'd told the major she was going to remain in her room, sleeping and weeping, until the next morning, and that under no circumstances was he to disturb her. Jessamine was loath to go out, even to the privy, for fear of running into him.

On waking, it had occurred to her that there was only one way to simplify her problem. Tomorrow morning she would tell Major Harding goodbye. She would be polite and distant and unswerving. If necessary, if he drove her to it, she would tell him the unvarnished truth—that she couldn't bear the sight of him, the touch of his hand on hers, the touch of

his lips on hers, the thought of marriage to him. And if he had any pride at all, he would let her go. All she could do in the meantime was wait. Wait, and keep Lee and the major apart.

"I don't feel like going out," she said. "Let's play poker."

Lee raised an eyebrow. "You got any money on you, Jessie?"

"All I've got are the clothes on my back."

He began shuffling the cards. "Stud poker, little girl. Deuces wild," he said, the cards fairly flying from his deft fingers. He looked at his hand. "I'll open with my left boot."

Chapter Seventeen

Jessamine lost all her clothes twice, thoroughly enjoying the consequences of both defeats, though she hotly accused Lee of cheating when he beat her with four aces in three consecutive hands. Now the victor was sleeping soundly, his backside against hers.

She was thinking of Thomas, one floor up, and rehearsing her lines for the morrow, when she saw the linen curtains gust into the room. She got up to close the window, then stood with her hands on the sill, transfixed by the angry orange glow in the sky to the north. A flame shot up above the tree line about a quarter mile away. It couldn't be anything but— The prison! It was burning. "Caleb," she whispered.

Her pantaloons were draped over the foot rail. Jessamine slipped into them as quietly as she could, looking frantically around the dark room for her dress. It was under the bed on Lee's side. She crawled till her fingers touched the cool sateen, and pulled it toward her with a rustle. There wasn't time for her corset, even if she could find it. Sitting on the floor, she slid her legs into the dress, and buttoned it as she ran down the stairs.

"The prison's on fire," she said to the desk clerk as she raced past his rolltop desk.

" 'Bout time," was his sleepy reply.

There were others on the road that led from the town to the prison. They made a strange procession—men carrying torches, women with their skirts hiked up, chattering children with dogs running little circles around them. A wagon full of rain barrels clattered past. All the while the sky grew brighter as the flames licked higher.

Armed Union soldiers met them at the gate, and while they argued with the raucous, curious crowd, Jessamine slipped through.

The yard was bright as day—a red, hellish day. Nearly every building was on fire, some with flames rushing up the walls, some with burning patches on their roofs, one already collapsed and smoldering. Ashes, sparks and shingles were wafting upward and falling back to the ground. The conflagration seemed to have created a weather of its own, with hot, swirling winds, dark clouds of smoke and wave after wave of heat.

Jessamine stood with her arm up, protecting her face. Then, in the wild orange light, she saw the wooden leg and cane of Colonel Evan Moore, and she ran to him, calling his name.

"Colonel Moore! My brother—Caleb Dade. Where is he? Is he safe?"

The handsome colonel looked down at her, without surprise, as if this hell were to be expected, as if her presence were nothing out of the ordinary. "Miss Dade," he said. "The prisoners have been gathered at the east end of the compound. Your brother is not among them."

"Not— But, Colonel, if Caleb's still in there—" she pointed toward the fiery barracks "—you've got to do something."

Colonel Grove stepped from behind the shoulder of his Confederate counterpart. His countenance was hard, im-

placable. "Madam, we have done everything humanly possible to alert him. I'll not send a healthy man to risk his life for a man who is capable of saving his own."

"Capable! Caleb is ill. He needs help. Do something," Jessamine shrieked. "You must do something."

"It is in God's hands now," said the Union colonel.

"God doesn't care about Caleb," Jessamine said. "I'll just go get him myself." She turned from the officers and faced the burning buildings.

Colonel Moore took a step in her direction, but the Union colonel put a hand on his shoulder. "It's too hot," he said. "She won't get but a few feet before she turns back."

The officers returned to their supervision of the weary bucket brigade of soldiers who were trying to wet down the headquarters, the sole building not in flames.

Jessamine locked her eyes on the third building on the left, the one where Caleb sat on the second floor. The lower part of the building was intact, but the roof had begun to burn. With each step she took toward it, the heat became more intense. She raised both her arms and averted her face, but kept going. She had to keep going. Caleb was in there. Nobody would help him. Nobody would help her.

There was a muffled explosion on her right, and a chunk of burning wood rolled against the hem of her skirt. A bright flame licked up the red satin. Jessamine screamed and beat at it with her hands, and then something fell against her, hard as a wall, knocking the breath out of her as she hit the ground and was rolled over and over.

"Jessie, what the hell are you doing?" Lee howled at her as he knelt on one knee beside her.

She blinked at him, his white shirt glowing with the flames behind him. He wasn't supposed to be here. It was too dangerous for him, but she had to put that out of her mind now.

She had to concentrate on her brother. "Caleb's in there. I have to help him," she said.

"You can't go in there," he said.

"I have to," she wailed. "Nobody will help. I won't let my brother die."

"Jessie." Lee gathered her against his chest. "It's too late."

And then, through all the popping and roaring of the fire, Jessamine heard the sound of shuffling feet, heard the distinct click of a pistol, and then the flinty voice of Colonel Grove.

"We were alerted to your presence in these parts, Mr. Kincannon. Will you stand, sir? You are under arrest."

Lee stood, with Jessamine still in his arms.

"Unhand the woman, sir," demanded Colonel Grove, the firelight glinting on the brass buttons of his blue coat.

Jessamine looked wildly from Lee to the Union officer. Behind him, she saw the sad, defeated expression of Colonel Evan Moore.

"Leave him alone," Jessamine said.

Lee shook her. "Be still, Jessie. This woman has a brother in great peril, Colonel."

"That is not your concern, sir."

Then Jessamine felt every muscle in Lee's body clench, every nerve quicken.

"Which building?" he whispered against her ear.

She turned and stared at him. Then he gave her a shake, the question burning in his eyes.

"Third on the left," she whispered.

Without another word, Lee shoved her into the Union colonel and turned and ran toward the burning barracks.

She heard the soldiers' guns lifting to their shoulders, felt Colonel Grove's hands setting her away from him with deliberation.

"No," she screamed.

"Put down your arms, men," said the colonel. "Let the bastard burn."

Jessamine started running after him, but Colonel Moore yanked her back with the hook of his cane.

His face was grim, tinted orange in the firelight. "The fence has burned on the other side of the compound, Miss Dade. He's got a fighting chance to get away," the colonel rasped as Jessamine struggled against him. "Let him go. Let God go with him."

Sparks were falling in Lee's hair. His sleeve caught fire, and he swatted at it furiously, cursing, squinting his eyes against the blistering heat.

When he reached for the doorknob of the third building, it burned his hand as he gripped it, so he brought back his leg and kicked the door in.

"Caleb! Caleb Dade!" he shouted once inside.

The only sound he heard was the roar of the fire at the far end of the barrack where flames slithered up the wall.

"Caleb!" he called again, looking around frantically till he saw the flight of stairs. He took them two at a time.

The roof had burned through at the far end, sparks falling and starting little fires on the floor. Lee could look up and see the stars against the black sky.

At the far end of the room, a figure sat on the edge of a cot. He, too, was staring up at the stars.

As Lee walked toward him, a chunk of a crossbeam hit his shoulder. He glanced at it, knew it must have injured him for his shirt had burned away, but he didn't feel anything.

He stood looking at Caleb for a moment—into the depths of Jessie's big pansy eyes, at the soft waves of her raven hair. Then he grasped the man's upper arm and tried to pull him

up. Caleb's body was rigid, his fingers twisted around the edge of the cot and his feet planted firmly on the floor.

"Caleb!" Lee shouted at him.

There was no reaction at all.

"God damn it!" Lee stood helplessly a second. Then another chunk of the roof crashed to the floor. "I'm not dying in this fire, Caleb, and neither are you," he said, drawing back his fist and ramming it into Caleb's jaw.

Lee hoisted the still figure onto his shoulders and headed for the stairs.

"Do you believe in heaven and hell, Colonel Moore?" Jessamine asked quietly as they stood watching the inferno.

"I believe in hell, Miss Dade. I've seen nothing resembling heaven so far," he said.

"I have," Jessamine whispered. "I have." It was a prayer of sorts as she stood there fighting back her tears. Godspeed, my love, she thought, as she wished him over the fence and safely far away, as she prayed for a quick and painless end to Caleb's living death, as she let go all her dreams of Riverbend, because nothing, nothing on this earth, was as important to her as Lee.

The colonel edged forward on his cane. "Holy Christ!"

"What? What is it?" Jessamine's eyes searched the fiery perdition, but she saw only flames. "What? What do you see?"

"Over there," said the colonel, pointing with his cane.

There was someone stumbling through the smoke, tripping over the charred shaft of a wagon, going down, then rising with a burden on his shoulders and stumbling forward again.

"Lee!" Jessamine cried, breaking free of Colonel Moore's grasp and running toward him as far as she could

before the hot blast of the fire stopped her like an invisible wall.

When he reached her, Lee went down on one knee, rolling Caleb off his shoulders as he coughed and gasped for breath.

The Confederate colonel signaled to one of his aides. "Help these men," he said. "Let's get them back where there's more air."

Two corporals picked up Caleb's listless body. Another assisted Lee to his feet, locked an arm around him and led him back. Jessamine scurried along beside him, her eyes flashing from Caleb to Lee and back.

The soldiers put both men on the steps of the still-undamaged headquarters. Caleb sat staring. Lee was bent over, elbows on his knees, coughing. Jessamine placed a soothing hand on his back, and soot and grit came off on her fingers.

"Jessie," Lee said, trying to speak.

"Hush," she crooned. "Just hush. Just breathe."

Colonel Grove walked toward them, his bearing stiff and straight.

Jessamine glared at the Union officer. "You leave him alone," she said. "Stay away."

The colonel stood still, his arms crossed, his eyes trained on Lee. "Well done, sir. I commend you. I hope you display the same courage with a rope around your neck." Colonel Grove snapped his fingers. Two Union corporals came forward and, lifting Lee by the arms, dragged him away.

Jessamine flew at the blue-uniformed colonel, her fingernails going for his face, her feet for his shins. Colonel Moore and his aide pulled her away as the Union colonel straightened his shoulders and walked up the steps of his

headquarters, his pant leg just brushing Caleb's immobile arm.

"Do something," she hissed at Colonel Moore.

"I can't, Miss Dade. I can only promise you that he will be well treated," he said.

"Before they hang him?" Jessamine shrieked.

He nodded sadly, leaning harder on his cane.

Jessamine whirled around. "Come on, Caleb. We're going back to town to get Major Harding."

Her brother only stared.

She closed her eyes a moment, her gentle love for her brother at war with her fierce desire to save Lee. Then she slapped Caleb as hard as she could with the flat of her hand. "Now you get up, Caleb Dade, before I pull you up by the short hairs of your neck. You get up and you come with me."

Caleb got to his feet and stood staring at the ground.

"All right," said Jessamine, stiffening her backbone. "Now you just walk with me." She picked up her charred skirt and strode toward the gate, with Caleb shambling behind her.

Jessamine sat Caleb down on the bed in her room at the hotel. She smoothed his dark, sooty hair back from his eyes, speaking to him softly but firmly.

"I want you to stay here, Caleb. I have to leave for a little while to do something very important, but I'll be back. I'll be back, Caleb, and then I'm going to take you home." Jessamine kissed his cheek, then turned to the door.

She starting running up the stairs, but her knees quit on her, and she sagged against the handrail, biting back her tears, praying silently that Thomas was in his room, that there was something, anything, he could do.

There were four doors in the second-floor hallway. She knocked on them all, smashing the palm of her hand against the wood, calling his name.

The first door opened a crack, then wider. Major Harding came out in the hall, fumbling with the buttons on his blue pants. He was shirtless, the coppery hair on his chest echoing the hair that was falling in his eyes.

"Thomas!" Jessamine cried when she saw him. "Oh, Thomas, I need your help."

"Jessamine, what is it? What's happened to you?" He put his arm around her. "Come. Sit down." He walked her into his room, leaving the door open the proper fraction.

"You must help me, Thomas," she said in a rush of breath as tears began streaming down her cheeks.

He walked her toward the bed, sat her down, then sat beside her, stroking her arm. "Where have you been, dearest? Your face is streaked with dirt and your skirt is— Is it burnt, Jessamine?"

"The prison . . ." she said. "The prison is burning."

"What?" He leapt to the window and looked out at the fiery sky. "Good Lord! You must have been out there, Jessamine. What a foolish thing to do. Why didn't you wake me?"

"I had to get Caleb," she said.

He sat beside her again. "Of course you did, dearest. Of course."

Her tears were falling freely, wetting her mouth and her hands as she wiped them across her cheeks. "No one would help. Nobody would help. Oh, Thomas, please . . . I need your help. They've got him."

"Who, dearest? Caleb?"

She shook her head. "No. I have Caleb. I brought him back with me. The soldiers took him away."

He petted her arm, her hair. "Who, Jessamine? Who is this you're speaking of, dear?"

"They're going to hang him!" she wailed.

The major stood up. He stared at Jessamine as his blue eyes iced. Then he drove a fist into the palm of his hand. "That son of a bitch!" he thundered. "He's here. He followed you, didn't he?"

"Lee helped me, Thomas. He saved Caleb's life. And now they—they've taken him away."

The major glared at her tear-stricken face. "What is this man to you, Jessamine?" he asked in a voice as thin and cold as a sheet of ice. "What is he to you? I demand to know."

"Lee is . . . Lee is my friend," she whispered.

Major Harding just stood there, hands clenched at his sides.

Jessamine raised her wet eyes to his implacable face. "He saved my life, Thomas. He brought Caleb out of the fire." She slipped off the bed and wrapped her arms around his knees. "I beg you. For all that is holy and decent, help me. If you love me, Thomas, help me save his life." Her tears spilled down the coarse, dark blue fabric of his pants.

He didn't answer for a moment. Then he placed his hand on her head as she knelt there. "I love you, Jessamine," he said, in a voice thick with sorrow. "From the first moment I saw you. Perhaps too much."

"Then help me, Thomas, please," she sobbed.

"If I help you, Jessamine... If I help you, you must make me a promise in return."

"Anything. I'll promise you anything," she said.

His hand moved from her hair to the side of her face. "You must give me your word that you will never see this rebel cur again, and that when we return to Riverbend you will marry me."

Jessamine clung to him. She would have promised her soul to Satan for all eternity to keep them from hanging her Lee. "I promise," she said.

"Stand up, Jessamine," commanded the major.

He let her struggle to her feet to stand before him, her face wet and soot-streaked, her damp hair sticking to her cheeks. "Look at me, Jessamine," he ordered.

She raised her eyes to his cool blue gaze.

"Tell me what I want to hear."

The devil take me, Jessamine thought. And she didn't bat an eye as she said, "I love you, Thomas. I will be honored to be your wife."

The prison compound was a smoldering wreck. The haze above it blotted out the morning sun. Small fires still burned here and there, but for the most part everything that could burn had burned through the long night, except for the headquarters, where the Union flag sagged on its pole, where Major Harding had disappeared over half an hour before.

Jessamine sat in the back of the wagon with Caleb, holding his hand, touching his face every now and then, talking softly to him. She hadn't slept. The major had told her to go back to her room, where he would come get her at first light. She had sat on the floor with Caleb, both of them leaning back against the wall, their eyes fixed on nothing in the dark hotel room.

Now, waiting for Thomas to come out of the prison, Jessamine fought down the desire to run to the back of the building, where she saw a few windows with iron bars, resisted the urge to stand up and try to see or be seen in her tattered scarlet dress.

The major had told her to sit there. She had taken him at his word. She would sit till hell froze over, if need be.

She saw Colonel Moore limp down the steps, cast a grave and tired look toward the wagon, and walk away. Major Harding and Colonel Grove came out of the building a short time later, talked briefly on the steps, and then the major saluted smartly and walked briskly out the gate.

"Sit up here with me, Jessamine," he said.

She climbed over the seat and sat beside him, settling her skirts.

He whipped the reins over the horses, and the wagon jolted forward.

"I forbid you to look back," he said.

Jessamine bit her lip and stared straight ahead, her face as blank as Caleb's. The wagon hurtled down the road for several miles before she dared turn to look at the stern, coppery profile.

"Tell me, Thomas. Please."

"Everyone has a price, Jessamine," he said coldly. "How dearly we must pay for what we want."

"Thomas, please." What about Lee? she wanted to scream, though she knew she didn't dare.

"Colonel Grove's price is two thousand dollars."

"What are you saying?" Her eyes grew wide and wild. "I don't have two thousand dollars. We must go back."

He swatted the horses again with the reins. "Mrs. Alpha Parker will pay eagerly, I assure you, Jessamine, for her lover's release. I telegraphed her last night and received her immediate reply. I shall speak with her personally in St. Louis on our way back to Riverbend. The sum will reach Colonel Grove at Coulterville on or about our wedding day," he said. "And then the prisoner will be allowed to escape."

Jessamine hardly dared look at him when she asked, "And is he to be treated well until then?"

The major waited a moment to reply. "I understand the prisoner suffered some burns. Medical supplies should be arriving from North Carolina in the next week or so. The subject is closed now, Jessamine."

"Yes, Thomas." Closed, she thought. But alive. Lee was alive. And she would keep him so, no matter what she had to do.

Chapter Eighteen

Charlotte Dade's finely drawn eyebrows pulled together, and her Cupid's-bow mouth flattened out.

"I was disappointed with the meringue last evening, Maisie. Clarence—Mr. Dunlap—ate it, but I could tell he found it much too sweet."

"Sorry 'bout that, Miz Dade," said Maisie, letting the thin peelings from the carrots she was scraping fall into a bowl.

Charlotte picked up an orange curl. "You do wash these before you peel them, don't you?" she asked, peering at the scraping.

"I washes everything, Miz Dade," said Maisie.

The widow went to the window. "Where's that Sampson? I asked him to get the surrey ready for me over an hour ago. I'm due at the dressmakers at four o'clock. What time is it now, Maisie?"

"Don' know, Miz Dade."

As she passed the kitchen table, Charlotte picked up another carrot scraping, inspected it closely before dropping it back in the bowl and rubbing her hands together. She was just walking into the hallway when Sampson came flying through the back door.

"Mama! It's Miss Jess. She done come home, and she got Mr. Caleb with her, too. She coming up the drive right now, with that major holding the reins."

Maisie dropped her knife, wiped her hands across the bosom of her apron and stood up. Charlotte stepped back into the kitchen doorway, blocking her path.

"You needn't go to the door, Maisie. I'll see them in."

The big black woman pushed a chair out of her way. "That my baby girl comin' home, Miz Dade. Ain't you nor nobody else goin' to keep me from greetin' her."

Jessamine had to tear her eyes away from the sight of the big house in order to look back at Caleb.

"We're home, Caleb," she said. "Go ahead. Say it. Home."

"Home," he said.

"Did you hear that, Thomas? Caleb said 'home.'"

"Indeed," said the major. "You'll be an excellent mother, Jessamine. I haven't a doubt."

A shadow flitted across her face as she looked up the long drive again. There was Maisie coming down the steps, Sampson just behind her. And there, standing in the door like Lady Dade, was Charlotte. As bad as Jessamine felt, she smiled at the prospect of bidding her sister-in-law a less than fond farewell.

It had taken them over a week to get home. Thomas had driven them across Georgia to Savannah, where they had boarded a steamship for New Orleans. She'd been sick after the first hour, and Thomas's sympathy had been cool and restrained as Jessamine lay in her small bunk, not caring if she lived or died. The sole pleasant moment had been when Caleb came in, touched her cheek, and walked out.

In New Orleans the major had hired a dressmaker to put together a quick traveling suit for her. While the woman

measured Jessamine, Thomas had looked through bolts of fabric and carried his choice, a gray poplin, behind the curtain. "I believe this will..." Major Harding had fallen silent upon seeing Jessamine in only her pantaloons and corset, a measuring tape clinging around her narrow hips.

There had been a time, Jessamine thought, when the major would have blushed, stammered an apology, and turned briskly on his heel to leave. Instead, he had stood there staring, a glint as hard and bright as a diamond in his eyes. It was Jessamine who had blushed and stammered then, beneath his possessive gaze.

"Is . . . is that the fabric you've chosen, Thomas?"

She hated it. It reminded her of the rat gray dress she'd left behind on the *Delta Princess*.

His eyes had been riveted on her. He had seemed unable to speak.

"Will it be the gray, then, Major?" the dressmaker had asked as she let the tape fall from Jessamine's hips.

"The gray?" Major Harding had asked, his eyes moving from Jessamine to the woman kneeling on the floor beside her. "Oh, yes. The gray. I believe this is suitable for an officer's wife, don't you?"

"Indeed, Major," she had said. "But since the young woman isn't an officer's wife yet, I might suggest that you step out now, sir."

They'd come up to St. Louis on the *Mississippi Queen*. Once there, Thomas had rented a wagon and driven straight to the Imperial Hotel, where he'd conferred with Alpha Parker while Jessamine and Caleb waited outside in the early-July heat of the city.

"Did you see her? What did she say?" Jessamine had asked when he got back in the wagon.

"I will not discuss this with you," he'd said sharply.

It was the only time Jessamine had lost her temper. "And I won't take your abuse, Thomas. I will marry you and I will try hard to be what you want in a wife. But I will not be treated like a simpleton or a fool or a piece of dirt on the sole of your polished boot. Do you understand me?"

He had turned on her then, his blue eyes hard and cold, his copper hair fiery in the summer sun. "I understand, Jessamine. Do you understand that I am trying to forget that my love for you has made me a blackmailer and the accomplice of a murderer and his redheaded whore?"

They had barely spoken on the long drive west along the Missouri River. Jessamine thought about the price they all were paying in the name of love—what Lee had done for her, what she had done for him, the fine and honorable vision of himself the major had sullied for her sake. She never questioned that saving Lee's life was worth any price. She only hoped, that as time went by, her heart would ease.

The sight of Riverbend cheered her. She'd brought Caleb home to claim his inheritance.

"Welcome home, Miss Jess," said Sampson, helping her down from the wagon.

She threw her arms around his neck. "Oh, Sampson, it's so good to see you. And Maisie. Oh, come hug me, Maisie."

The mountainous woman swiped at her eyes. "My baby. And you done brought Mr. Caleb home. Ain't you somethin', Miss Jess. Ain't you jus' somethin'."

Charlotte met them at the door. "Jessamine," she said, kissing her on the cheek and giving a quick, disparaging look at her gray dress. She extended her hand to the major. "You look well after your long journey, Major," she said.

"Thank you, Mrs. Dade."

She patted a spit curl back in place on her forehead, then gazed at Caleb. "And this must be my dear Louis's brother, Caleb. How do you do?"

Caleb simply stared at her.

Charlotte stared back, then turned to Jessamine. "Is he all there, dear?" she whispered.

"Caleb's fine, Charlotte. He just doesn't like you," Jessamine said, walking in the front door.

Dinner that evening was unpleasant, to say the least. Jessamine had seated Caleb at the head of the table, herself at the foot. When Charlotte walked in on the arm of her frequent companion, Clarence Dunlap, she stood by the table a moment, clearly bewildered. Major Harding quickly pulled out the chair beside his. The attorney took the chair across from them.

"I've asked Maisie to fix Caleb's favorite dishes," said Jessamine from her end of the table. "I'm sure you'll enjoy this, Charlotte." She rang the little crystal bell by her water goblet, and Maisie appeared with a plate of hot biscuits and a bowl of steaming gravy. Sampson followed, with a platter of sliced ham and one of scrambled eggs.

Charlotte's nose turned up. "This is a very inappropriate meal, Jessamine. We have guests, after all."

"I only see two guests, Charlotte. You and Mr. Dunlap."

"I beg your pardon?" Charlotte's hand jerked to her throat, where her fingers twitched at an ivory brooch.

Jessamine stood beside Caleb and helped him to everything. "Here's your fork, Caleb. Maisie's fixed your favorite food. Go on and eat now."

"Jessamine has worked miracles with your brother-in-law, Mrs. Dade," said the major, helping himself to a slice of ham.

"Does he speak?" asked Clarence Dunlap.

"Say something, Caleb," commanded Jessamine.

"Caleb," he replied.

"See? Of course he speaks, Mr. Dunlap." Jessamine walked back to her chair and sat down. "Shall we discuss the ownership of Riverbend now, or would you rather wait until after dessert? We're having blueberry grunt."

Charlotte dropped her fork.

Clarence Dunlap cleared his throat. "I'll have to look into it," he said. "Considering Caleb's condition."

"What condition?" asked Jessamine innocently.

"Well, he...uh..." The attorney's face reddened.

Charlotte pushed her plate away. "I'm not afraid to say it. Caleb's an idiot. It's perfectly obvious."

Jessamine was out of her chair in an instant, and in another instant she had Charlotte by the hair. "My brother is not an idiot, Charlotte."

The major rose and unclenched Jessamine's fingers from the blond curls. "Jessamine, please, this behavior is most unbecoming," he said.

Charlotte stood up, water goblet in hand. "I have never been treated so rudely in my life," she said, "so I see no reason not to do this." She tossed the contents of the goblet directly into Jessamine's face.

There was a great howl from the head of the table, then Caleb stood up, his hands flat on each side of his plate. "Y...you," he stammered.

Everyone stared at his tortured expression. His eyes were squeezed half-shut, and his lips were pulled back, as if he were in terrible pain. He banged his fists on the table, then roared, "Y-you leave my sis-sister alone."

"Oh, Caleb," Jessamine cried. "Oh, Caleb, welcome home."

The east field was still dry when Jessamine inspected it the next morning, but there had been some rain during her absence. The hemp looked as if it could go until the next rain,

anyway. Jessamine pulled up a plant to inspect the roots. They appeared healthy enough.

"Did that derelict Eamon Dobbs come back?" she asked Sampson.

"He did. Then she kicked him out again. Don' know if he's still in Newton drinkin' or if he's gone."

"Well, we've been through droughts before, haven't we, Sampson? This isn't the worst one." Though it couldn't have happened at a worse time, she thought, with all their debts.

Sampson angled his head back toward the house. "You s'pose she gone now, Miss Jess?"

"Who, Charlotte? She said she was going as soon as Maisie got the crystal packed."

"Nasty woman, that Miz Charlotte," he said, shaking his head. "We sure glad you found Mr. Caleb."

Jessamine smiled. "I'm still waiting for Maisie to tell me she was wrong."

"Don' hol' your breath, Miss Jess. I'm still waitin' for when she was wrong ten years ago."

They walked along through the tall green plants. Jessamine remembered Maisie's words the night she'd left for St. Louis, how she'd gone on about Lee not wanting any part of her. Then she thought about all the parts of her he had claimed.

"When you and the major gettin' married, Miss Jess?"

"What?" She'd been so lost in thoughts of Lee that she had almost forgotten Sampson's presence.

"I asked you when you was plannin' on gettin' married."

"The major has gone back to his commanding officer today to discuss his tour of duty. Perhaps he'll have some idea soon."

"You be livin' here after the weddin'?"

"I don't know, Sampson. I doubt it. Whatever the major wants."

Sampson stopped, looked down at her through slatted eyes. "You ain't all a-twitter about this, Miss Jess."

"No, I'm not. But being a-twitter and doing the right thing are entirely different matters." Like the difference between heaven and hell, she thought.

"I'm thinkin' of takin' myself a bride," he said, staring down at his feet.

"Sampson! You're not!"

"You remember that pretty little Deely Jones over at the Harlan place?"

"You mean the girl with the big brown eyes and the big . . ."

Sampson nearly blushed. "Yes'm. That's Deely. She's all a-twitter about me."

"Well, it doesn't surprise me one bit," Jessamine said. "You're a tall, good-looking young man. You're smart, too, Sampson."

"Yes'm. Smart enough to know you're makin' a big mistake about this weddin', Miss Jess. Mama think so, too."

Jessamine tore a delicate leaf from a hemp plant. "I don't want to discuss it," she said. "And you can tell Maisie I said so." The less said, the better, she thought. And the sooner the wedding, the sooner Lee would be set free.

Two months after Charlotte's departure, and after weeks of near-perfect weather, Riverbend offered up a bumper crop. Jessamine was eager to dispose of it. Personally.

Caleb was leaning against the mantel in the parlor. "Absolutely not, Jessamine. Thomas is coming back from Ohio tomorrow. You two haven't seen each other in almost two months. You'll have a lot of catching up to do. And you're

going to be busy planning your wedding. Too busy to be worrying about selling some hemp."

Jessamine dropped her hands in her lap. "Caleb Dade, sometimes I wish you hadn't found your tongue."

"Well, I had some help," he said. "I have expressed my undying gratitude, haven't I, sister?"

"About twice a day," Jessamine said with a smile. Then she frowned. "Caleb, you don't know the first thing about the hemp market. Please let me..."

"I'm learning, Jessamine. And the answer is no. You stay here and plan that wedding of yours."

"There's nothing to plan. We'll just marry and have done with it."

"I thought all brides-to-be dreamed of fancy trousseaux and romantic honeymoons," he said.

"Not all." Besides, Jessamine thought, I've already had my honeymoon—three days in a brothel in Georgia.

"Are you well, Jessamine? You haven't been very cheerful since we've been home, haven't even had a temper tantrum. I've barely heard you yell at Maisie."

"I've grown up since you left for the war, Caleb. Grown-ups don't go around giggling all the time, or screaming and yelling. And don't forget I'm about to become an officer's wife. I must be cognizant of my place in society."

Caleb laughed, his violet eyes sparkling. "Your place in society, my ass. I was in New Orleans, if you'll recall, when you took your place in society by running away and then attending the ball with some handsome devil twice your age."

"Oh, Caleb," she said, tears filling her eyes.

"What'd I say to upset you, Jess?"

"Nothing. You just reminded me of happier times, that's all."

* * *

Maisie pulled the sheets off the bed. "Miss Jess, that the third day in a row you done throwed up your breakfast. If I didn't know better..."

Jessamine closed her eyes and held a cool cloth to her forehead. "Oh, hush, Maisie. I just want to die. Leave me alone."

Maisie cocked her head, put her big hands on her hips. "You and the major done spent any time 'tween the sheets, Miss Jess?"

"Maisie! Good Lord, no."

"Well, then, you is the first virgin since ol' Mary to be with child. 'Cause that what you is, Miss Jess. I seen all the signs."

"Well, it's impossible," Jessamine said. "It just isn't true. Oh, Lord, Maisie, where's that pail? I'm going to do it again."

"Oh, yes, you is, child," murmured Maisie as she stroked her hair while Jessamine threw up.

"Anyone home? I knocked and nobody—" Major Harding rushed into the room. "My dearest, what's wrong? Are you ill?"

Jessamine coughed. "No, I'm all right, Thomas."

He looked at Maisie. "How long has she been ill, Maisie? Has the doctor been here?"

"She been doin' this awhile, Major. We ain't sent for the doc."

"Well, I believe we should."

Jessamine began to tell him not to, but then she got sick again.

"I would never forgive myself, Jessamine, if you were seriously ill and I just stood by and did nothing. Where is the nearest doctor, Maisie?"

"That'd be Doc Ferguson over in Newton, Major."

"I'll have him back here within the hour," he said, striding from the room.

Jessamine's curse echoed inside the pail.

"I feel fine now," Jessamine protested as Doc Ferguson eased himself onto the edge of the bed, taking her wrist in his hand.

The white-haired doctor was quiet a moment, his lips moving, as he felt the pulse in her wrist. He pressed his hand flat against her forehead. "Nice and cool," he murmured.

"I told you—"

Maisie swatted Jessamine's leg under the sheet. "You jus' be still and let the doc be 'bout his business."

Jessamine glared at her.

"Open your mouth, Miss Jessamine, and let me have a look inside. That's it. Turn a little toward the window. Uh-huh."

"What you see, doc?" asked Maisie.

"A tongue, Maisie. Plenty of good teeth."

Jessamine glared at Maisie again. "See. I'm fine."

"Now you just lie back, Miss Jessamine, and I'm going to poke around on your tummy a little bit. I won't hurt you." He pressed his fingers into her abdomen, moved them farther down. "That hurt you any?" he asked.

"No," she said.

Doc Ferguson scratched his head, then crossed his arms. "Your bosom been tender of late, Miss Jessamine?"

She didn't answer, but stared at her feet beneath the sheet.

"How about your monthlies? You been having them or not? Answer me, Miss Jessamine."

She averted her eyes.

"You answer him, Miss Jess," said Maisie. "An' you tell the doc the truth now."

"No, I haven't. Not July, August or September."

"Uh-huh," he said. He slapped his crooked hands down on his knees. "You coulda done this, Maisie. Don't know what that soldier was in such an all-fired hurry to get me out here for." He stood up. "You're gonna have a baby, Miss Jessamine. I expect you'll be calling me out here next March sometime."

Maisie swatted her leg again. "What I tell you, Miss Jess?"

"I'm going downstairs now," Doc Ferguson said. "You don't have to stay in bed, Miss Jessamine, unless you feel like it. You aren't sick."

When Doc Ferguson opened the door, he walked directly into the major, who had been pacing outside the bedroom.

"Is it serious, doctor?" Major Harding asked.

"I'd say having children is a most serious endeavor, son," the doctor said. "Congratulations."

The major's face expressed his complete shock and bewilderment.

"It's always a shock the first time," the doctor said. "'Course, if I were you, I'd move the wedding day up a bit. But I wouldn't let it distress me none. Hell, half the people in this county carried a baby down the aisle."

The late-afternoon sun slanted through Jessamine's window as she heard hoofbeats approaching the front steps and recognized Pepper's distinctive snort. She heard Thomas's boots on the steps, then on the stairs, before he knocked on her bedroom door.

"Come in, Thomas," she said. She was propped up in bed, not because she didn't feel well enough to get up, but because it seemed the best place to hide for a while, to hide and place her hand on her belly, touching Lee's child.

The major carried his hat in his hand. He walked in like a stranger paying a sick call under duress. His face was flushed, and his eyes were red.

"Are you feeling better?" he asked awkwardly.

"I'm feeling fine. I'm not ill, Thomas."

"Yes. I know."

There was a horrible silence between them—horrible for Jessamine, who had no idea what to expect, and horrible, she assumed, for the major, judging from the twisted expression on his face and the moisture clouding his eyes.

He took her hand, then dropped it. "I can't marry you, Jessamine. I've agonized over this. It wasn't an easy decision, believe me. But I simply can't do it."

She sat up straighter. "But, Thomas, what about—?"

He paced along the side of the bed. "I can't be a father to another man's child. I would forever be resentful, perhaps even cruel, knowing as I do who the father is." He stopped pacing, and his eyes at last met hers. "How you could allow yourself to submit to the craven attentions of such a beast, I'll never know. I'm... I'm extremely disappointed, Jessamine."

Was she free? she wondered. Jessamine's heart leapt at the very idea. Free of the gray future that marriage to him meant to her? But what about Lee? The two thousand in gold was to reach Colonel Grove on their wedding day. She was afraid to ask. She was afraid of the answer, afraid she'd have to get down on her knees and plead with him to marry her.

"I'm sorry, Thomas. I'm sorry to have disappointed you so. But... well, what about..."

He laughed bitterly, using a knuckle to brush a tear from his cheek. "Our bargain, Jessamine? Is that what you're asking me?" He began pacing again, or rather stalking from one end of the bed to the other. "Our little pact with the

devil and his whore? It fell apart a week after we left Georgia.''

"What are you saying, Thomas?" She stared at him, at the sudden brutal twist of his mouth, the hard blue of his eyes.

"Your lover escaped from Coulterville before any money changed hands, Jessamine. Mrs. Parker informed me by letter. He arrived in St. Louis not long after our return to Riverbend."

"That's not possible," she said. Lee would have come to Riverbend if he had escaped.

"Not possible, Jessamine, because you can't believe he wouldn't come for you? You think the father of this child loved you, do you?" he spit. "Let me tell you how much he loved you, my dear. Mrs. Parker's letter informing me of his escape also informed me that the rebel had finally made an honest woman of her. They were married soon after his return."

"I don't believe you," she said.

"I have her letter, if you'd like to see it."

"I still wouldn't believe it," she said.

"Believe whatever you wish. It doesn't matter. He won't be coming for you." He bent and kissed the crown of her head. "I did love you, Jessamine. I wish you well—you and the unfortunate child."

When the door closed behind him, Jessamine curled her body around the child within her and wept.

It was true. Oh, God, it was true. If Lee had loved her, he would have come to her. What had ever made her think he did? He had never said he loved her. He had never spoken of a future with her. They had lived in the moment, for the moment.

And now he was married to the woman he had been in love with for so many years. The hurt of losing him was as

keen as it had been the day she had ridden away from the prison with Thomas.

But this child. His child. Jessamine curled tighter, protecting it. This child was all she had, all she would ever have, of Lee.

Chapter Nineteen

Nora Fleming got out of her hansom cab in front of the Imperial Hotel and adjusted the fox skins around her neck. Giving the doorman such a look that he wouldn't have dared bar the way of St. Louis's most infamous madam, she opened the door herself and strode to the registration desk.

She gave the desk clerk the same menacing look.

"May I help you, Mrs. Fleming?" he asked with icy politeness.

Nora whisked off her black kid glove and tapped a long red fingernail on the marble counter. "You get Alpha Parker, and you get her now," she said.

The clerk's Adam's apple bobbed as he swallowed. "Mrs. Parker is on the *Delta Princess* this morning. It's tied up at—"

"I know where the hell it is," she said, turning and striding outside, with one more glare for the doorman.

Moments later she stalked up the gangplank of the *Delta Princess*. When she failed to see anyone around, she stood on the first deck and yelled, "Alpha Parker, I'm looking for you."

Alpha lifted her head from Deuce Barnett's bare shoulder. "What the hell does she want?" Alpha snarled.

Deuce parted the curtain of her tumbled hair to reveal her face, its sensual flush now heightened by anger. "Better go see, Red. Nora's liable to yell the paint right off the decks," he said.

"Alpha!" Nora bellowed again.

With only a bed sheet around her, Alpha shoved open the window on the third deck. "Hold your damn horses, Nora!" she called. She tossed the sheet over Deuce and stalked around the small cabin, gathering up her lace undergarments, shaking out each one with a blistering curse.

"What the devil are you smiling at?" she asked as she looked at the aging gambler, seeing the upturned lips nearly hidden by the gray of his beard and mustache. Alpha could remember when those rough whiskers had been black as midnight, making Deuce Barnett the meanest looking gambler on the Mississippi—or any other river, for that matter. She preferred the gray. It gentled him somehow.

"I'm smiling at you, Red," he said in his whiskey-deep voice as his eyes roved over her shapely form. "You're one hell of a woman, you know that? And I'm waiting with great anticipation for an answer to my question."

Alpha frowned as she adjusted the stays of her corset. "You've been asking me to marry you for going on twenty years, Deuce. Seems to me your anticipation ought to be a little frayed at the cuffs by now."

"Nope," he said. "Nothing's changed. My heart still goes pitty-pat each time I look at you." He drummed his fingers on the soft gray hairs of his chest.

"Oh, hell, Deuce. You're either blind or the biggest damn fool on the Mississippi River. Everything's changed. These past few years, with the war and all... I don't know." Alpha stabbed her arms into the sleeves of her apricot silk dress. "The hotels aren't doing the business they used to. The riverboats lose ten passengers for every railroad spike

they drive. I don't know what we're going to do. It just about kills me to see all this go under.''

"It's killing you to see the boy go under," Deuce said quietly.

"The boy," Alpha murmured, straightening the seams of her long sleeves. "Wonder if you'll ever stop calling Lee that."

"Prob'ly not. Just like I'll never stop calling you the prettiest girl in all creation."

Alpha shook her head, smiling, then felt her mouth pull down once more.

Deuce pummeled a pillow and stuffed it behind his head, then crossed his arms over his chest. "How many times has the boy asked you to marry him, Alpha?"

She threw him a black look. "You know the answer to that. Never."

"How many times have I asked you? You can't even answer that, can you, 'cause you don't have enough fingers or pretty little toes to keep count. What does that tell you? Which one of us do you think loves you more, Red? Me or the boy?"

"Lee needs me now," she said, doing up the two small mother-of-pearl buttons on her collar. "I've never seen him this low. Not even right after the war."

"He needs somebody, all right, but it's not you, Red. It's that dead girl, that Bessie or Jessie or whatever the hell her name was. It's her that's pulling him right into the grave."

Alpha's full lips trembled. "I did a terrible thing, Deuce, telling him she was dead. I never thought he'd take it so hard. I thought..."

"You thought he'd finally get around to asking something he hasn't asked in all these years."

"Only he didn't," she said, wiping a tear from her cheek.

Deuce reached for her hand to draw her down on the bed. "Only he didn't," he echoed softly. "He loves you, Red, but it's not that special love that makes a man want to just pluck out his heart and place it in a woman's hands." He pressed her palm over his heart. "Take my heart, Red. I'm asking you again."

The redhead blinked through her tears. "I've done something terrible, Deuce. I know I'll go to hell for it."

"Honey, on judgment day, old Saint Peter's gonna take one look at you, then take your hand and say, 'Come along, Miss Red. Let's you and me go sit on that cloud awhile, just the two of us.'"

Alpha laughed wetly. "You old coot. I do love you. But I have done something awful. That girl, that Jessie, she isn't dead, Deuce." Alpha searched his eyes for his reaction.

"Go ahead, honey," he said softly. "Get it all out."

"I made a bargain with this soldier who wanted to marry the girl himself. He wanted Lee out of her life as much as I wanted little Miss Pansy Eyes out of Lee's. I had him write me a letter telling how she died. He wrote it right at the desk in my suite in the hotel, while the girl was sitting outside in a wagon waiting for him. I helped him with some of the details. He posted it later from a town called Newton. I knew Lee wouldn't just take my word for it if I told him she was dead. I had to have something for proof."

Alpha's voice dropped to a whisper. "He cried like a baby when he read it. Oh, Deuce, I felt so bad, but it was too late then. I only did it because I wanted him to get her out of his heart. I never meant to hurt him so bad."

The bearded gambler stroked her hand. "You've got to set things right by him, honey. And right away, too. You want ol' Deuce to come with you?"

Alpha looked at him then as if she were seeing him for the first time. "Yes," she said. "I need you, Deuce. You know I do."

Deuce laughed from deep within his chest and wrapped his arms around her. "Well, of course you do, Red. I been tellin' you that for years."

The sound of Nora's voice floated up to them. "Alpha Parker, you get your talcum-powdered ass out here now."

It was the middle of November, but Indian summer had turned the sky a bright, deep blue and the sun was golden and hot. Deuce and the two women walked up the herringbone-brick path to the front door of Nora Fleming's gaudy limestone mansion, with its turreted corners and fanciful gargoyle drainpipes. Nora yanked off her circle of fox skins halfway up the path and let them drag on the walk.

"You shoot those critters yourself, Nora?" asked Deuce from behind her.

Alpha gave him a twinkling grin, and Nora tossed her hennaed curls and stuck her nose in the air.

"I remember you, Deuce Barnett, when you were twenty years old and didn't have two nickels to rub together," she said tartly.

"Prob'ly 'cause I kept giving those nickels to you and Red," he said.

Nora snorted. "That was a long time ago."

"We're not getting any younger, that's for damn sure," said Deuce, climbing up the steps to the front porch.

With her hand on the doorknob, Nora turned to both of them. The hard slant of her mouth softened. "You have to get him out of here," she said. "He's drinking my cellar dry. He started a fire in bed with one of his damn cigars, then he bloodied the noses of Cletus and Mack both when they tried to escort him to the door. And my girls all feel so damn

sorry for him that they're walking around all sniffly and red-eyed half the time. This isn't a house of pleasure anymore. It's a goddamn funeral parlor." Nora shrugged her shoulders helplessly. "I know he's grieving, damn it, and it pains me to see him that way, but Lee Kincannon is ruining my business, and I want the son of a bitch out. Now."

She opened the door into a dark paneled vestibule with a marble floor and a wide, sweeping staircase. A stained-glass window on the landing cast a jeweled light on the glossy marble stairs.

Deuce sucked in his breath. "Damn, you two girls have done all right for yourselves, haven't you?"

Alpha and Nora exchanged the smallest of smiles before Nora pointed up the stairs.

"There," she said. "The door to the left of that cranberry-glass lamp. He's got it locked from the inside. At least he did when I left."

"Is he alone?" asked Alpha.

"He's the most alone man I ever saw," Nora said.

Alpha rapped on the walnut-paneled door. There was no answer. She rapped again with her gloves off. "Lee, it's Alpha. Open the door."

From the other side of the door, Lee slurred, "Leave me alone, Red."

Alpha and Deuce looked at each other.

Deuce stepped forward and banged his fist on the wood, then bellowed in his deepest, whiskiest tone. "Lee. It's Deuce. You hear me, boy? Open up."

"Go away."

Deuce pounded again. "You don't want me to put my shoulder to this, do you? I'm gettin' too old to be breakin' down doors. But I will. We're comin' in, one way or the other, you hear?"

They heard a glass shatter, then the key as it rasped in the lock, and a bolt as it was rammed back. Deuce twisted the knob, and Alpha preceeded him into the room.

She sighed. "Aw, Lee."

The room looked as if a tornado had come in the door and gone out the window, leaving havoc behind. There were two broken brandy snifters on the floor, empty bottles and burned-out cigars, one of them with a charred line of carpet beneath it. The red satin drapes hung loose, their tie-backs undone. The red velvet tester above the bed drooped like bunting down one side. Below that, white linens were bunched up in the middle of the scorched, brandy-stained mattress, as well as the ripped ticking of several empty pillows. Feathers were everywhere.

"Damn," murmured Deuce, leaning against the door-frame.

Lee sat on the edge of the bed, his elbows on his knees, trying to light a cigar. He broke two wooden matches before the third one blazed under his thumb. His hands trembled so violently that he could barely touch the flame to the end of the cigar.

With a cool hand, Alpha steadied the match, caressed his unruly hair and picked a feather or two out of the dark curls. He muttered something she couldn't understand. "What, honey?" she asked, touching his unshaven cheek.

"I'm not leaving, Red. You tell Nora I said so. I plan to stay. Here. Sitting in a whorehouse all the goddamn day."

"You can't stay here, Lee. Come on. Let me take you home." Alpha took his elbow, but he wrenched it out of her grasp.

"Leave me alone, Red."

Deuce pushed himself off the doorframe. "She is going to leave you alone, boy. Red's going to marry me, just as soon as we can find a preacher. Now you get yourself to-

gether. She's not going to be around to run your hotels and boats for you like she's done all these years.''

Lee turned his bloodshot eyes on Deuce. ''What took you so long, old man?'' he asked, attempting a grin.

''I had a little competition,'' Deuce said dryly. ''Now, Red, you've got something you want to tell this boy, don't you?''

The redhead knelt before Lee, her hands on his knees, and he shifted his bleary gaze to her upturned face.

''Congratulations, Red.'' He reached out a trembling hand to brush a tear from her cheek. ''I couldn't love you enough, you know. Just not near enough, honey.''

''I know that now, Lee,'' she said as more tears fell. ''We had our good times though, didn't we?''

He nodded.

She reached up to pluck a feather off his shirtfront. ''What are you doing with all these damn feathers, darlin'?'' she whispered.

Lee closed his eyes. ''Remembering a snowfall in Georgia,'' he said huskily.

''Go ahead, Red,'' urged Deuce. ''You say what you have to.''

''I lied to you, Lee,'' she said.

''Doesn't matter now, Alpha. You go on and be happy. Both of you.''

She got up further on her knees, leaning closer to his face, demanding his attention. ''Lee, I lied to you about the girl—about Jessie.''

He looked at her without expression, his mouth slack and his eyes blank.

Alpha pressed her lips together, then continued. ''She didn't die of a fever like I said. That letter was nothing but a pack of lies. I had that major write it, 'cause I knew you wouldn't take my word all by itself.'' A tear slid down

Alpha's cheek. "I wanted you to forget her. I wanted to get her out of your heart, and I thought if you thought she was dead, you could forget." She stroked his hair. "But you can't. I see that now. And I'm so sorry, Lee. I'm just so damn sorry."

Still, Lee just stared at her.

"Alpha is telling you your Jessie is alive, boy," said Deuce.

"She's alive," said Alpha. "I can't say whether she married that high-hat of a major or not, but I do know the girl didn't die."

Lee's voice was hoarse. "Where is she?"

"That I don't know," answered Alpha.

"Why don't you just clean up and go find her, boy?" grumbled Deuce. "Shouldn't be too hard for a fella as sharp as you—findin' one little girl in this big ol' country."

Lee bent his head. His shoulders began to shake, and his breath became ragged. Before Alpha could reach out for him, Deuce took her by the arm and led her toward the door.

"We'll be waitin' for you outside, boy," he said softly.

She isn't dead. Jessie isn't dead. Alpha's words sounded again and again through the thick brandy haze inside his brain—like the sweet, throaty whistle of a riverboat moving through dense fog. His last clear memory was of reading the major's letter telling how Jessie had succumbed to a fever on the way home from Georgia. After that, he hadn't cared anymore. About anyone or anything.

He stood up and walked gingerly to the window, surprised to see the bright sunshine and deep azure sky. What the hell? Had he drunk himself clear through autumn and winter and into the next year's spring?

The sharp light hurt his eyes so he leaned his head against the window frame, remembering his last glimpse of Jessie in her tattered red dress as she'd clambered over the wagon seat to sit beside her major. After that—because he was burned and blistered and could already feel the noose around his neck—his thoughts of Jessie had been a stew of despair and desolate desire.

But those emotions had fueled his escape and driven him back to St. Louis at a reckless pace. He intended to go to Riverbend and— And then Alpha put the letter in his hand.

A lie! Lee opened his eyes again. Or maybe they were lying to him now, bringing his Jessie from her little grave just long enough to get him out of Nora's place. It didn't really matter, he thought. Either way—alive or dead—he was going to be with her soon. And forever.

Chapter Twenty

The bacon wasn't done quite to Jessamine's liking. The wavy ribbon of fat was still glistening and a little too transparent. But when she saw Maisie pulling the last pillowcase off the line and snapping it as if to scare the very wrinkles out of it, Jessamine took the four strips of bacon from the cast-iron skillet and plopped them on the bread, which was already slathered with apple butter. She placed another slice of bread on top, hunkered down at the kitchen table and bit into it, letting the soft bread shield her tongue and the roof of her mouth from the hot bacon grease.

Maisie saw her through the window, so by the time the big woman wrestled her laundry basket through the back door she was already well into a snit.

"Is you eatin' more lard, Miss Jess?" she asked, then looked at the greasy skillet on the cast-iron stove. "You is," she said.

Jessamine continued to chew, her eyes nearly closed with the pleasure of satisfying her craving, her mouth delighting in the salty heat of the bacon and the cool sweetness of the apple butter.

Maisie dropped her basket on the table with a resounding thump. "You know what's gonna happen to you, don't you?"

Jessamine, unable to speak, raised a curious eyebrow.

"You're gonna turn into one o' them swine layin' on a platter with a apple stuffed right in your mouth. That baby o' yours prob'ly already done turned into a squealin' pig." Maisie stalked to the stove, curved her apron over her hand, and removed the hot skillet. "I's gonna hide this, Miss Jess. An' don' you be looking for it neither. Or fryin' up pork fat in one o' them other pans."

Jessamine took another glorious bite, and another. When she was done she licked her fingers, and her lips for the last dab of salt. "Didn't you ever have cravings, Maisie, when you were carrying Sampson?"

Maisie shook out a pillowcase and began to fold it. "No. I et what was good for me an' that boy, an' he done turned out awright, too. Your child's gonna be a little porker, Miss Jess, with apple butter for a brain."

Jessamine was wishing she had cooked eight pieces of bacon rather than four. Sighing, she got up from the table, searched through the laundry in Maisie's basket, and pulled out a large white bath sheet.

"I'll be home about sunset, Maisie. If Caleb wants his supper early, you just go ahead without me," Jessamine said, heading out the door.

Maisie dogged Jessamine's heels down the hall. "Where you goin' with that bath sheet?" she demanded.

"Swimming, Maisie. It's such a fine day, and I can just hear Chinaman's Branch calling to me." She made a trumpet of her hands. "Hey, you, Jessamine! Wouldn't a nice cool swim feel good on this hot old day?"

"It's November, Miss Jess," Maisie reminded her sternly.

"It's ninety degrees, Maisie," said Jessamine.

"You cain't do no swimmin' in your condition."

"Why ever not?" asked Jessamine, looking in the gilded mirror over the library table and tying the chin ribbon of her

straw hat into a big blue bow. "I'm so fat I expect I'll float like a big old pink balloon."

"You jus' wait til Mr. Caleb get home an' you ask him why not," said Maisie.

Caleb stepped into the vestibule from the front parlor. "Mr. Caleb is home. What's all this hollering?" He looked from his sister's calm expression to the black woman's frenzied face.

"Miss Jess is plannin' on traipsin' down to Chinaman's Branch for a swim, that's what the hollerin' is," said Maisie, throwing up her hands. "You go on an' handle her, Mr. Caleb. I's goin' back to my kitchen."

"A swim, Jessamine?" he asked, raising an eyebrow.

"A swim, Caleb." She folded the bath sheet with deliberation and placed it on the library table, then stood with her fists on her hips, her violet eyes locked on her brother's.

"Do you think that's wise? Walking all the way to Chinaman's Branch in your...well, with your..."

"With what, Caleb?" she snapped. In the two months since Doc Ferguson had happily pronounced her pregnant, Caleb had been silent on the subject. He had been sweet to her, even solicitous of her health, insisting that she get her rest while he took over the entire running of Riverbend, from clearing ten acres of bottomland for next years wheat to tuck-pointing the chimneys.

"With what?" she repeated. "With my dress pulling away at the seams and my stomach sticking out? Are you afraid I'll pass somebody on the road and they'll cluck their tongues and say what an awful girl your sister is?" She had, in fact, endured such a scene only the week before, in Newton, when Charlotte—now Mrs. Clarence Dunlap—had passed her on the sidewalk. Jessamine's voice broke. "Oh, Caleb, are you so ashamed of me?"

He wrapped his arms around her. "Oh, my sweet sister, no. I was only worried about the distance, and about your swimming all alone. I don't give a tinker's damn what people might say or think." He hugged her hard. "And I could never be ashamed of a sister who brought me back to life after everybody else gave me up for dead."

"I love you, Caleb," Jessamine said, hugging him back. "Uncle Caleb! Won't Riverbend be a wonderful place when there's a child tearing around?"

He laughed. "I confess I'm looking forward to it, Jess."

"I'm glad," she said.

"Why not let me walk with you at least part of the way to the branch? For company, if nothing else."

"You get back to your books, Uncle Caleb," she said, her hand resting on the outcropping of her skirt. "I have all the company I need right here."

"Where are you sneaking off to, Sampson?" Jessamine said teasingly when she encountered him coming around the side of the barn, dressed in a crisp white shirt and carrying a fistful of crimson sumac.

"Well, Miss Jess, when Mr. Caleb went in to do his figures, he said to me, 'Sampson, it's too pretty a day not to go see that Deely of yours,' so that's where I'm headed."

She put her arm through his. "I'm headed for Chinaman's Branch. I'll walk partway with you."

They walked in silence for a while, enjoying the unseasonable warmth of the sun and the soft breeze blowing from the south.

"When are you and Deely planning to marry, Sampson?" she asked, holding her big straw hat against the tug of the breeze.

"Deely wants a Christmas wedding, though I'd just as soon get it over and done with."

"Did Maisie tell you I asked Caleb and he agrees that the front parlor would make a lovely wedding chapel? We'd like to share in your happiness, Sampson. Yours and Deely's."

"That's kind of you, Miss Jess. Deely will be thrilled down to her toes to be married at a fine place like Riverbend."

"Then it's all settled. You tell her to come see me one day soon and we'll make some plans."

They reached the dirt road that led on to the Harlan place, where Deely lived. Sampson took Jessamine's hands in his.

"You lookin' fit and happy these days, Miss Jess," he said.

"I am, Sampson. Maybe more fit than happy, but I'm feeling fine."

"Maybe you be usin' that front parlor as a chapel yo'self one of these days."

Jessamine shook her head. "No. I won't ever marry, Sampson. I plan on just raising my child and looking after Caleb. I'm sure that will keep me well occupied."

"You never know, Miss Jess. That what Mama always says. Each day be a whole different day from the last. The sun never do come up the same way twice, 'spite of what most folks think."

She watched as he turned up Deely's road, his stride long, the feathered red sumac branches swinging at his side. Jessamine was happy that Sampson still regarded life as a series of sunrises. For herself, it seemed more like a prolonged twilight, with the exception of a few lovely afternoons like these.

Lee shifted his weight on to his right leg. Caleb Dade was going on at length about the war—stressing the fact that he and Lee had been enemies in name only, blue against gray, never Caleb against Lee. And when Caleb proceeded to thank him for saving his life, Lee could hardly stand still.

Maisie had told him Jessamine was swimming about a mile and a half away.

He was about to interrupt the talkative Caleb when Maisie did it for him.

"Mr. Lee, Miss Jess done forgot her bath sheet. You don't mind takin' it to her, do you?" She handed him the folded sheet.

"Not at all, Maisie." He took it from her. "Well, I best be on my way before Jessie gets out of the water and freezes her...well, before she takes a chill."

"It's good to finally shake the hand of the man who nearly broke my jaw," said Caleb with a smile.

"Miss Jess gonna be mighty surprised to see you, Mr. Lee," Maisie said. Then she added, "An' you gonna be mighty surprised when you sees her, too."

Caleb interrupted her with a withering look. "All right, Maisie. Let's just let the man get on his way, shall we?"

His coal black thoroughbred couldn't take the road fast enough to suit him, but the day was so hot that Lee felt obliged to slow him to a walk as he neared the swimming hole. He was so close to Jessamine now, he could afford some restraint.

He'd lost his courage back at the house, though, with Caleb and Maisie. He hadn't been able to bring himself to ask them about Major Harding. And now, as his stallion ambled down the road, Lee decided he was in no rush at all to discover that Jessamine was betrothed or, worse, married.

His head was clear, and he felt strong. He'd slept for a full twenty-four hours after Red and Deuce had gotten him out of Nora's and back to the hotel. Then he'd eaten a blood-red steak, washing it down with a tall glass of chilly water. He'd had a bath and a shave, and then a little family dinner with Red and Deuce in the main salon of the *Delta Prin-*

cess, which Deuce had sold earlier that afternoon to the Northern Mississippi Steamship Line.

"They're gonna take her upriver, poor ol' girl," Deuce had announced over dinner. "She'll freeze her pretty stern off, runnin' from St. Paul to Dubuque."

Deuce had been preparing to leave the next day for San Francisco. Alpha was to follow, after she took care of all the paperwork for the sale of the hotels in New Orleans, Memphis and St. Louis, and the two remaining riverboats. Lee had been adamant that they split the profits fifty-fifty.

"Hell, Red," he'd told her, "if it hadn't been for you, I'd have sold the *Delta Star* for a quick thousand and lost it all to some four-flusher the very next day."

Alpha hadn't disagreed. She'd raised her wine goblet. "To us," she'd said, her eyes pausing on Lee with a hazy mixture of longing and regret before settling on Deuce with love.

Lee had set out for Riverbend just before dawn the next day.

Jessamine gripped the limb of a fallen sycamore, and with her face in the water let her body float quietly for a moment, enjoying the feeling of lightness that her swelling body had begun to deny her.

She had spent a long time just paddling and splashing in the creek, talking to the child within her, teaching him how to backstroke, describing the brilliant sapphire of the sky overhead, telling him how when he was old enough she'd take him on a picnic to the bank of the wide Missouri. She told him how the Missouri flowed east to meet the big Mississippi, and how the Mississippi rolled on to New Orleans and the Gulf of Mexico.

Jessamine hadn't decided what she'd tell him about his daddy. But she had years to go till he even thought to inquire, and she hoped that by then she would know exactly

what to say. Hoped that by then her heart would have healed enough not to tear apart when she spoke about it.

She kicked her legs again, laughing out loud, wanting to prolong this lovely Indian-summer day, to treasure it, for by next week the skies over Riverbend might be leaden and heavy with snow, and she might have to stay indoors.

"You best get out of that water before you get all wrinkled like a prune, Jessie."

Her heart held still. She turned her head to the gravelly bank of the river branch, where Lee was standing—tall, lean, clad in black, and booted like a French marquis. There was a warm rush through her body, and then she sharply reminded herself that he was now somebody else's husband. He held out the bath sheet for her.

"Come on, Jessie," he urged.

"Isn't it customary to say hello to somebody you haven't seen in five months?" she asked, trying to keep her heartbeat from drumming in her words.

He squatted down on his haunches. "Hello, Jessie."

"Hello, Lee," she said, and began kicking at the water again, just to distract her feet from their desire to run to him.

"You look beautiful, Jessie, with your pretty backside all gleaming in the water and the sun."

Good Lord, she hadn't even thought about that. Then Jessamine realized her true predicament. She was far from the slim little girl Lee had last seen in Georgia. Her bosom wouldn't even fit in a corset anymore, and her stomach... Well, she just wouldn't get out of the water. At least not until it was dark. There was nothing else she could do.

"What brings you out to Riverbend?" she asked, forcing a casual note into her voice.

Lee took off his hat, tossed it and caught it again twisting the brim through his fingers. "Well, it was such a fine morning that I took a notion to go out riding. I was trotting along, admiring the colors of all the trees and the bright golden sunshine and the long strings of geese flapping their way south, and the next thing I knew, here I was."

She frowned. Happy as she was to see him—thrilled to her toes as she was—this couldn't be good. It wasn't right. Lee was married to Alpha now. He had no business toying with another woman.

"So," she said with false brightness, "here you are."

"Come on out of the water, Jessie," he said, a bit more forcefully than the last time.

"I haven't finished my swim yet, Lee."

"How long do you intend to stay in there?"

"Oh, I don't know. Quite a while, I should imagine."

Lee pulled his long legs out from their squatting position and sat, Indian-style. His patience was real, nearly as tangible as the white sheet in his hand. His Jessie was very much alive, and it was enough for now just to gaze at her, drink her in. Better than the finest brandy, he thought. More necessary to him than water itself, or even air. "I'll wait," he said pleasantly. "I love just looking at you, Jessie. Your pretty little rump, with the water lapping at it. Your pearly white spine. Your—"

"Stop it, Lee. Married people shouldn't be having conversations like this."

Lee's joyous grin slid right off his face. "Oh, hell, Jessie. Damnation! Why'd you do it?"

"I didn't do anything," she said.

"You said married people shouldn't be talking this way."

"You shouldn't," she said. "It isn't right."

"I shouldn't!" Lee said, outraged, dejected, and now thoroughly confused. "I'm not the one who's married."

"You're not ... but Thomas said ..." Now it was Jessamine's turn to be bewildered.

Lee picked up a handful of gravel and threw it toward the water. "And I suppose you believe whatever your husband tells you, Jessie, as every good little wife should."

"My husband?"

"Well, that's what he is, isn't he?"

"Who?"

"Your husband, goddamn it!" he yelled.

"I don't have a husband, Lee. I'm not married. You're the one who's married, or have you forgotten?" she yelled back.

Lee stood up. "Jessie, last time I looked, I wasn't married."

She held still in the water. "You and Alpha Parker ... you aren't ... you didn't ...?"

"Hell, no. She's going to California, with my blessings," Lee said. "You aren't married to your major, then? Or betrothed?"

A slow smile began to spread across her mouth. "I keep telling you he's not *my* major," she said. "And anyway, he abandoned me."

"I always knew that bluebelly was a fool," snarled Lee.

Jessamine felt light as a feather as she floated on the water. "Well, he had his reasons, Lee. One in particular."

Lee picked up the bath sheet. The patience he had enjoyed earlier had been obliterated by his need to hold her in his arms. "Jessie, you come out of that water right this minute. I want to wrap this around you, and then wrap me around you so tight you can't breathe."

She didn't need to breathe, she thought as she tucked her knees in and got ready to stand up. "Do you love me, Lee?" she asked. She had to know, needed to be sure that it was love, not duty, and that Lee was free to be hers, not forced.

"Jessie, I love you so much I'm about to ruin a good pair of boots by coming in there and getting you."

"Don't be flippant," she said. "Tell me properly." Her heart was soaring.

Lee's expression turned serious. "I love you, Jessie, with all my heart, with all my blighted soul, with every yearning inch of my worn-out body." He lifted the bath sheet. "My flag of surrender, darlin'." Lee bowed his head dramatically. "Another gallant rebel bites the dust."

Jessamine forced her legs not to run, made herself stay under the water when every muscle, every fiber of her being, cried out to race into his arms. "Is that a proposal of marriage, Lee Kincannon?" she asked.

Lee splayed his hand over his heart. "For want of further eloquence, Miss Jessamine, yes. You may consider that a proposal of marriage," he said.

"Well, in that case..." She gathered her legs beneath her and began to stand. The water rushed off her shoulders, and Lee smiled. The water slipped over her swollen breasts, and he stared. The water at last washed over her distended belly, and he gaped as the muscles of his legs lost their strength and his knees gave way and he dropped to them.

Jessamine walked up the gravelly riverbank toward him. Her heart was whole again. She knew because it was beating wildly, as only a whole heart could. She was alive again. Truly and completely.

Lee slid his arms around her, pressing his face into her swollen belly. Jessamine threaded her fingers through his dark, curly hair, glorying in the feel of it.

"Jessie, Jessie," he murmured against her skin.

She slipped to the ground, fitting her body to his. Their lips met in a slow, luxurious kiss. "Oh, Lee, I'm alive again," she murmured, her violet eyes meeting his.

"Twice alive, Jessie," he said, his hand moving to feel the life inside her. "And so am I," Lee whispered, "Jessie, Jessie, so am I."

* * * * *

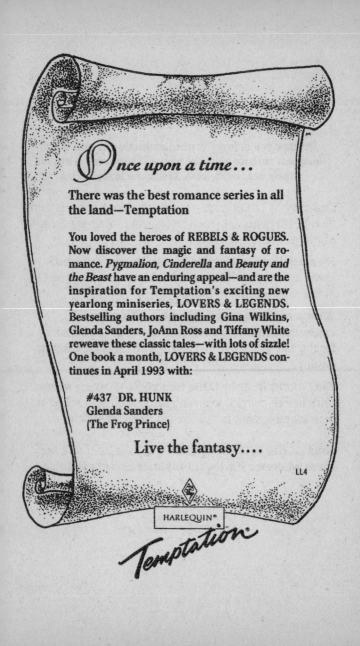

Once upon a time...

There was the best romance series in all the land—Temptation

You loved the heroes of REBELS & ROGUES. Now discover the magic and fantasy of romance. *Pygmalion*, *Cinderella* and *Beauty and the Beast* have an enduring appeal—and are the inspiration for Temptation's exciting new yearlong miniseries, LOVERS & LEGENDS. Bestselling authors including Gina Wilkins, Glenda Sanders, JoAnn Ross and Tiffany White reweave these classic tales—with lots of sizzle! One book a month, LOVERS & LEGENDS continues in April 1993 with:

#437 DR. HUNK
Glenda Sanders
(The Frog Prince)

Live the fantasy....

LL4

HARLEQUIN®

Temptation

Harlequin® Historical

We hope you enjoyed your introduction to our March Madness authors and that you will keep an eye out for their next titles from Harlequin Historicals.

Castaway by Laurel Ames—A British shipowner gets more than he bargained for when he becomes "heir-apparent" of a large and zany family.

Fly Away Home by Mary McBride—The story of a half-breed Apache and the Eastern-bred woman who proves to him that their love can conquer all.

Silver and Steel by Susan Amarillas—The western expansion of America's railroads serves as the backdrop for this tale of star-crossed lovers who can't escape their destiny.

The Unicorn Bride by Claire Delacroix—A young woman finds herself married to an enigmatic nobleman veiled in secrets and legends in this French Medieval setting.

Four stories that you won't want to miss. Look for them wherever Harlequin Historicals are available.

Where do you find hot Texas nights, smooth Texas charm and dangerously sexy cowboys?

COWBOYS AND CABERNET

Raise a glass—Texas style!

Tyler McKinney is out to prove a Texas ranch is the perfect place for a vineyard. Vintner Ruth Holden thinks Tyler is too stubborn, too impatient, too... Texas. And far too difficult to resist!

CRYSTAL CREEK reverberates with the exciting rhythm of Texas. Each story features the rugged individuals who live and love in the Lone Star State. And each one ends with the same invitation...

Y'ALL COME BACK... REAL SOON!

Don't miss *COWBOYS AND CABERNET* by Margot Dalton. Available in April wherever Harlequin books are sold.

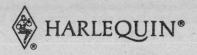
HARLEQUIN®

THE TAGGARTS OF TEXAS!

Harlequin's Ruth Jean Dale brings you
THE TAGGARTS OF TEXAS!

Those Taggart men—strong, sexy and hard to resist...

You've met Jesse James Taggart in FIREWORKS!
Harlequin Romance #3205 (July 1992)

And Trey Smith—he's THE RED-BLOODED YANKEE!
Harlequin Temptation #413 (October 1992)

And the unforgettable Daniel Boone Taggart in SHOWDOWN!
Harlequin Romance #3242 (January 1993)

Now meet Boone Smith and the Taggarts who started it all—
in LEGEND!
Harlequin Historical #168 (April 1993)

Read all the Taggart romances!
Meet all the Taggart men!

Available wherever Harlequin Books are sold.
